# THE NIGHT OF
# THE FLOOD

# THE NIGHT OF THE FLOOD

## A Novel in Stories

EDITED BY
E.A. AYMAR & SARAH M. CHEN

DOWN&OUT
BOOKS

Down & Out Books
3959 Van Dyke Rd, Ste. 265
Lutz, FL 33558
www.DownAndOutBooks.com

Cover design by Page Godwin

ISBN: 1-946502-51-0
ISBN-13: 978-1-946502-51-3

# CONTENTS

# GUEST EDITOR INTRODUCTION
## Hank Phillippi Ryan

This book is so ridiculously terrific I can't begin to tell you, but being a writer of course, I will try.

What makes it so brilliant? It's three books in one.

First, of course, it's an anthology of short stories. No dearth of those around, of course. Like Mickey Rooney and Judy Garland (with me here?), writers will get together and say—let's write all some stories about detectives, or aliens, or famous crimes.

But this anthology is wonderfully unique. Each short story reveals a moment in time in a super poor Pennsylvania town called Everton. What would happen, these thriller writers asked, if a massive dam was town-destroyingly blown up by a group of zealots? More I cannot say, but that's the jumping off point. If your world was about to be deluged with millions of tons of uncontrollably rushing water, how would you react? What would you do? What decisions would you make? How would your "friends" behave? Who would you save? And—with law enforcement as overwhelmed, terrified (and wet) as you are—would any laws apply? What could you get away with—and what would you try?

Whether these authors collaborated and divvied up the people and timing I don't even want to know—because that's the fascination. But each short story is a personal jewel, a look deep inside the characters' motivations and fears and unleashed desires. These are thriller writers, after all, so there are no stories where someone says, "Oh, golly," then packs up the family albums, puts them in the Pontiac and heads for the—less soggy—hills. Each of these is a pitch perfect little story of raw emotional choices—sometimes violent, sometimes shocking, and sometimes hilarious. Each is an investigation into the impossible-to-predict process people would go through when faced with a cataclysmic event. If you simply read it story by individual story, it's fun and fast-paced and imaginative and surprising. But that's only part of it.

It's also a second book entirely—because somehow, like an Altman movie or a photo developing in a chemical bath (you remember that, right?) each individual tale isn't just a story in itself, but the piece of an emerging bigger picture. In this about-to-be-obliterated little town, each person, suddenly *mano a mano* with destiny, is pitted not only against the relentless water, but their own personal demons. Each person struggles not only to survive, but also understands this disaster may offer the opportunity to do something they always wanted to do. Get revenge. Even the score. Leave someone behind. Take what they want. Form unlikely alliances. Reveal the truth. Start over.

And as you read, a comprehensive portrait of the whole town emerges, a twisted Spoon River or a sinister Grover's Corners—or maybe more like Rod Serling's suspect-your-neighbors Maple Street. You begin to realize that what's happening in the bank is happening at the same time as what's going on in the Wetherbee's house, or at the auto mechanic, or on the river. The stories work together—and as we read, we become more and more invested in this increasingly believable and realistic drama.

But there's yet another element. *The Night of the Flood* is also a master's class in storytelling and voice. An illustration of why when we say "thriller" it could mean so many things—suspense, horror, caper, procedural. Each author's voice is eloquently individual, each story imaginative and unique. And if you notice, as I did, a certain dark cynicism about the state of our world these days, well, that's probably your imagination.

I'm happy I don't live in Everton. But trust me—it's a pretty amazing place to visit. Just bring an umbrella and a rowboat.

# DEAR TOWNSPEOPLE OF EVERTON

Jenny Milchman

Dear Townspeople of Everton:

First, I want to say I'm sorry for what's about to happen to you tonight.

I gotta admit that my sympathies lie with Maggie Wilbourne, and I guess that don't make me a—what would you call it? Unbiased observer. But all we're asking is for the governor to grant a stay of execution, or the judge to overturn the verdict, better yet.

I'm not saying Maggie didn't do it, mind. I'm saying she had a good reason to.

You already know about what she done. It was in all the papers, ones we just heard the names of but never read, plus the *Everton Early*, of course. Those slick reporters talked about it on the news—our local little channel six, all the networks, and on cable too. Even when there was nothing new to say, they kept rehashing every gory, grisly detail. Gore and gristle sell. And when even those start to get old, begin stinking like a bad piece of meat, then people speculate there's more to it than we was hearing about, make all sorts of things up.

There wasn't more to it. Maggie Wilbourne went to get justice from the law, and when the law didn't give it to her, she took her daddy's rifle and shot the heads off two men whose names you already know: James Manning and Trevor Daw. And when James saw Trevor's face go flying, he didn't turn around and run or try to hide, that's how shocked he was. He just stood there, staring down at what was left of his friend, till Maggie blew him away too.

Why James Manning and Trevor Daw? Because Maggie said they raped her pretty bad. One at a time so the other could watch. Helpless on her daddy's couch in that house he has by the Big Dam. Did you ever wonder why we call it the Big Dam like there was a smaller one? But the Big Dam's the only thing we got in Everton. Powers all the towns downriver, people fear that one day, nothing will be left for us.

Won't matter if we do what we're intending on tonight.

My daddy brought me to Everton when I was twelve years old and my momma had just walked out on us. He found work here at the dam, and that was reason enough to stay. So I'm not from around here, and sometimes it seem like folks can see that about me, hear it in the way I talk, smell it on me almost. But I love this town same as if my good-for-nothing family lived here for four generations. This town took me in when I was nothing.

I love it enough to destroy it.

Maggie told Chief Wilcox what James and Trevor done, and the chief did what he was supposed to, wrote up a report, started an investigation. I guess it was Maggie's lawyer couldn't make a good enough case. Or maybe the jury started feeling some sympathy for those two blown apart boys.

It'll be a fitting follow-up when we blow up the Big Dam tonight, won't it? 'Cause if Maggie Wilbourne dies with needles poking into her veins, sending in poison that's the only thing could be strong enough to wipe her memories away, we're going to make sure everything else here in Everton gets washed away too.

And if the house Maggie grew up in, her daddy's house that sets right on the hillside over the Big Dam, is the first to go when we let that big wave of water free? Well, maybe that's fitting too. Maybe Maggie's lawyer couldn't think of anything to say when that other lawyer made the truth about her daddy come out in that court-house. Maggie didn't start crying, you know, never even blinked.

She sure was crying, screaming too, that night on her daddy's couch when James and Trevor went running to see what was the matter. Maggie's daddy just slinked away. He came straight to my house, which is where he always does go, nights when Maggie sleeps so hard, she can't be woken, or those times when Maggie's momma, my auntie, decides to stay home.

Too much blood has flowed in this town, too many tears have been spilled. Time for us to wash it all away.

From,
The Daughters

# THE ORPHANS

E.A. Aymar

The dam blew up ten minutes after six, then we emerged. It wasn't what you see on TV. You hear about riots and looting and you expect a mob tossing rocks through windows, snatching TVs. But we were smart. A plan had circulated through text and email, going to all us folk in the south side, the poor, the angry, the ones on the edge of breaking. We'd hit homes first, wait for the Everton cops to help out those victims, then target the stores.

We went to the houses on the hill. That's the rich part of Everton, where the folks who have more bedrooms than family members lived, where they stayed, where they looked down on the rest of us. Their houses were built around the dam, but none of those houses were damaged. None of those houses stood in the path of the rushing water. Those people never suffered the way we did.

The looters stole through Everton. My sister Callie and I avoided the flood and stayed on the outskirts of the town. Here the ground was higher and, for now, dry. We rode my motorcycle north, occasionally stopping to stare at the submerged town below, some of the families already perched on rooftops to watch the water rise. The

9

men and women were shocked or sad. The children, excited or scared.

It took a half hour to reach the hill, and we figured we had an hour before everyone else showed up. We wanted to get here first, before the riots started and blood spilled. The homes here were all spread apart, not clustered together like the south side. The house we targeted was at least three stories, but so dark it looked abandoned. Every other house had people standing out front, staring down at the drowning town. The porch on this one was empty. Trees curved around it like a crown.

"Vic, check it out," Callie said to me, her long knife hanging at her side. "They started the fires."

She was right. Fires flared to life through Everton, five, ten, more. The town was pitch black since the power had gone out, so someone had texted that we should set the trees on fire.

"I'm going to miss this after tonight," I told her. "Just kidding."

"Still want to leave, huh?"

"There's been nothing for us here. And there'll be even less after tonight."

"Then let's do this."

I pulled my 9 mm semi out of its holster, used the handle to smash the small glass window next to the door. I listened to hear if anyone was inside.

Silence.

I reached through the broken glass, unlocked the door. Pulled my ski mask down over my face. Looked back at Callie.

"Where's your mask?"

Callie shook her head. "My hair looks really good tonight."

She opened the door and stepped inside. Tossed her mask behind her.

I picked it up and followed her in.

Callie and I had lived in Everton since I was six and she was three. We'd been born in Baltimore to a crack addict and a hooker and ended up in foster homes, until James Whitlow of Everton—a lifelong bachelor desperate for a family—adopted us and moved us to western Pennsylvania. We were the only adopted kids in the town. The adults called Whitlow a saint. Kids called us The Orphans.

Whitlow wasn't much of a saint. He was a moody drunk and, when the plant closed in 2007, he went over the edge. He ended up putting his fists on me and his fingers in Callie. I didn't know he was doing anything to her until almost a year had passed.

"He promised he'd kill me if I said anything," Callie told me one day at school, as we sat by ourselves at lunch. "That's why I haven't said anything until now."

My insides felt like rocks sliding down a hill.

"When?"

"When did he start or when does he do it? He comes into my room at night. Really late. Since January."

My shoulders hurt. I hadn't realized my body was so tense.

"Should we run?" Callie asked. "Go somewhere else?"

I glanced at the crowded tables in the cafeteria, listened to the conversations around us, the sudden shouts of laughter and happy exclamations.

"I don't want to run. I want to do something else."

Callie smiled. "Me too."

We waited until later that night, when Whitlow was passed out drunk, and dragged him to the garage. He was a large man, probably two-fifty with a protruding belly. It took both of us, but we finally got him into his car and started it up. We stuck a hose in the exhaust, fed the other end through the window.

They found him the next night, gray and bloated and dead. Everyone called it a tragedy. Everyone pitied us. One of our neighbors, a librarian named Natalie Moreno, offered to take us in. I was seventeen, Callie fourteen, and after a year I moved out and took Callie with me. Natalie didn't hurt us the way Whitlow had, but she was mercilessly strict and I worried Callie would kill her. When Natalie took away her phone because Callie had stayed out all night, and I saw Callie eyeing the kitchen knife rack, I made my decision. We left days later.

I got a terrible job at Woods Automotive and a small apartment. Callie and I lived there for the next three years.

No one bothered us. People had always given me a wide berth. "It's because you never smile," Callie told me, but Callie was legitimately crazy so I didn't put a lot of stock in her opinions. Most people couldn't put their finger on it, couldn't figure out what exactly about my sister, a thin pale brunette, made them nervous. But I knew the reason.

Callie didn't have limits, didn't even know what limits were. I tested that the night we murdered Whitlow. Killing him didn't bother me, not after I learned what he'd done to Callie, but she couldn't care less. When the cops took away his body the next morning, she told me she dug her nails into her palms to stop herself from smiling.


The house was darker inside than outside so I turned on my flashlight, kept my gun in its holster. I figured people were less likely to shoot at an unarmed man. Besides, if I needed my gun, I could have it in my hand in two seconds, maybe less.

I'd always been a fan of westerns and, for the last three years, I'd spent at least thirty minutes a night drawing my gun, trying to get faster. Not that I sought violence but, eventually, violence sought everybody. I wanted to be ready for the next James Whitlow to cross us.

But I didn't want to shoot a cop, and I had a feeling the police would be here soon. Especially once they found out the people down south had come up.

Callie and I walked underneath two giant chandeliers, past furniture and even a silent fountain, and headed into the living room. Walking through the living room reminded me of a class trip I once took to some art museum in Philly. Like that museum, this living room had little sculptures on high tables, paintings behind glass, actual statues in the corners. But Callie and I didn't care about any of that and didn't bother examining it closely; I had no idea how to pawn that stuff without getting caught. And I figured that after tonight, all the cops in western Pennsylvania would be on the lookout for fenced valuables. Cash was the smart play.

We checked the bedrooms and didn't find anyone.

"They're probably on vacation," Callie said bitterly, as she went through the closet in the biggest bedroom, pulled out different shirts, and tried them on.

"Seems like it."

"So next house?"

"Next house."

I felt like we had to take something, on principle, so I broke open a locked jewelry case. Callie draped a long necklace around her neck. I shoved some plain silver rings into my pocket.

At the next house, a woman screamed when I broke a window to get in.

Callie grinned.

"Sounds like money."

This second house was about the same size as the first but, where the first house had a massive living room, this one had an expansive kitchen. There was an island in the middle long enough to house castaways, and two refrigerators. Callie and I looked in them and they were both stocked with food. We couldn't tell the difference between them, couldn't imagine why anyone would need two.

We headed up a wide marble staircase. At the top, the hall stretched in either direction. All of the doors were closed.

"I take one hall, you take the other?" Callie suggested.

I shook my head. "Could be a gun waiting on the other side of one of those doors. And you just have your knife."

"Pretty sure I'll be okay." A few months ago some guy followed her into a restroom in a Pittsburgh bar, tried to move in on her. Callie left him unconscious on a toilet, cuts all over his stomach and chest, bleeding into the bowl. "I like using a knife," she'd said nonchalantly on the drive back home. "Makes a point. Get it?"

"I know you'll be fine," I told her now. "But I'd rather stick together."

Callie grunted.

We went left. Callie reached for the first knob. I put a hand on her wrist, an ear to the door. Didn't hear anything inside so we moved on. No sense making unnecessary noise. And after the scream we'd heard earlier, I didn't think anyone hiding in one of those rooms could keep quiet.

Callie grabbed my ear, pulled my head down close to her mouth.

"Maybe they're hiding in a panic room, like that movie."

I thought about it. "What's your point?"

"I've always wanted to see a panic room."

"Honestly, our odds of finding it aren't great. If they even do have one."

"Don't be a downer, dude."

We found her hiding in the last room in the left hall. An older woman, probably somewhere in her forties, standing in a corner of a study between a desk and a tall plant.

"Please," she said, speaking slowly, deliberately, "I'll give you whatever you want. Just don't hurt me."

I wasn't planning on hurting her, but no sense sharing that information. "We're just here for money. We get that, we're gone."

"I, I don't have any money on me."

"Is it in your panic room?" Callie asked excitedly.

"I don't have a panic room."

"Damn."

I was disappointed too. Kind of wanted to see that.

"Is this about Maggie Wilbourne?" the woman asked. "Because I support the Daughters."

Callie turned toward me. "Who's Maggie Wilbourne?"

I ignored her. "Where's your money?"

"I don't keep cash on me. Everything's credit."

I definitely didn't want her credit cards. Figured the cops would arrest me the minute I used one.

"You don't have anything on you?" I asked. "And no cash in the house? Like, hidden behind a picture or something?"

"Nothing. I'm so sorry. Please don't hurt me."

"We're not going to hurt you."

"Well, I might," Callie said.

"She might," I corrected myself. "What I meant was, we don't want to hurt you."

"But we're going to need something," Callie added.

"You can take anything you want," the woman said. "Except my life."

Callie shook her head in disgust. "Christ lady. Over-dramatize much?"

I gazed at the woman, wondering how much time we had before a neighbor or the Everton police stopped by to check on her. I figured the cops would be up here soon, making sure the rich people were safe.

I knew this lady was lying about her money, and I hated the thought that Callie and I were going to leave this house empty-handed. Leave this lady thinking she'd pulled one over on us. Even if she begged for her life, she'd count it as a win. End up telling her friends at some dinner party years from now how she outsmarted a pair of looters. Like that's all Callie and I were.

I shined my flashlight on her left hand. Saw a glint.

"Where's your husband?" I asked.

"He's on the road. Traveling for work."

"How much is that ring worth?" Callie asked.

The woman's hand tightened. "I don't know."

"Come on, lady," Callie pressed. "You didn't have it insured?"

"I think it was five thousand, maybe?"

"Maybe, huh?"

"Got anything else?" I asked.

"Not in the house, I promise."

"I'm going to take a look around. My sister will keep you company."

She looked like she wanted to say something, but didn't. Just closed her eyes.

I left them there, the woman murmuring something, Callie smiling, her long knife at her side. I walked down the hall and peered into a couple of rooms. Didn't see anything but an orderly office in one, an empty bedroom with no sheets on the bed in another.

I found the boy in the third room I checked, a kid's bedroom that looked like a zoo had stopped spending money on cages. Giant toy stuffed animals crowded it, their silhouettes visible as my flashlight's beam darted around the room. A giraffe that was nearly my height, an elephant the size of a small car, monkeys hanging in different playful positions, a couple of zebras. If there was a bed or dresser in here, I couldn't find them.

The kid was huddled in a corner of the room.

I walked over to him, knelt down.

"What's your name?"

"Max." His voice was faint.

"You got some cool stuff in your room, Max."

He was terrified. Big eyes, breathing fast. I remembered I had the ski mask on and pulled it up. Showed him my face.

"If I wasn't robbing you," I said, "I'd ask if I could come back and play."

"Is my mom okay?"

I nodded. "You got any brothers or sisters, Max?"

He shook his head.

"Anyone else in the house?"

Another shake.

He was trembling.

I hated seeing the kid scared, hated even more that I was the one scaring him.

I remembered being that afraid, and no adults had been there to make me feel better.

"Hey buddy, I promise you'll be safe."

"Is my mom really okay?"

"Absolutely." Callie wasn't going to do anything to her, just scare her a little.

Max and I stared at each other for a moment. Something about the way he looked at me reminded me of Callie at his age.

"Let me ask you something, Max," I said. "Your mom or dad, they ever hurt you? Do something to you that doesn't feel right? Touch you someplace and ask you to keep it a secret?"

He shook his head.

"What about anyone else? A teacher, sitter? You can tell me."

"No, no one."

"If anyone ever does, you know what to do?"

"Tell an adult?"

"Yeah, that's a good idea too. But you know what works even better?" I reached down, touched his Achilles heel. "Stabbing them right here. It'll hurt so much they won't be able to chase you. You stab them there and then you run. Run like hell, Max, because they're going to try and catch you. Then you can tell someone, but do that first. Otherwise, you might not get to do it later. Don't want to regret that later in life."

"I don't have a knife."

I reached into my pocket, pulled out my keychain, took off the small folding knife I kept on it. I pressed the knife into his hand.

"Oh, brother?" Callie sang from across the hall. "Where art thou?"

"Come on," I told Max. "Let's go see your mom."

We headed back to the other room.

I should have walked in first, made Max wait in the hall. Then he wouldn't have seen what Callie had done to his mother.

I pulled him out of the room, closed the door and left him in the hallway.

"Who's that?" Callie asked.

I locked the door and hurried over to Max's mother. She was still in the same corner of the room, but sitting. Her shirt was off and stuffed into her mouth. Her bare stomach was crisscrossed with bloody cuts.

I pulled the shirt out.

"Max?" she said, distantly.

"He's okay," I told her. "I promise."

Max's mother seemed like she was in shock. She didn't try and stand, didn't move at all. Just stayed sitting, staring.

"She wouldn't tell me where anything was," Callie said. "Even when I started carving."

"That's because she was hiding her son from us."

Callie was playing with something on her hand. She was wearing the woman's wedding ring. "Maybe he can tell us."

"No," his mother said. That seemed to snap her back to her senses. She looked at each of us, struggled to stand. "Is he okay?"

"For now," Callie said.

"For good. We're leaving." I glanced at Callie. "Cops and robbers are probably on their way."

Callie wiped her knife on the carpet, sheathed it, shrugged. "Let's go."

I took off my shirt, gave it to the woman. "Don't let him see your stomach."

She pulled the shirt on.

We opened the door, let Max in. He ran over to his mother, fell into her arms.

We left them in the study. I stopped in the master bedroom, pulled out a man's shirt from the closet. He was smaller than I was and the shirt was tight, but it'd do.

Callie and I headed out into the night.

"What happened with that kid?" Callie asked, as we walked down a dark winding street, the loud rush of water and fire in the distance.

"Nothing. I gave him my knife."

"The Swiss Army one on your keychain?"

"Yeah."

She nodded approvingly. "Every kid should have a knife."

"New plan. The houses up here aren't going to have piles of cash lying around, and they'll take forever to go through. And the cops will be up here quick. I've been thinking about those looters. They're probably hitting the stores now."

"So you want go after the stores with them?"

"Nope. Those looters left their own houses empty. Let's rob them."

We rode my motorcycle back south, sticking to the outskirts of the town. Sirens from cop cars flashed red and white in the night sky. Even though the water hadn't topped the banks, it was threatening. Callie and I finally reached the south side's rough roads, the one-story houses stretched out like rows of dominos. We parked the bike and headed into the town, splashing through ankle-high water. I ditched the ski mask; figured there was no reason in looking suspicious when you're walking around a neighborhood you're planning to rob. We headed toward a home we knew, owned by a guy named Billy Johnson who Callie had gone on a few dates with. He'd been the most excited of anyone about looting the town, already had run-ins with the law, wasn't opposed to having more. I figured he'd be out all night.

We walked around the back. I boosted her to the top of a chain-link fence, then climbed over.

"He probably took his money with him," Callie said.

"No chance. He's not going to risk getting arrested and having the cops keep it, or getting jacked in the riot.

Trust me, he left his roll here."

"Or in the bank."

I took out my gun, sized up a back window pane, smashed it open. I reached inside, undid the lock, lifted the window open. "Poor people don't have banks."

This house couldn't have been more different than the last one we'd broken into. We stood in one long room facing two closed doors, a hallway that led to a bathroom, a small separated kitchen, and a front door. That was it.

"Where's Billy's room?" I asked.

Callie headed to one of the doors, opened it.

"Who's there?" someone called out.

My gun jumped into my hand. Callie looked at me.

"What are you doing?" she hissed.

"Didn't you hear that?"

"That's his grandfather in the other room," she explained. "He's ancient. Can't even get out of bed on his own."

"You didn't tell me his grandfather lived here."

"Yes I did."

"No, you didn't."

"Maybe I didn't."

"Just hurry up."

I kept watch while Callie searched the bedroom. Billy's grandfather called out a couple of more times, but otherwise the house was quiet. It took Callie five minutes, but she emerged from the bedroom with a handful of bills.

"Two hundred," she said, proudly. "Found it under the mattress."

"Not a bad start."

We left the way we came, headed to another house we figured would be empty. It was.

An hour later Callie and I had a pretty good streak going. Ten houses and thirteen hundred dollars. But we ran out of homes owned by people we knew.

"We need a big one," I told her. "My goal's to get two grand before we leave."

"So we hit the stores?"

"Nah. We go to Woods."

Callie grinned.

The owner of Woods Automotive and my boss, Ken Woods, was a walking, talking pile of vomit. Ripped off customers whenever he could, harassed any women that worked there, paid his employees shit wages. I didn't fool myself into believing I was Robin Hood or anything, but I wouldn't feel guilty at all about robbing his store.

Callie and I approached the shop straight on. The street around us was silent, the water a distant hum. A massive F150 was parked in front.

"The good thing is," I told Callie, as I tugged my keychain back out of my pocket, "we don't even have to break a window this time."

Woods Automotive was a giant garage, with two car lifts and the overpowering smell of rubber from stacks of tires lining the walls. We walked in, pushed over a couple of signs advertising car parts and cleaning supplies. Headed toward the payment desk in the back.

"So we just empty the cash register, right?" Callie asked. "We don't want to hock any of these shiny rims?"

"Just the cash."

That's when we heard a click.

"Thought that was you, Vic."

Ken stepped out of the shadows.

I saw the shotgun in his arms before I saw him.

"You robbin' me?" he asked.

Ken Woods was a big man. Massively overweight with small black eyes and curly black hair, and he always wore jeans, a white shirt, and suspenders. The shotgun looked small with him holding it.

"Just wanted to make sure everything here was okay," I said.

"Yeah, bullshit. Stay where you are. This shotgun could tear a hole in your faggot ass so wide your sister could step through it."

"That's gross about the hole." Callie turned toward me. "You're gay?"

"I don't know where he got that."

"It's okay if you are," she said.

"I'm not."

"Are you sure?"

"Positive."

"I made out with another girl once."

"Hey," Ken said. "Remember me? Man with the shotgun?"

"What's that behind you?" Callie asked.

I hadn't seen him at first, but now I did. A kid standing behind Ken, peering around his hip.

"Christ, Ken," I said. "You have your son with you?"

"You think I'd leave him at home tonight?"

It wasn't a bad point.

"We'll go," I told him. "This was a shitty idea. I get it."

"Knew the looters would be out tonight," Ken said, as if he hadn't heard me. "Knew I had to wait here. People want to step over boundaries, break rules. Just looking for an excuse. Tonight gave it to them."

Callie and I stared at him. I was trying to see his finger, see if he had it curled around the trigger. I didn't think he'd shoot us in front of his son, but something seemed different about Ken tonight.

"Everyone wants to rob, rape, kill," Ken went on. "Deep down, that's all they want to do. Just looking for an excuse."

"Not us," I said. "Well, not two of those things."

"Plus killing's not that great," Callie said. "Trust me."

Ken looked toward her. "Heard you were a crazy bitch."

I looked at his kid. He hadn't moved.

"Sounds about right," Callie agreed.

"We can all walk away." I tried to soften my voice, make it soothing. "None of us has to die."

Ken glanced in my direction. "You're not getting any money."

"I know."

"And your faggot ass is fired."

"Figured that out too."

"Go on," he said. "Turn around, get out of here."

"I'm not turning my back to you," Callie said.

"Leave however you want," Ken said, impatiently. "Just leave."

"I don't like your tone. Or the way you've treated my brother. Or the way you called me a bitch. Or, honestly, your attitude about gay people."

"Door's right there." Ken pointed behind her with his left hand.

When he pointed, the hand holding the shotgun lowered.

Callie turned into a blur. She was rushing Ken when his gun exploded, but she'd already passed the gun. I saw his mouth open, then grimace, and I saw Callie sink her knife into his stomach. She grabbed the knife with two hands and yanked it sideways.

I was a second behind her. I ran past them, picked up Ken's son, sprinted with him to the back of the store and blew through the door.

I set the boy down in the back lot, filled with broken cars and scrap metal.

"My dad!"

"He's going to be okay," I told him. "He'll be okay. But you need to stay out here. You understand me?"

He sat down, his head bent over his thin legs. "My dad."

I went back in, locked the door. Callie was standing by the cash register, peering at it intently. Ken was crawling to the front door. The shotgun lay on the floor behind him.

"Why'd you do that?" I asked her.

Callie looked up from the cash register, puzzled. "I thought I just explained why."

"My son," Ken said, his voice high, frightened.

"He was letting us go!" I told her. "He didn't want this."

"And you trusted him not to tell the cops about us?"

"Please..." Ken moaned.

"He didn't deserve what you did," I said to Callie.

"You had no reason to do it. Not with his kid there. The world has enough damaged kids running around."

"My son."

"You heard what he said to me," Callie retorted. "And you told me how he treated you."

I shook my head. "Wasn't enough."

Ken rolled to his back. Breathed loudly, wetly.

"To be honest," Callie said. "I don't really trust his kid either. He's out back, right?"

"He's staying there."

Callie and I faced each other. I was suddenly very conscious of the gun in my hand. And Callie's knife in hers.

"Why did you do it?" I asked.

"My son," Ken said, softly.

Her voice was hard. "I told you why."

"You're lying." My voice came out just as hard.

"I did it so we could get out of this town. Get the rest of the money we need. Take one of the cars out back that's not too dinged up instead of your old motorcycle. Find somewhere else to live. Somewhere we can start over."

"That's not it. Why?"

"I'm telling you! Because I don't want to stay in the same town where James fucking Whitlow raped me, and it feels like everyone here knows it. And no one cares, because I'm some crazy bitch."

"Why?"

Our voices had both risen.

"Because no one cares what made me this way, just that I am this way. And you killed that fucking monster for me, so I did this for you. And I know what else I have to do. Out back. For us."

"I won't let you hurt him."

"There's no other way."

I couldn't hear Ken breathing anymore.


The kid and I walked back to my motorcycle. We didn't say a word the entire way. I walked ahead of the kid because I couldn't bear to look back at his face. And I didn't want to give him the chance to ask any questions.

I climbed on the bike and helped the kid up. Sat him on my lap, his back to my chest. He leaned forward, like he was doing his best not to touch me.

I stayed on the outskirts, made a few stops.

One to try to stop shaking.

One to throw up.

And then I made one last stop.

I parked just outside the town and the kid and I headed back in. It took about ten minutes of sloshing through ankle-high water until we reached Ken's house. The kid looked up at me.

There was nothing I could say that would help.

I knelt anyway.

"I'm sorry."

He was crying too much to hear me.

I rang the doorbell and hurried away, splashing loudly. The kid stayed by the door, crying harder. I turned a corner and hid, waited until I saw the door open and the kid hugging someone.

I watched the hug, watched the kid ushered inside, watched the light vanish as the door closed behind him.

I thought about Callie, remembered the shock and

pain in her face after I'd shot her in the leg, moments before she fell to the ground. She wasn't going to die; I'd made sure of it by waiting until I heard sirens screaming, waiting as she begged me not to leave her.

I left her as the cops were parking, as she was dragging herself across the floor, desperately trying to come with me.

I started the motorcycle.

And then I left Everton, consumed by flood and fire.

# ANYTHING WORTH SAVING

## Wendy Tyson

He said his name was "Big Earl" King. With Aunt Lena, there was always an Earl. Sometimes he was a business-man temporarily down on his luck and thinking my pretty aunt would bring some sunshine back into his world. Sometimes he was a two-bit hustler with more *chutzpah* than morals, money, or common sense. This Earl looked like the latter. Dimpled smile. Mustachioed. A lanky six-foot-plus frame encased in funeral black that brought to mind an exclamation point, his red suede dress shoes the dot on the bottom. Big Earl eyed me side-ways after giving me a misspelled business card—he was an "entreprenur"—and a firm handshake. A handshake that said *I'm the man*. And he would have been made to *feel* like the man. That was always Lena Bloom's way.

No doubt Big Earl thought he was using Lena, but it would have been Lena using him. She'd spend time poking holes in his plans to get rich while he was busy poking her. Had Lena lived, Big Earl would have woken up one day with his bed empty, his cash missing, and whatever was left of his half-baked scheme misappropri-ated and reimagined by Lena. Big Earl would have real-ized he'd been played a Big Fool. Just like the rest of us.

The thing was, Lena Bloom *intended* to do right by the people in her life. That's what made her dangerous. She was believable. So when the screws finally came, you didn't see them coming. I almost felt sorry for Big Earl, sitting back there across the aisle from Pastor Lewis, smoothing his mustache with one calloused finger, his eyes runny and red. But being done with Lena Bloom meant being done with pity for the people she broke. We all should have known better. What a collective bunch of assholes we were.

I sank into the pew at the front of the empty Everton Unitarian Church and turned to study the mourners. Fourteen of us total—and only nine if you didn't count the pastor, his wife, and their three sour-faced teenage sons. Besides Earl, I saw five older women in courthouse gray—probably former coworkers, a husky woman in army-issue green, and a girl in a white dress. White to a funeral service seemed an odd choice, but maybe the black tattoos snaking their way down her bare arms like vines around a tree trunk were her way of showing respect to the deceased. Maybe, but I didn't think so.

Pastor Lewis said prayers over Lena's cremated body, contained as it was in a pewter urn. No one except the pastor and his wife sang. I left that church before dusk, the off-key voice of Marietta Lewis mutilating "Amazing Grace," the smell of acrid smoke from a nearby factory a fitting tribute to the only person in the world who'd cared if I lived or died.


The shower head in my beige bathroom at the Sleepy Time Motel was too short. I'm nearly five-foot and ten inches, so I had to squat to get my head under the water. That detail matters, because if I'd been standing straight I might have heard some noise that would have stopped this night from veering out of control. Instead, oblivious, I let the hot spray wash the regrets from my mind just as poorly as it removed the cheap shampoo.

Lena Bloom. Dead. And just two weeks ago she'd called me to say we needed to talk. "This is the big one, Casey," she'd crooned. "I'm gonna make it up to ya. All of it. The house, your momma. I promise, Case. This is it."

Of course, she couldn't have made any of it up to me. Losing our house in a "sure thing" wager with a previous Earl would have killed Momma if the stroke hadn't. As it was, it was me who nursed Momma for three long years in that cramped sorry excuse for a bedroom at the back of a trailer, cleaning the drool from the shell left of Barbara Bloom. Not Lena. Lena, who said she'd make it right again but could only afford a rundown single-wide in North Pocono Sunrise Park. Lena, who Momma looked up to like the converted look to Christ. Heartbreak killed Momma. Not three jobs. Not having my daddy leave when I wasn't even born yet. It was Lena, and she couldn't fix what she'd done then. And she surely couldn't fix it now.

But she wanted to try.

"Just come to Everton," she'd said. "I'll explain it all when you get here. I promise, Casey. You won't be hurting for money no more."

I'd been to Everton and I had no intention of returning. I wanted to tell Lena to go to hell, but no one could tell Lena to fuck off. Maybe it was that sultry voice that got excited when she was sniffing out a scheme. Maybe it was the way she made you feel like you were the only person in the whole damn world who mattered. Maybe it was the fact that *I* had nothing to lose. Who was I fooling? I'd take whatever hope Lena was giving. Living in an apartment over a bakery in Harrisburg meant waking up at two every morning when the bakers started clanging in the kitchen. And writing for the *Harrisburg Gazette* meant I couldn't afford anything other than a studio over a bakery in the seedy section of town. A section not unlike the block of Everton that housed the optimistically named Sleepy Time Motel. The banging and screaming from the room next door told me my neighbors were doing more than sleeping. I turned off the water, pissed at Lena. Pissed at the world.

She'd sent me here. Even in the end, dead as the fucking nearby factory, contained in that urn, she'd had her attorney send me a package with her living will, her burial wishes, and even the name of the damn pastor I was to contact for services. When I called that lawyer, he'd said she'd just wanted to be prepared. Make it easy on me, should something happen.

Something happened, all right. Damn you, Lena.

The lights in the bathroom flashed off, then on. I stepped out of the shower, into the hot steam, hearing only my neighbors and the television blaring from my bedroom. The floor seemed to move. I felt a shock like an earthquake run through the joists of the building. Bending to grab a towel from the rack, I stared in horror at the mirror, my breath catching in the back of my throat.

Someone had been in the bathroom while I was in the

shower. They'd written "CHAOS" in the steam in the mirror above the sink in big, scrawling letters.

I ran out of the bathroom and into the bedroom, awash in anger and confusion. While my hands groped for clothes, my eyes cased the room, combing for the intruder. Mid-search, the newscaster's voice grabbed my attention and I let the towel drop to the floor. There, on the screen, was a picture of Everton's Big Dam, which turned the Monongahela River into power for Everton and a half-dozen nearby towns. Someone had blown it up. The reservoir behind it was pouring forth, retribution from Hell itself. The newscaster was calling it a terrorist act. "Right here in Everton," she said, as though that were the grand prize and she was awarding it.

I considered my location. Sleepy Time Motel was up by the old plant, on the south side of Everton—not directly in the path of the dam, but close enough. But that wasn't worrying me at the moment. I was too busy thinking about the word "CHAOS" written in blocky capitals across a picture of the dam flashed up there on the television screen. The terrorists were a group called The Daughters. NBC broadcast pictures of the known members. I recognized one face—a sturdy woman in army green whom the reporter was calling Betty. She'd been at the funeral.

Oh, Lena, I thought—what have you done this time?


It took me three minutes to get dressed, one minute to find my phone, and another thirty seconds to spot the girl crouched in my closet, behind the ironing board. This time, she wore the starched pink uniform of a

Sleepy Time Motel maid. Her tattooed arms gave her away as one of my aunt's mourners. The gun was my clue that she was hostile to my interests.

"What do you want?" I asked.

Her gaze skirted toward the television. "You know."

"No, I don't know." I looked at the images of raging river waters, finally seeking their revenge on the town that contained them. "You're one of those? The Daughters?"

She hesitated, then nodded. The gun shook in her hand. She seemed more scared than I did.

"You know we need to get out of here," I said. "It's only a matter of time before the water reaches this side of town. There'll be looting and blackouts. My car's outside. If we leave now we can—"

"No." The girl stood, holding the gun out in front of her, and climbed out of the closet. "Not without the information."

"What information? I seriously have no idea what you're talking about."

The girl raised her head, listening. I thought about how to wrestle that gun from her grasp; she seemed to be waiting for some cue from outside. I didn't think she'd shoot me purposefully—despite the tats, she looked more Girl Scout than gangsta—but I was nervous she'd pull the trigger accidentally. She seemed easily spooked.

The lights flashed on and off, then stayed off. The sun had gone down, and I used the cover of darkness to dive at the gun, pulling it from her grasp and slamming her against the bed.

"What the hell are you thinking?" Pulling her straight,

I ran my hands along her sides and down her legs, searching for another weapon. Satisfied, I pushed her down on the bed and walked backwards toward the door, gun pointed at my new friend. "Stay put."

"There're more of us," she said.

"I have no doubt. It must've taken a small army to pull off what you did."

"It was for her. Maggie." She sniffled. "I knew her. She babysat me sometimes, growing up. She was sweet. Didn't deserve what those men did to her. Or what the state did, either."

I didn't want to say that no one deserved what those men did. It wasn't that I didn't care about Maggie, the Big Dam, or the cause that had militant women flooding backward-ass towns outside of Pittsburgh. But right then, my main priority was getting the hell out of Everton—and figuring out what mess Lena had pulled me into.

I waved the gun. "Get up."

"No."

"Seriously? Don't fuck with me. Get up."

"It's not loaded."

"Goddamn." I checked the gun—she was right. I tucked it into my jacket anyway. "What the hell are you doing here? Why me?"

"You know."

"Stop saying that!" I took a step closer, holding my cell phone flashlight toward her face. She winced. I noticed the scar that ran alongside her mouth. Someone had slammed their knuckles against her jawline, hard— hard enough to shatter bone. From the look of the scar, it had happened long ago, when she was just a kid. I felt my anger toward her waning. The tag on her uniform said her name was Bonnie. She's been too dumb and green to remove it. "Come on, Bonnie. Let's get out of here."

"I can't."

"Look, the river—" I had my hand on the doorknob when I felt the lock give way and the door slam open, pushing me with it. "What the hell—"

Two more women rushed inside. The taller one held a flashlight, the shorter one pressed me up against the wall. I saw black trench coats, tall galoshes, and the orb of light that blinded me, then bounced around my room.

The tall one barked at Bonnie: "Did you get it?"

"Says she doesn't have it."

The taller one nodded. With surprising force, the shorter one rammed me down on the ground. I felt a knee in my back, metal against my spine, then something made of burlap was slipped over my head.

"Get her out of here," the tall one said. "We don't have long before this area will be flooded—with water *and* cops."

"The boat?"

"No. Where we're going, we'll need the car."


It took the better part of an hour to get where we were going. I couldn't see out of my burlap bag, but I could hear enough to know the panic and looting had started already. I felt the car stop, the tall one yell "Move!" before a gun shot rang out.

Bonnie murmured, "Fuck, Roe. Don't draw attention to us."

The short one pressed the gun harder into my ribs.

"Don't even fucking think about it," she said.

I pushed myself against the seat, willing my racing heart to stop squeezing the air from my lungs. Damn Lena. My mind swirled, thinking about my conversations with my aunt. Had she said anything to indicate what this was about? Anything I could grasp on to as a negotiating tool? Clearly they thought I had something of value—but what? I needed to focus.

But all I could think about was Momma. "Play it safe, Casey. Bloom women are the supporting cast. We're not meant to be the stars. Accept that and you won't get hurt." Even after Lena lost the house: "Head down, Casey. Work hard. It's high expectations that make people miserable. Just look at poor Lena." Momma with her house cleaning jobs, sewing drapes and matching bedspreads at night for the rich folks from New York and Philadelphia who bought second homes in Pocono developments called Tall Pines or Lake Serene. Momma with her bleak outlook and timid smile. I loved her, but life with Momma was gray.

I hated myself for it, but I sure looked forward to Lena's long stays. While Momma was working, Lena would teach me stuff Momma never did: how to apply eyeliner, bluff in poker, use tampons. She loved puzzles—word puzzles, jigsaw puzzles, you name it. We'd sit at the kitchen table with one of those two thousand-piece puzzles in front of us for days on end. All those pieces would overwhelm me, but before long, Lena would have a picture of a horse or a meadow or some puppies put together. She'd smile and say "Well done, Casey," as though I'd figured out more than a piece or two. Before bed, she'd comb my hair and tell me I was smarter and prettier than anyone she knew. And with that voice of hers and those soft kitten eyes, I believed her.

I so wanted to believe her.

I felt the gun press hard, tearing into tender cartilage between my ribs, and I knew we were stopping again. The car rocked, a man yelled. Another bark from Roe, a blast of cold air, and a gunshot followed by a long howling man-scream.

"Damn it, Roe, get there already." The short one jabbed me three times, let out a biting sigh of frustration. "Stop shooting people. She's waiting."

"I know. Just shut up, okay. Make sure Casey doesn't try anything."

With the window down, I could hear it—the sounds of a town dying. Screaming came bubbling up from somewhere beyond. Even through the burlap, the air smelled of smoke, garbage, and Bonnie's drug store perfume.

Roe slowed. "Shit. They're cops at the top of the hill. Push her down. Keep her quiet."

The short one twisted my head, thrusting me to the ground between the seats. "Shut it, bitch," she growled. She needn't have worried. I wasn't going to say a word.


The house was a mansion on the edge of town. It sat alone on a ridge, overlooking the wooded banks of the Monongahela and beyond, the beginning chaos below. They'd removed my hood. Up here, they must've figured, no one would hear me scream.

The tall one shoved me toward the garage. I wore no coat, and the cold November air bit into bare skin. I thought about running, but where to? I let them lead me inside. At least there it was warm.

She met us in the kitchen. Her hair was long and flaxen, the kind of blonde that women of a certain stature pay salons of a certain stature hundreds of dollars to create. Her face was heavily lined, her limbs long and elegant. I recognized her face from somewhere, but couldn't place it. She drew a mug of something to carefully painted lips and watched me over the rim. She was studying me, measuring my worth. I knew the look.

"Sit." She pointed a manicured finger at one of the stools that lined an island. Papers were spread out atop the granite, and I realized she had electricity. Noting my surprise, she smiled. "Generator. One thing the ex did right. It's really his house." With a dismissive glance at my three bedraggled captors, she said, "Put the guns away. We're not thugs." She smiled at me again. "Right?"

Bonnie looked relieved. The one called Roe lowered her gun but kept it in her lap. The short one disappeared into a bathroom.

"Where are my manners? My name is Maria. You're probably wondering why we brought you here. But first, would you like some coffee? It's fresh."

I shook my head no. Bonnie said "Yes, please." Maria ignored her.

"I'm sorry you had to go through this. But it was unavoidable, all things considered. Just hand over what we need and you're free to leave."

"I don't know what you're talking about."

"Lena's papers. The materials she gave you."

"Aunt Lena didn't give me anything."

It was then I realized who she was, what was happening. With mixed feelings of horror and admiration, I said, "You're Maria Bendroit."

"I am indeed." I saw the flash of fear and it gave me courage.

"Lena was blackmailing you."

Maria didn't deny it, nor did she agree. She put her coffee down on granite and walked to the window, looking out at what would soon be the carnage below.

"We don't have time for negotiations, Casey Bloom. I know who you are, you know who I am." She turned slowly, and I saw the condescending stare for which she was famous. "Let's not play games. With a night of absolute chaos like this one, people will lose their lives. One more body is not going to surprise anyone. Is that how you want to go?"

"You killed Lena."

Her over-plucked eyebrows arched in surprise. "I most certainly did not."

"She was blackmailing you and you killed her. You were looking for whatever it was she had on you and you made it look like a failed robbery."

The condescending stare was back. "You graduated from Mount Hope High School. Spent over three years taking care of your invalid mother in the dump of a trailer you called home only to have her kill herself with a handful of pills pulled from the bedside table when you weren't watching." She pressed her lips together, an expression meant to convey carefully crafted sympathy. "After another six months of depressed mourning, you enrolled in community college, then finished a degree in journalism at Penn State, living all the while on a shoestring. But alas, the Bloom family tradition continues, and you find yourself back where you started—nowhere."

This time she didn't bother with the pretense of warmth. "Do I have that right, Casey Bloom? I did my own research, you know."

I watched her, wondering how she knew that much about me. I shouldn't have been surprised. Maria Bendroit had made millions as a defense attorney before retiring from the law and turning her passion to environmental causes. Surely she had resources I could only imagine.

I said, "What do you have to do with the Daughters?"

"Poor Maggie. We all sympathized with her plight."

"Lena wouldn't be blackmailing you for sympathizeing. She must have discovered another connection."

Maria put her cup down, hard. "Come now. For an intellectual powerhouse like yourself, that should be obvious."

Bonnie snickered. The short one reentered the kitchen and helped herself to an apple from a bowl by the prep sink. "Has she given up the goods yet?"

Maria didn't answer. She nodded instead at Roe, who lifted her gun and pointed it toward me. "This is getting tiresome."

Only I was starting to see what had happened. "The Daughters couldn't have pulled this off on their own. The dam was secure. The Daughters would need financeing, someone with connections to get past security and monitors. Someone like you."

"They have money," Bonnie protested. "That woman up here, Wheelhouse—"

Shortie silenced Bonnie with a look.

I pursed my lips, feigned confusion, all the while keeping my eyes on that gun. "I wouldn't have seen you for a bleeding heart, Maria. Why Maggie? You didn't represent her. Had you, she would never have been killed."

"True."

I could see the logic now. "You had other reasons for wanting The Daughters to succeed. The Big Dam. It's long been an eyesore, a concern for environmentalists. Helping the Daughters helped your cause."

Maria's smile blossomed, long and slow. "You're definitely Lena's niece."

Lena. How'd she fit into all of this? But before I could ask any more questions, the sound of sirens acted like a trigger. All at once, the four women started clamoring.

"Roe, outside. Keep watch." To Bonnie, Maria ordered, "Tie her up in the basement. There's a tarp set up down there. Hurry. We'll need another means of getting this information out of her."

Maria started collecting papers and notebooks from the island. She strolled past me, arms full, reeking of the kind of confidence only those who never knew hardship can have, and headed toward the fire burning in the fireplace, at the other end of the cavernous room. She threw the papers into the fire. Real wood, lots of smoke. She waved her hand, gasped at the fumes, and took a step back.

"Easy for you to be holier than thou," I said, anger boiling. "Up here in your fortress, away from the riffraff. You could house three families in this place, easy. That's a lot of consumption for someone so concerned about the environment."

Maria's jaw set. "What are you two idiots waiting for? Get her down there, now."

44

Bonnie grabbed my hands from behind, pulled me up off the stool. Roe kept the gun steady. Is this what they'd done to Lena? All in the name of two righteous causes.

"She's using you," I said. "You want Maggie's death to mean something, but I bet Maria pulled strings behind the scenes. Made sure Maggie was executed. She wanted you to blow that dam."

"That's enough." Maria's voice—a warning growl.

Bonnie shoved me. I landed on my knees. As the short one yelled at Bonnie, I lunged forward, plowing into Shortie's legs, bowing her knees backwards. She screamed, toppled, and the gun flew from her hands. I scrambled for it, stood. Sidling backwards, I kept the gun steady, aimed at one head, then another. I backed toward the kitchen door.

"You don't want to do that," Maria said. "Calm down. Be smart." That condescending half-grin. I wanted to rip that smile off Maria's face. "There's no need to panic. We're all on the same side."

But I knew there was no way in hell they were going to let me go now. I'd end up like Lena, a casualty of whatever crazy war Maria and The Daughters were fueling.

Shortie dove for me. I aimed for her legs, pulled the trigger. Shortie went down.

I waved the gun, feeling crazy make its way up my spine, into my brain. Maybe crazy had been there all along, a genetic link to my beautiful aunt. "You two, in the basement." I herded Maria and Bonnie into the stairway, flicked off the light from outside the doorway, and locked the door from the kitchen. I pulled up a stool, wedging it beneath the handle. Forcing myself to stay calm, I grabbed a coat off a hook by the mud room, a flashlight from the counter, a paring knife from a kitchen drawer—and gloves, plus the gun. And the car keys—which were sitting by an espresso maker on the island. I had my phone. I'd need it.

The basement door was rattling. Bonnie and Maria were screaming, kicking. I tuned them out. I knew who I needed to talk to. If only I could find him.

Roe gave no resistance. Mainly because I clocked her on the back of the head before she saw me coming. The tall woman went down, her body hitting the pavers with a thud. Below me was the town of Everton, set out like a giant chess board. Emergency lights and fires flashed, reflecting off the dark, swirling water. The river would be cold. I shivered, climbed into the car, and floored it. I wanted distance from Maria's home. The car hugged a winding ridge. I felt thankful to be alive.

A few miles away, I parked in a dark lot behind a billboard touting the benefits of "clean coal" and pulled out my cell. Digging Big Earl's business card from my pocket, I dialed his number. No answer. I tried again. And again. It was hopeless, I knew. If Maria and her minions were following me, they might know about Earl. If the flood or the looters hadn't gotten to him, they might have.

I was about to hang up when someone answered. The voice was low, gravelly, but distinctly his. "You trying to get me killed?"

"Earl, this is Casey. Lena's niece."

"Yeah?"

"We need to talk."

He snorted. "Now isn't a good time."

"It's about my aunt. Some people grabbed me tonight. They thought I had something of theirs."

A long pause during which I heard more sirens, shouting.

"You know there's a fucking flood, right? I'm on a fucking cruise ship. Heading downstream, toward the hills section."

"Can you get to dry ground?"

Silence. Then, "Yeah, I think so. Know where the Midas is? On Pine? I can pull out if you can get there."

I knew the section he was talking about. It was on the edge of the business district, not far from the neighborhoods on the hills—where I was now. "I'm on my way."

More shouts from Earl's end, water splashing. Even from my spot up here in the woods, above the mayhem happening in Everton, I could hear the river raging, taste the burnt air. Smoke smelled a lot like desperation.

"Don't fucking forget, Casey. I may have some answers for you."

I hung up, tucking the gun in my pocket, the knife in my sock, and headed out of the beautiful homes in Neverland, toward the hell that was Everton proper.


Big Earl looked flattened, broken—just like the Big Dam. He glanced around furtively before climbing into the borrowed Chevy, his Adam's apple bobbing to the beat of his anxiety. He was soaked. His cruise ship was a decrepit canoe he must have stolen.

"I never thought they'd do it." He sat back, stared

straight ahead. "I didn't think those nut jobs would go through with it. Lena said they would. I didn't really believe her."

"You knew about this?"

"There was a letter. From some crazies call themselves The Daughters, or some such nonsense. Anyway, they threatened to blow the dam, just like Lena said they would. She knew. She fucking knew."

I started the car and headed south, away from Everton, away from the stench and the smoke and the sirens. I didn't trust Earl, but I didn't much think he'd try to overpower me. We drove in silence, weaving our way past fire trucks and ambulances and cop cars and vehicles parked along the side of the road. In the distance, I saw the National Guard. I let the heft of that sink in. The National Guard. In Everton. And I was in a stolen car.

When we were far enough from Everton that I could think, I asked, "What was Lena up to?"

Earl was watching out the window, his skinny claw-like hands clutching his knees. "Like I said, she knew about this mess before it happened."

"How?"

He shrugged. "How'd Lena know anything? Talking to people, deducing things. Screwing around."

He said the last words like he was spitting out poison, and I knew right then that he'd made the ultimate mistake: he'd fallen in love with Lena. Like that, my gut turned sour, my head began to pound. No good came of loving Lena Bloom.

I said, "She must have had some connections. Who'd she know in Everton?"

"She didn't tell me nothing. Just to put my things on high shelves. Anything worth saving."

I pulled up alongside an embankment and waited while an ambulance passed.

"Earl, do you have any idea who killed my aunt?"

His eyes shifted, he grabbed his knees with those claws. "Someone who wanted what she had, I suspect."

"And what was that, Earl? What did Lena have?"

This time, Earl met my gaze. "I don't know."


We'd driven around in circles. Earl didn't want to stray too far from Everton, and I was, by this point, a fugitive in a stolen car. Only the chaos of the night had prevented the police from tracking me down, but the farther I got from Everton, the more likely no one would buy my story of kidnapping and escape. Especially from Everton's beloved Maria Bendroit. If she dared tell, that is.

We had to ditch the car. I needed my own car, still parked by the Sleepy Time Motel. And I needed to ditch Earl, especially because his questions had become far too personal and on point.

"Whose car is this?" Earl glanced around the interior of the Chevy. "Not yours. Smells like cigarettes. Lena said you didn't smoke."

Now he gets smart. "Belongs to a friend."

"What friend? Lena said you didn't know anyone in Everton."

"Lena told you a lot about me."

Earl shrugged. He'd changed from his funeral garb to a flannel shirt and khaki pants, and the hem of the pants were soaked and sooty.

"She told me she was making amends. Penance for something bad she'd done."

"Yeah, well, some things can't be undone."

"She wanted to try."

I ignored Earl as we approached Butler Avenue, near the old plant. I pulled along the road as far as I could go—about a block from The Sleepy Time. The street ahead was cordoned off by emergency workers in yellow gear, and it looked like everything beyond—including the motel's parking lot—was submerged under water.

I jammed the car in reverse and started to turn around. I was three-quarters through the K-turn when I felt his hand on my thigh. It wasn't a lascivious touch. He was outlining the edge of my gun through my jeans with one finger.

Voice low and menacing, Earl said, "Who grabbed you tonight, Casey?"

"Some people."

"Who?"

All pretense of playing nice gone now, Earl squeezed my thigh. "This ain't your car. I saw your car at the funeral. You're packing a gun. Lena said you was a straight arrow, not the kind to steal cars, carry a gun."

I didn't trust Earl any more than I believed Maria was involved in this mess for the good of disenfranchised women. I pounded on the gas, heading once again away from Everton.

Forcing a steady voice, I said, "Some people grabbed me. Women. I fought back, stole the gun and the car." I glanced at Earl. "I'm trying to figure out why."

Earl's mouth twisted into a frown. "I may know the why of it." He paused, that Adam's apple bouncing in his throat. "Can I trust you, Casey?"

My turn to weave and bob. "Of course."

"Lena left me her papers. I can't make no heads or tails of them, but maybe you can."

"Where are they?"

"In my house. But it's flooded. Not so bad as some others—" he looked down at my sneakers, up at my stolen coat, "—But we'll need some waders. Or that canoe."

I stared at the horizon, wishing there was another way. Finally, I nodded. "Let's go, then."


Earl lived in a brick row home on the outskirts of the business quarter of Everton. Getting there was a challenge. The canoe was gone, but we hitched a ride on a motor boat under the pretense of saving Earl's cat.

We waded through what was left of the living room— a sopping brown velour couch circa 1972, a floating stool, an empty liquor cabinet (apparently the booze had been worth saving), and the detritus you might expect of a single man with a misspelled business card, including beer cans, the soppy remnants of a *Penthouse*, and Chinese food takeout containers bobbing along the water like drifting luminarias. Earl ran upstairs and came back with a box. Inside was a manila envelope, secured by rubber bands. He handed me the contents, which I perused with my stolen flashlight.

Lena had housed her materials in a blue, thin, plastic cover, the kind you would use to protect a report. Inside lay a small stack of papers, pulled together with a binder clip. I paged through the materials, a random collage of

photocopies and notes. News articles on the environmental impacts of big hydroelectric plants. Photos of
Maggie and her defense counsel. Pictures of the court
house. A handwritten note with Pastor Lewis's name on
it. Publicly available information on Maggie, her family,
the rapists, and the events that led to her incarceration.
A few other scraps that made no obvious sense.

"See? It's all shit." Earl jabbed a finger at the picture I
was holding, of James Manning, one of Maggie's so-
called victims. There was also a photo of the judge pre-
siding over the case, and he grabbed that from my hand.
"She was crazy as those liberal nutters who blew the
Dam. Blackmailing people with nothin' to show for it."
He shook his head violently. "Damn woman."

"It is crazy," I agreed.

"So this don't make no sense to you, either?" Earl had
a gleam in his eye, one that made me think about that
knife tucked in my sock.

"No, afraid not."

I thought about Maria Bendroit and her merry band
of kidnappers. Surely they were out of their makeshift
jail by now. Maria was desperate to keep Lena quiet. But
for this? Lena couldn't prove anything with this hodge-
podge of documents.

"Is this all she left?"

"Crazy." Another head shake. Earl seemed to be
thinking hard, an act that appeared painful. "Damn
woman. I can't fucking believe it."

"Can't believe what?"

Earl didn't respond. In that silence, I heard water
dripping in the kitchen, smelled charred wood and mil-
dew and damp, rotting plaster. I shoved the papers back

in the plastic casing, hugging the file to my chest, and pushed away from the wall toward the door. I suddenly wanted out of that row home. Now.

Earl reached out. "The file, Casey."

"I'm keeping it Earl. Lena meant for me to have it."

"She gave it to me."

I clutched the file harder. "But there's nothing here. Nothing worth saving."

Earl lunged, but I was younger, quicker, and fitter. I cleared what had been the floor of his living room and put the couch between him and me. We stood there, dueling stares across a murky abyss. I reached for my gun, tucking the file inside my coat. Earl pulled a switchblade from his pocket.

"Doesn't need to be this way, Casey. We can be partners, just like me and Lena was."

The flashlight danced shadows across Big Earl King's face, and I knew he was lying. I knew because what lay inside this folder was a puzzle of mismatched, seemingly random pieces that only someone who understood Lena's brand of jigsaw crazy could put together. This was code, and if Lena had trusted Big Earl, there'd have been no need for code.

"You killed her."

"Give me the file. And tell me who the fuck jumped you tonight."

"When Lena wouldn't tell you what she was up to, you attacked her. Figured you'd get the goods and finish the blackmail scheme yourself. Only after the so-called robbery, you realized you have no idea what's in here, what this means." Sirens wailed. Yellow lights from the flooded street outside the house poured into the living room, a jarring reminder of what was going down in Everton. "You murdered Lena for nothing."

"Give me the file, Casey."

"No."

"She was my girl. Would want me to see this through."

Such a sad, disillusioned man. This part of the puzzle came together with startling clarity. Lena would have made her contacts in this town, sniffing around for an angle. With her job at the courthouse, it wouldn't have taken her long to realize something was up. Some research, a few harmless conversations, maybe a friendship or two, and Lena would have pieced together what was happening. She'd have seen her opportunity to cash in—and make amends. Blackmailing a woman like Maria Bendroit was genius. It was also utterly stupid. But then, that was Lena.

Poor Earl...again, I almost felt sorry for him. Almost. He may have been a connection to this town, or a place to sleep, or who knew, maybe under that skinny frame was a hell of a lay. Whatever Lena's reasons for her liaison with Earl, he hadn't been her partner. And she hadn't trusted him—or anyone else. If he'd been her partner, he'd have known he was holding a puzzle. If he had been her partner, Maria and her goons would have come after him. Like the other Earls, Big Earl was a chess piece, to be used and discarded when the time came.

Only Lena misjudged this Earl. He wasn't quite as easy to snow as the others.

Earl lunged across the couch, aiming his knife at my face, his own frozen in a snarl of hate and vengeance. I reacted quickly, pulling the trigger, feeling the reverberations course down my arm and across my shoulders. Earl's body flopped down on the couch, a flaccid reproach to this night of violence.

I didn't need to feel for a pulse. The hole in his chest said Big Earl wouldn't be faking any more robberies, killing any more women.

I waited only a moment before making up my mind. After wiping the gun clean of prints, I tucked it in the couch, by Earl. It had been Roe's gun, and if it was still here once the waters finished rising, the police could sort that out. I doubted they'd have any sympathy for a Daughter, and I doubted even more that Maria would want to shine a light on her connection to The Daughters' baser elements.

Shutting off the flashlight, I left the row home in the cover of darkness, wading back out into the frigid Sea of Everton. The water was up to my chest, so I carried the file above my head, keeping it safe. It wasn't long before I was rescued, all that I needed clutched in my hands.


Lena's final puzzle was a doozy. It took me weeks to piece together all the clues, but once I realized that Pastor Lewis was the key to another store of information, the rest was easy. Lena had, in the end, trusted a man of God with her funeral *and* her personal belongings. Once Lena had realized she was in danger, she'd asked him to keep a lockbox for safe keeping. The good pastor had done so, succumbing, no doubt, to Lena's charms just as surely as Adam had fallen for Eve. Little did he know he had the makings for one hell of a blackmail scheme stored up in his attic, where the flood waters couldn't go.

55

Maria Bendroit was only one of Lena's marks. She had dirt on the judge, Maggie's rapists, Chief Wilcox, even Maggie's defense counsel and the Everton Energy Company. The picture she painted was one of deceit, graft, and greed—with poor Maggie at the center.

I left Everton the day after the flood, Harrisburg five days later. Mexico suits me, with its sunny shores and spicy men. I received the advance for my exposé in time to buy my own house, but the greatest satisfaction will be unmasking the full depravity of the train wreck that was Maggie's trial and execution—and the revenge that followed. Lena was right. This was the "big one."

I should have known she'd come through.

# THE COPY MAN

J.J. Hensley

*Problem:*

*Three women are pointing loaded rifles at your head. You're holding a revolver that may or may not function. Water from a massive flood is filling the room like sand accumulating at the bottom of an hour glass. Time is running out and you can't stay here. The assailants, hurling a mixture of commands and threats, won't let you leave. You can't wait to be rescued because the police are not your friends. One false move, one misconstrued twitch, or one hiccup may cause anxious trigger fingers to contract. Oh, and you have an unconscious man bound and gagged behind the counter of this print shop.*

*Solution:*

*Change the math.*

"Put the gun down!" screamed the tallest of the women for the third time. Her upper body was mostly dry, but she was soaked from the waist down. While I would have liked to have thought my steely demeanor, my five o'clock shadow that I'd been growing for two weeks, and the silver gun I was choking to death had frightened her to the point she'd wet herself, I considered this possibility unlikely.

She yelled again. I kept the pistol trained on her while using my peripheral vision to keep track of her two associates who were sloshing their way through ankle-deep water to opposite corners of the room. The battery-powered lantern next to the cash register seemed to emit as many shadows as beams of light, causing me some difficulty in tracking the women flanking each side of my position. The husky woman sliding to my right wasn't the alpha of the pack, but the way she seemed to glide by side-stepping, never once crossing her feet, hinted of tactical prowess. Her smooth motions kept the barrel of her gun steady and betrayed a history of military or law enforcement training. Training I'd gone through a lifetime ago.

The woman stumbling around on my left was a different story, and I knew I could wait to deal with her. With no cover and no hostage in my grasp, I figured I was going to catch a bullet any second. It wouldn't have been the first time I'd been shot, but I don't like picking up bad habits.

"Ten pounds of pressure," I said calmly to the alpha I had lined up in the sights of the revolver.

"What?"

"This is a hammerless Smith & Wesson .38. Without the hammer visible, you probably can't gauge how much pressure I'm applying to the trigger. It's about ten pounds. It fires at twelve, I think. I just wanted you to know. If something was to happen and I'm subjected to a sneeze, a cough, or a bullet in the head from your friend maneuvering around that Xerox over there, I might accidentally find those other two pounds of pressure. Of course, I'm kind of guessing on the twelve-pound pull. It might be eleven."

The alpha forced a grin, her eyes shifted to her left. She said, "Hold your position, Betty." Her eyes flicked to her right. "You too, Lisa."

The husky woman, Betty, floated to a stop at a diagonal angle from my position behind a counter that I was certain wasn't bulletproof. Lisa, obviously the youngest of the trio, froze inches short of a concealing shadow, confirming my suspicion that this was all new to her.

"Are you Snyder?" asked the alpha.

"That's what the sign above the door says."

She took a step in my direction, unconcerned with giving me an easier shot.

"You're going to help us," she said.

"Sure. Color copies will cost you a dollar each, unless it's a bulk order. Or, perhaps you ladies are updating your resumes. We have a fantastic selection of resume paper. What is it you do for a living?"

"Jesus Christ, Megan," said Betty as she took a half-step my way and adjusted her grip on the rifle, which was attached to a sling draped across her body. "I told you this was a mistake. Let's forget this and rejoin the others."

Megan, apparently not appreciating the challenge to her alpha status, glared at the other woman before turning her attention back to me.

"You deal in papers," she said, punctuating the statement by jabbing an assault rifle a few inches forward.

I stayed silent and waited.

"Don't play dumb with me either, copy man. You

know what I'm talking about."

I did know what she was talking about. I knew all too well what she was talking about.

"Who are you?" I asked.

The three women exchanged glances and Megan and Betty found amusement in my question. Lisa, the church mouse, faked something between a giggle and snort before shifting her weight uncomfortably.

Megan lowered her weapon and asked, "Is that supposed to be funny?"

I shook my head.

Betty straightened up and said, "We're the Daughters, you idiot."

"Oh," I said, not comprehending. Betty squinted and seemed to expect more of a reaction from me. "So...do I know your mother or something?"

Legitimate snickering started and then abruptly stopped from Lisa's side of the room.

"Don't be cute," Betty spat. "You know who we are and you certainly never knew my mother."

"You never know," I said. "I'm not proud of it, but I slept with one or two strippers in my younger days. What was your mother's stage name?"

Betty stepped forward with surprising quickness and positioned her rifle across her body in an obvious attempt to club me with the butt end. When she was less than three feet from me, I swung my arm in her direction, shot her in the head, and immediately brought the gun back to Megan as the two of us resumed aiming at each other. Lisa joined in by willing her trembling hands to point the gun at my skull. None of us spoke. None of us pulled a trigger.

*Problem:*

*Two women have guns pointed at your head. You have a revolver that now contains one less bullet because you sent one through the brain of your aggressors' colleague. Both tensions and the water level are rising rapidly. Even when taking into account the apparent timidity of one of the assailants, you appear to be outnumbered and your options are few. Oh, and the unconscious man you have restrained behind the counter is starting to wake up.*

*Solution:*

*Talk and keep your enemies talking. People rarely pull triggers while they are talking. Rarely.*

"She caused me to find those two pounds of pressure," I said. "This is a five-shot revolver and I have four rounds left. I don't want to use any of them but I will."

Keeping the gun pointed at Megan, I slowly drifted around the counter until I reached Betty's body. With one hand, I grabbed the sling attached to Betty's rifle and slid it over her head. Dangling the rifle by the sling, I retreated behind the counter and placed the rifle on a shelf underneath the countertop. In addition to the water that was now well above my ankles, I sensed some motion around my feet. The source of that motion was going to be another issue in a room full of serious issues.

Megan, who had been at a loss for words, seemed to have dug around in the lost and found and retrieved a few. "You son of a bitch!" she bellowed.

"What?" I asked.

"You killed her. You...you just killed her."

"Of course I did," I said. "You're welcome."

Pressing the stock of the rifle to her shoulder and leaning forward, she said, "You're welcome? You killed one of us and you think I should be thanking you?"

"Yes," I said. "Come on, admit it. I saw it in your eyes when she questioned your decision to come here in the first place. Part of you knew this would never work with her on board. Whatever it is you ladies did, you want to get away free and clear and you need false identity documents. My services don't come cheap and I don't work with people I don't trust. I didn't trust her and I don't think you trusted her. She was a hothead. In the end it's all about maintaining your poise, right?"

Megan's protest wasn't quite strong enough and it came a beat too late.

"She was one of us," Megan finally said.

I stole a glance at Lisa to see if my words had had any impact. In that fraction of a second I saw it. The seed had been planted.

"Like I said, whatever you did must have gotten law enforcement on your trail. You should probably get going."

Megan was incredulous. "Whatever we did? Whatever we did? You're standing in what we did. You're witnessing the reckoning that has occurred since this state chose to execute Maggie Wilbourne. We warned all of you that this would happen and the destruction of the dam was only the beginning."

I had no idea what she was talking about. They blew up a dam? Well, that would explain why I was feeling nervous about not having my water wings with me.

"That doesn't make any sense," I told her.

Lisa seemed to be coming unglued and was pacing the wall to my left. She traveled a little further every time she walked toward the back wall. If she kept this up, that could create another problem. While I kept the pistol pointed at Megan, my attention was starting to drift toward Lisa.

"Hey!" Megan snapped.

"I'm sorry, what?"

"What the hell is wrong with you, Mr. Snyder? Am I boring you?"

"Malcolm," I said. "You may as well call me Malcolm."

Her mouth gaped and I thought she was going to scream at me some more, but then she said, "While you were zoning out, I asked you what you meant when you said what we did didn't make any sense."

"Oh, that," I said.

Lisa splashed another path through the water, pivoted, and headed toward the back wall again.

"Actually, two things don't make sense," I said. "The first is that you didn't approach me sooner to get new driver's licenses, birth certificates, and passports. Which is what I assume you want. You should have come to me before you blew up the dam. Now you're screwed."

The anger on Megan's face started to transition to concern. "Why is that?"

"Look around," I said. "I can't do a damn thing for you—no pun intended."

"What pun?" she asked.

"I said 'Damn.'"

"Yeah. And?" said Megan.

I blinked.

"Never mind," I continued. "The point is, your group knocked out the power. No electricity means no fake IDs. The special computers and printers I use aren't powered by hamsters running on wheels. I need power."

She grinned, which suddenly made me nervous.

She said, "Nice try, Malcolm."

Lisa was still strolling around and running one hand through tangled black hair and holding an SKS rifle with the other. She was nearly even with the counter and would have a clear view from the side at any moment.

"I did my research on you," Megan spat. "You have a generator for the special equipment you need and all of it is in the building out back, just up the hill."

"The generator," I said dumbly.

"Uh-huh," she said confidently.

Trying to reassert myself, I said, "Creating the papers you need takes time. I have to take your photos and make sure all the right security measures are in place. If you want passports, it's better if I create ones with new identities and with realistic stamps that show some moderate travel. These things can take weeks."

Looking around and the water surrounding us and doing some sort of rough calculation in her mind, she said, "I'm guessing you have thirty minutes before the building out back is destroyed."

"I won't do it," I replied.

"You will," she said, holding up a walkie-talkie. "Or I'll call in the cavalry and you'll have to deal with dozens of us."

"Megan," said Lisa almost inaudibly.

Ignoring her friend, Megan said to me, "So, you will do this."

I thought about the trio's arrival after the act of terrorism and the disagreement Betty had voiced before I'd helped resolve the argument. All of this had the feel of something off-script.

"No. You can't call anyone," I said. "Because running wasn't part of the deal, was it?"

Her expression soured.

"Megan," Lisa said again, but Megan's eyes stayed fixed on mine.

"You were supposed to be martyrs," I said. "This was a one-way trip, but the three of you decided to call an audible. Your group doesn't know you're here and you can't call them."

I had her. I'd won. I'd observed, reasoned, deduced, and prevailed. All in all, it was quite a bloodless coup. Well, minus Betty's corpse now floating around and banging into the Coke machine.

"You're right," Megan admitted. "This was a suicide mission for my team. Coming to you was the only way we were going to get out of this alive."

I smiled with confidence.

"If you aren't going to work with us, then I suppose Lisa and I can't escape clean. We decided from the start that we wouldn't want to live as fugitives. So, we'll have to revert back to our original mission." Megan turned her head to her friend and nodded. "Lisa, get ready. If he gets me first, you take him out."

I smiled with less confidence.

*Damn.*

You can reason with criminals. You can bargain, haggle, and persuade.

Suicidal zealots are a different matter altogether.

From somewhere out of my view, Lisa said, "Megan, there's something—"

Tilting her head toward the rifle, Megan said, "I'm sorry we couldn't do business Mr. Snyder."

I stopped smiling altogether. In fact, I couldn't remember why I was smiling in the first place. Smiling is stupid.

"Wait, wait," I said as I lowered my gun to my side. "Maybe we can work something out."

It was Megan's turn to smile. "I was hoping you would see it my way. Now, what was the other thing?"

I gave her a questioning look.

"You said there were two things that didn't make sense. Us not contacting you in advance was the first. What was the second?"

I inhaled deeply and tried to recall what I'd been thinking. Then it came to me.

"You said the name of the woman who was executed was named Maggie?"

"Yeah," said Megan.

"Are any of you related to her?"

"No," she replied.

"Then why is your group called the Daughters?"

Her smile vanished and she said, "What difference does it—"

"Megan!" Lisa yelled so loudly that I worried we were all going to shoot each other simply out of astonishment.

"What?" Megan shouted in annoyance.

"Mr. Snyder has a man tied up behind the counter. He's on the floor and the water is up to his chest. I think the guy might be dead."

Megan's eyes returned to me.

I pressed my lips together and hoped the moment of curiosity would pass for the visitors. It didn't.

Megan cocked her head. "Mr. Snyder?"

"Malcolm," I said.

"Malcolm. Do you have a man tied up behind your counter?

I nodded. "Just one."

"I see," said Megan.

We all stood in as much silence as there can be when water is flowing around your knees.

Finally, Megan said, "Malcolm?"

"Yes."

"Is he dead?"

Right on cue, the man let out a deep moan. I shook my head in response to Megan's question.

She asked, "Who is the man tied up behind the counter?"

"Oh. That's Cyprus Keller," I said. "He's a customer too."


*Problem:*

*Two suicidal women have guns pointed at your head. They are intending to force you to create false identity documents for them. The man you have tied up and gagged is slowly starting to come to, and his participation in this gathering could become a serious issue. Actually, his waking up will probably get you killed.*


*Solution:*

*Introduce doubt, which creates hesitation, into your adversary's plan and misdirect to create opportunity.*

"You have a customer tied up? I don't think so," said Megan.

"He's not a legitimate customer. His interests are similar to yours," I explained.

Megan's face showed a trace of amusement. Lisa's expression conveyed confusion. Another groan from beneath the counter told me to hurry the hell up.

Megan said, "I have to question your definition of customer service, Mr. Snyder. I doubt the man you are holding captive will want to give you any repeat business."

Noting the growing fatigue in my right arm, I switched the revolver to my left hand while never taking the business end of the weapon off Megan.

"I never have repeat customers for that portion of my business," I said. "My work is beyond reproach and the people I assist have no reason to return." This train of thought made me think of something else to say. "How did you hear about me? My document customers come through trusted referrals."

Megan seemed to weigh my question with the care of a bomb technician disabling an IED.

"Timothy Sutton."

*Yahtzee!* I thought. I had finally caught a break.

In an intentionally suspicious tone, I asked, "Is he still working out of that bar on Dashofy Street in Pittsburgh? Showing off that damn Captain America tattoo to anyone who passes by?"

Megan smirked. "Tim never really worked a day in his life. But he still inhales whiskey and exhales cigar smoke in the corner booth at Drake's Pool Hall at the intersection of Martin and Tremel. And his Ironman tattoo is hideous."

I gave an approving nod, letting her know she had passed the test. Lisa slid in behind the other end of the counter. She was eyeing the man slouched near my feet and appeared to be growing concerned. Her eyes darted between me, him, and some papers splayed out on a ledge behind the counter.

"The water is getting up toward his chin," said Lisa. "He's going to drown."

Megan looked like she was about to dismiss her friend's concern for the semiconscious man slumped on the floor, but curiosity got the better of her.

"So, what's with this Cyprus Keller guy."

I noticed Lisa take another glimpse at the papers behind the counter.

"He's dead," I said.

"I heard him groan," Megan replied.

"No," I explained. "He got himself in a bind and is believed to be dead. Keller and I had arranged everything and he came in today to pick up the finished products. I had the documents for him and his wife, he had the cash, but the transaction went south."

"I can see that," said Megan. "Explain."

I took a deep breath, as if gathering the strength to explain a situation that I found to be an inconvenience was every bit as great as dealing with the aftermath of a group of nutcases blowing up a dam and wiping out a town to avenge some woman who probably deserved the gas chamber. Lisa crept closer, but was still out of reach. Her full attention was now on the folded newspaper and handwritten notes on the shelf that was only a couple of feet above the waterline.

I began giving my explanation of the business. "The

prices I set for my illicit commerce are based on several factors: Costs of raw materials. The intricacy of the work. The need for an expedited completion date. The overall depth of a legend, or background, for the new identity." I paused for a moment and hesitantly added, "And, I admit, the perceived need of the customer can come into play when I'm determining my fee."

Megan picked up on my reticence. "You mean you'll jack-up the prices if they're desperate."

I shrugged. "I make adjustments for those who are involved in high-profile matters that garner press attention."

Megan's expression became a scowl. "That's low," she said. "You're low."

From the periphery, I saw Lisa lean down closer to the papers, inspecting the partial article from the *Pittsburgh Tribune-Review*. She reached down to the counter as if she was going to unfold the paper, but retracted her hand when I turned my head her direction and spoke loudly.

"Hey, I'm not a bad guy!" I protested. "Keller was high-profile. I didn't even know who he was at first because I don't ask questions about real identities. But I happened to find out Keller came with a lot of unwanted attention and that increased my risk level. It's only fair that I adjust my prices when I become aware of the increased exposure to my business."

I had to admit, I was impressed with my businesslike rationalization. Extremely impressed.

Megan was unimpressed. With no shortage of animosity, she said, "You tell people you'll help them and you give them a set price. But when you pick up on the scent of desperation, you extort them. I know the whole 'honor among thieves' thing is a load of crap, but that makes you the worst kind of parasite. We ought to kill you now and carry out our original mission."

I looked down the barrel of Megan's rifle, swallowed hard and wondered if my next gulp would help pull one of her bullets down my esophagus. My grip around the pistol at my side tightened and I made the decision that I was better off taking my chances and firing a round at Megan before spinning to confront Lisa—who very well could have killed me by that time. The only thing holding me back was the thought of my wife. I could almost hear her voice in my head telling me to be patient. She'd beg me to think things through and not simply react. Then, she'd tell me that if the time came and there was no other option, I'd have to kill these crazy bitches who were jeopardizing our future together.

That's why I love that woman.

My brain was calling my revolver-holding hand into action when Lisa spoke.

"He's telling the truth," she said.

The muscles in my gun hand relaxed and I resumed breathing.

"There's an article here about Keller. It's on the front page of the newspaper. And Mr. Snyder has some notes written out on a pad back here. It looks like Keller was referred by Tim Sutton, just like we were and that today was the pickup date. Since the newspaper article is laid out here like this, I think it went down like Mr. Snyder said it did. At the last minute, he must have figured out who Keller was and that his face was recognizable. So, Mr. Snyder raised the prices, like he said he does sometimes, and Keller must not have liked the deal being changed. They fought and Mr. Snyder knocked him out and tied him up until he could decide what to do with him." Looking at me, she said, "Isn't that right, Mr. Snyder?"

*Bravo, kid. Bravo.*

"That's right. You walked in on the tail end of a business dispute. That's all."

The man on the floor stirred again as the murky water lapped up on his bottom lip. His eyes opened and I delivered a hard kick to his jaw.

"What did you do that for?" Megan asked.

"He was waking up," I replied. "No need to have him complicating matters."

"Why haven't you killed him yet? There's gunfire erupting all over town. Nobody would have noticed the shot."

I thought about this and said, "Because I was still negotiating with him on a new price. I'd say I was winning the negotiation, wouldn't you?"

Megan sighed. "Well, now you have to haul him to the building out back. It would have been a lot easier to have him walk on his own."

"Sorry," I said. "I didn't think of that."


*Problem:*

*Two women have guns pointed at your head. You have no choice but to create false identification documents for them. Although you are no longer standing in water, your new location will be completely underwater in thirty minutes or less. Your opponents are in possession of high-powered rifles, capable of carrying multiple rounds of ammunition. You have a revolver with four unspent rounds, but also a rifle from a woman you shot. At most, you have twenty-five minutes to create two false driver's licenses, passports, and birth certificates. It's an impossible task and the only person who might be able to assist you is unavailable because you knocked him unconscious. Again.*

*Solution:*

*Humans have an instinctual need to band together and cooperate in times of stress. Demand help from those who share your suffering because some primitive part of the brain will compel them to assist for the good of the clan.*

While I executed a fireman's carry to get Mr. Dead Weight a few yards up the hill, Lisa waded through the water down below and retrieved a raft that had been tethered to the front of the building. Walking uphill with Betty's rifle slung awkwardly over my shoulder, a pistol tucked in my pants, and an unconscious man weighing me down, I huffed up the incline, playing the part of the eternally tormented Sisyphus, forever pushing a boulder up a hill as punishment for his clever nature and deceitfulness.

Megan, rifle in one hand, lantern in the other, kept an eye on me as I grunted my way to the secondary building that was as dark as the first. By the time Megan and I had managed to get to the building's entrance, Lisa had already dragged the inflatable raft to the still-higher ground on the opposite side of the building where Megan and I now stood. Gunshots sounded in the distance. A man screamed with terror and the echo hung in the air until it too was washed away by the omnipresent noise of the rushing water below.

I put the unconscious man on the ground and tried turning the knob. The door was locked.

"I left the key in the other building," I said meekly.

"So?" Megan said. "Kick it in, genius."

I took a step back, picked out a spot under the oxidized deadbolt, and slammed my foot into the door. In the movies, the wooden door and frame would have splintered and the dynamic duo and I would have simply walked into the now-open building. In real-life Everton, Pennsylvania, I bounced off the door having felt the impact from the sole of my foot all the way through my molars.

"Ouch," I said gritting my teeth and consoling my pride.

"Pansy," said Megan, who once again tightened the stock of her rifle against her shoulder and took aim. For a second, I thought she'd decided to write me off as a bad investment and carry on with her original suicidal plan. But then she used her AR-15 to fire a three-round burst past me, into the deadbolt. The door, being intimidated more by the high-powered rounds than my size-ten running shoe, decided to give way. My ears were ringing from the blasts as I pushed the door open. Megan gave the lantern to Lisa, who was still catching her breath from retrieving the raft, and the two corralled me into the building.

"Drag Keller inside and then go get the lights on, copy man," Megan commanded. "We don't have much time."

I squinted into the semi-darkness but couldn't see

more than twenty feet in front of my position. I let my eyes adjust for a moment and then pulled the heavy body through the doorway, letting him come to rest nearby against a wall.

I turned to Lisa and said, "Give me the lantern."

Megan nodded to Lisa who cautiously handed me the light. I maneuvered my way between desks covered with papers and laptops, printers, binding machines, and laminating sheets. A mammoth offset printer sat at the far end of the room. With rage and weaponry pushing me along, I made my way to a back room that had one small rectangular window for ventilation. I spied an exhaust hose heading out the window and my eyes followed it back to a portable red generator. I leaned in close and read the instructions printed in tiny black font on the side of the machine.

"What the hell are you waiting for? Fire the thing up already," said Megan.

"I don't exactly use this thing every day," I explained. "It's been a while, so give me a second."

Following the instructions, I moved a couple of switches into the proper position, pressed a primer, and yanked on a pull cord. The generator erupted on the third try and the building came to life with the beeps and whirls produced by rebooting hardware. In the main workshop area, a few fluorescent lights flickered into action and illuminated a space used for both legal and illegal enterprises.

"What do we do first?" asked Lisa, who seemed to radiate worrisome impatience.

I scanned the room until my eyes settled on the vertical white screen dangling along the wall near the offset printer. A wooden stool was centered in front of the backdrop and a digital camera fixed on a tripod stood a few feet away. I decided the photos would have to wait for a few minutes while I set the scene.

"First, I need to enter your bogus identifiers into the documents I keep on my computer," I replied.

I walked around a few desks until I got to the one with the appropriate name plate. I took a seat in an uncomfortable chair that had rollers on the bottom. The chair wobbled slightly and I adjusted the height before settling in to do my work. The laptop in front of me had not restarted when the power came back on, so I pressed the power button to get things going. Megan took up a post on the other side of the desk. Lisa looked curious as she coasted around the desk and watched the computer monitor come to life. As luck would have it, the template for the last false passport created was still on the display and a portion of the customer's photo was visible at the bottom of the screen. The eyes in the photo sat right above the bottom border of the screen and Lisa leaned in to view the electronic template of a U.S. Passport.

"I need the passport books," I said to her sharply. "The ones for U.S. Passports. Go get them."

For the first time, she seemed to be offended by my abruptness and furrowed her brow in response to my command.

"Go get them yourself," she replied.

"Hey, do you two want me to finish these quickly or not? If so, I'm going to need a little help here."

"Well, how am I supposed to know where to find them?" she said.

I glanced around the room and noticed the safe near

the rear exit. From my vantage point, I couldn't tell whether it was still open from the bungled transaction for the Keller IDs.

While typing on the keyboard, I jutted my head in the direction of the steel box. "Check the safe and see if it's still open."

"What's the combination in case it's locked?" she asked.

"Just check it," I answered.

Reluctantly, she moved away and I periodically took peeks away from the monitor to watch her progress. Megan kept watching me as I tried not to show much interest in what Lisa was doing.

"What are you typing on that computer?" asked Megan.

I did my best to look annoyed at the question, which wasn't hard to do since I was.

"Not that it matters, but I need to set up the passport template and enter in false information that will pass inspection. Then, I'll plug in your photo before printing the page. I'll cut out the page, and insert it into a passport book."

I took my eyes off the monitor and looked Megan over. She was wearing an olive green jacket that looked like something out of an Army surplus store. Once again, I thought about the photography area set up next to the offset printer. Then, I glanced around the room at the various items of November-appropriate clothing hanging on coat racks and over the back of desk chairs. It was the typical office clothing carnage one saw during Pennsylvania autumns when a day might start out as sunny and fifty degrees and plummet into the twenties with heavy snow by lunchtime.

"You need to change clothes for the photo," I said.

"This isn't a fashion show," she replied. "This will do."

"It won't," I said. "Cops everywhere will be looking for anyone associated with your group. If you want a clean escape, then you need to transform yourself into something more respectable."

"What the hell is that supposed to mean?" she asked.

I ignored the question as Lisa shouted from across the room.

"Here they are!" she announced proudly, while holding up a stack of passport books.

"Before you bring them here," I said, "you and Megan need to look at some of the women's coats and sweaters that are in here. Dress up a bit and make yourselves appear harmless for the photos I'll be taking." My eyes shifted to one item in particular. It was folded neatly on a desk with a nameplate reading *Cindy Wilton*. I pointed to the desk and said, "Megan, I think Cindy might be your size. Check her desk over there. The photos are basically head shots, so don't worry about your pants."

Keeping the rifle pointed at me, Megan walked backwards and diagonally until she reached the desk. She rummaged through a few items on a neighboring coat rack and took a few in hand. I was afraid she'd return with only those items, but then she spotted the folded accessory on the desk. To my relief, she grabbed it as well. Simultaneously, Lisa scavenged another area and came up with a black shawl. She laid her rifle and the passport books on a desk and wrapped the shawl around her. A hint of a smile became visible on her face but vanished when she made a closer examination of the booklets she'd taken out of the safe. She flipped one open and then another.

"Hey, these passports already have pictures in them! And some of them are beat up and worn in places." She snatched the rifle from the desk with her free hand and began walking my direction. Megan was paying little attention while she leaned her rifle against a wall, removed her drab jacket and replaced it with a pink sweater. Then she held out the item from the desk and after what to me seemed an eternity, put it on as well before retrieving her weapon.

"I said, these passports have photos of other people in them," said Lisa who had gone from meek to angry.

"Relax," I said, as if in the history of the human race any man had been able to say that word to a woman and have it actually work. "Of course they have other photos inside."

Lisa stopped short of the desk and tossed the booklets the rest of the way to me. "Don't tell me to relax." She looked toward the open front entrance. There was enough light coming from our building to allow all of us to see the building we'd left earlier was nearly submerged. "The water is getting higher. How are these fake passports for other people going to help us?" Now Megan was refocused on the task at hand and was glaring at me.

My mind searched for a way to articulate an answer that would pacify the two. I gained a few more seconds as their attention was diverted to the man who was tied up near the doorway. His eyes were fluttering open and through a duct tape gag he grunted something that sounded like a question. I thought I made out something like *What the puck?*, so he must have been waking from a dream about hockey.

"Because they're real passports?" I said, drawing Megan and Lisa back to me. "How do you think some fake passports get made?" I said condescendingly. Nobody had a good answer, so I continued. "I've got a guy who works airports all over the East Coast and Midwest. He steals genuine passports and, for rush jobs like this one, I use the real documents and stamps as a base before doctoring them up with the forged papers and new photo. That way, the passports look and feel real to customs officers. This method has the added advantage of using genuine stamps indicating previous foreign travel."

"I guess that makes sense," said Megan quietly.

"Of course it does," I said. "Now if there's any chance for me to get these finished before this building goes underwater, then you need to do exactly what I say."

Megan didn't want to relinquish any of her bravado, but part of her seemed to understand the urgency of the situation.

"I'm almost done with the template, but I need to take photos." I stood and moved to the digital camera. "Megan, can you sit on the stool in front of the backdrop?"

Megan's eyes narrowed. "I suppose you'll tell me I need to put the rifle down too."

I shook my head. "I told you, these are basically head shots and I'll crop them into the page for the passport. I don't give a damn if you're holding a rocket launcher. Now hurry up."

She still hesitated.

I drew the revolver from my waistband, causing both the women to react with their rifles. "Look," I said. "I'm putting my gun on the desk."

I started to place the revolver on the flat surface, but stopped when the man slumped against the wall startled me by speaking coherently. The duct tape had become unstuck from one side of his mouth and now the silver adhesive was dangling from his face like a reflective tusk.

"What's going on. Why are you using—"

I fired a round that struck six inches above his head. "Not another word," I said, staring him down. "Not one more word. I'm working and I don't have time for you."

Megan opened her mouth to say something, but I cut her off. "Come on, we're out of time. Get on the stool before the power goes out again. That generator only has so much fuel inside."

I unslung the rifle from my shoulder and placed it and the revolver on the desk before striding over and waiting behind the camera. Slowly, Megan made her way to the stool. Lisa covered me with her rifle, her eyes darting back and forth between me and the stunned crook sitting on the floor, who was craning his neck to view the bullet hole in the wall above his head.

"Keep your eyes on Snyder, Lisa," Megan ordered.

Lisa put herself behind me at a forty-five-degree angle. A strong tactical position, especially on an unarmed individual. Megan sat, played around with her straggly brown hair in an attempt to make it presentable, and I snapped a couple of digital photos.

"I'm going to need more light," I said.

I walked over to a floor light to the right of the screen,

equidistant from Megan and the massive black Heidelberg offset printer that appeared to be something out of the 1970s. We were on the side of the printer that had two exposed horizontal cylinders, one aluminum and one vulcanized rubber. The two cylinders were positioned so close together that maybe an inch of space existed between the two. I flicked on the floor light and Megan squinted against the sudden brightness.

"What are you doing you idiot? You're going to blind me."

My gaze found the man bound on the floor who was trying to comprehend the strange circumstances in which he now found himself. One minute, he'd been standing by a counter in the front office, talking about a deal, and the next thing he knew he was watching me work out an impossible transaction with two armed lunatics. Now that he was able to speak, I needed for him to understand at least part of the situation.

To Megan, I said, "I'm not going to blind you, you idiot. I'm doing you a favor, so shut up."

She stood up from the stool and held the rifle waist-high.

"Do I need to remind you what your options are, Mr. Snyder? Our group doesn't give a damn about anybody in this town. We'll kill every last one of you. Just because my team had a change of heart about becoming martyrs for the cause, don't think we won't kill you and anybody else around here if need be. We were prepared to die for what we believe in and we still might decide to go through with it if you don't do your job. In fact, I haven't decided whether I'm going to kill you regardless."

"Fair enough," I mumbled. I snuck a look at the man

and could tell he had heard every word. I knew he had to be ecstatic to not be in my shoes at this precise moment. Beside the man, I could see that the water had already creeped up to within feet of our new location. We had even less time than Megan had estimated.

Megan started to sit back down on the stool. I stopped her by saying, "Hold on. I need to adjust the lighting without you in front of the backdrop. There's a shadow messing things up. Move over here." I gestured toward the offset printer.

Without argument, she did as I asked and I made a show of scrutinizing the backdrop. Scrunching up my face in mock frustration, I sighed and walked backwards toward Megan and the printer. Keeping my eyes on the backdrop, I stumbled around Megan until I was behind her with the printer to my side.

"Do you see that shadow?" I asked the ladies, causing them both to look at the backdrop.

I made quick eye contact with the man who was across the room and while keeping my right hand to my side, raised my index finger toward a knob on the printer. It took a moment for him to comprehend my intent, but then he shook his head in a nearly unperceivable manner.

"I don't see anything wrong with it," said Megan. "Just take the picture," she said, turned to me.

"It's still not quite right," I said, taking another step back. "Look at the left side of the backdrop. It's more dim over there."

Megan and Lisa cocked their heads and examined the backdrop.

I said, "I'll have to shift the lighting around, if these are going to look legit."

I lifted my finger and pointed toward a button on the printer. The man on the floor gave me a restrained but definitive nod. I moved quickly back in front of Megan and picked up the floor light. I pulled it next to the printer and turned the bulb toward Lisa, who had been quietly observing the process from several feet away. Lisa covered her eyes reflexively and I took advantage of the opportunity by pressing the button on the printer, which caused Megan to spin in my direction. Without hesitation, I used one hand to grip the scarf wrapped around her neck—the accessory that had been folded neatly on the desk—while my other hand pushed the barrel of her rifle in a safe direction. Megan fired the rifle into a wall while I yanked down hard on the scarf and loaded the dangling ends in-between the offset printer's aluminum and rubber cylinders that were now spinning violently. The machine took over and slammed Megan's face into the horizontal workings of the printer. Megan's hands released her rifle as she used both hands to grab at the tightening scarf.

"Help us," I yelled to Lisa, who was still trying to regain her vision as I acted as if I were trying to free Megan and stop the act of strangulation playing out in front of us.

Lisa dropped her rifle and ran over to try to free her friend. While she struggled to release the gasping and gurgling Megan, I slowly stepped back and retrieved both the rifles that had now been abandoned. From the corner of my eye, I noticed the man on the floor slink out the front entrance. With his hands still tied behind his back, he took off running. When he conceived of that idea, he must not have noticed the water was up to the entrance, because I saw him fall face first into the murkiness. I have no idea if he managed to survive.

"Megan! Megan!" Lisa yelled as she tried to save her friend. The machine relentlessly continued its work.

"Mr. Snyder, how do you turn off the machine?" she asked from a hunched over position, assuming I was still standing beside her.

Eventually, Lisa raised her head and noted my absence. She did a double-take and scanned the room until she found me. Her eyes widened as she watched me calmly loading up my spoils. I had to put down my newly acquired rifles to sling Betty's weapon over one shoulder and tuck the revolver away. I gripped the other rifles in each hand.

*Problem:*
*Three women with malicious intent enter a building. They think they have three guns and you have one.*

*Solution:*
*From the outset, you have to know in your heart and mind that the second they walked in the door with their three guns that the math was in your favor. They didn't know it, but they never had the advantage. They never really had three guns to your one. No. You tell yourself that the moment they entered the building with three guns to your one, you had four guns.*
*That's how you win.*
*That's how you change the fucking math.*

Lisa stared at me in confusion with one hand on Megan's lifeless body. I started walking toward the back door where she had placed the raft on ground that wouldn't be dry much longer.

"No," she said, willing the circumstances to be different. "No."

"Good luck," I said, continuing on my path.

"But...the fake passports? The driver's licenses?" she said. "You have to finish making them for me," she pleaded over the racket of the killer printer.

"I couldn't even if I wanted to," I said, not breaking stride.

She ran over to the laptop on the desk and kept repeating, "No." She ran behind the desk and said, "You have to print something out for me. Something. Anything!"

I looked over my shoulder as she reached for the mouse attached to the laptop and clicked and scrolled madly, hoping to see some usable document. She froze and I knew what she was seeing. Her eyes were fixed on the passport template that had been on the monitor when we'd walked into the building. The template left over from the last false passport Malcolm Snyder had been working on before all hell broke loose. The template that included the photo of his most recent customer. The template that included my photo.

Her eyes came up and met mine as I turned and stopped in the doorway. I clinked with every motion, being loaded down with weaponry.

She said, "You're...you're not Malcolm Snyder."

"I never said I was."

"You're Cyprus Keller," she concluded. "You were robbing Snyder when we showed up?"

"No," I said. The printer made a grinding noise,

struggling to function after committing a homicide. "He tried to renegotiate his fee, pulled a gun, and things went sideways for him." I raised one hand to lift the butt of one of the weapons high enough to pat the envelope concealed inside my jacket. "Don't worry, I got my own documents from Snyder before you showed up. Two sets, actually. My wife and I will be fine."

"But," Lisa stammered. "You knew so much. You knew about making IDs. You know about Timothy Sutton, who told us about you...or rather Malcolm Snyder. You were typing something on this computer. You were working!"

"I made most of it up along the way," I said. "When you look back at this day, you'll realize that. As far as the reference goes, you saw the notes Snyder made. Sutton referred me to Snyder, just like you. I'm afraid what I was typing a few minutes ago is going to be a problem for you. I sent the Associated Press a quick email stating how you, Betty, and Megan had betrayed the Daughters and were attempting to get new documents in order to run. I'm sure your sisters-in-arms, if any of the group survives this day, will be extremely unhappy with your lack of conviction."

Lisa sank down into the chair behind the desk and covered her eyes with her hands. "What am I going to do now?"

I don't know for sure what happened next, but I assume she uncovered her eyes and saw the empty doorway. I assume she walked over to the doorway and noticed the raft she'd pulled to the dry ground near the rear entrance was gone. I assume her eyes went wide when she heard the sounds of an outboard motor starting near the front of the building and the raft speeding away with the current created from the flood she had done nothing to prevent. I assume she then came to understand the new arithmetic.

She was alone.

# THE CURSE
## Mark Edwards

"Ed, wake the fuck up."

I'm in the middle of a delicious dream. Princess Diana is crawling toward me across the bed, wearing a tiara and nothing else and telling me what she wants to do to my scepter. I realize there are two Dianas, like she's cloned herself, and they're both looking up at me through their eyelashes and one of them breathes, "You're the King, Ed, you're the bloody King."

"Ed, you stupid twat, wake *up*."

I open my eyes and there isn't even one princess on the bed, let alone two.

It's Rhi—and she's got a glass of water in her hand, like she's about to chuck it in my face.

"Leave me alone," I say, pulling the quilt over my head. I want to slip back into the dream, where Her Royal Hotness is waiting to do unspeakable things to my crown jewels, but Rhi yanks the quilt back and pours cold water onto my face.

"Jesus," I yell, scrambling into a sitting position and wiping my face. My ardor is well and truly dampened. "'Where's the fire?"

Rhi leans close to me. Her breath stinks of gin and her

hair is lank, hanging over what is still a remarkably striking face—all cheekbones and eyebrows and lips, like early Madonna—even after everything we've been through.

"Not fire," she hisses. There's a tremble in that hiss. "*Flood.*"

Now I'm fully awake. "Flood? What?"

She clutches at me, sharp nails digging into my bare arms. "He's come for us, Ed. Oh God, he's found us."


Rhi and I came to America two years ago. We came here to hide. Rhi wanted to go to Canada or New Zealand but the USA was really the only choice. It's vast, easy to get lost in, and there was a part of me that had always dreamed of living here—though in those fantasies I was strolling along Venice Beach or living in a Manhattan loft apartment. I didn't foresee myself living in a dying post-industrial shithole like Everton.

But there were two reasons we'd ended up here. One: we needed somewhere anonymous, the kind of place where no tourist would ever tread. A place where no one, not even a demon, would think to look.

Two: Rhi's dad had been a fanatical supporter of Everton, Liverpool's second-best football team. When we were scanning a map looking for somewhere to hole up, her eyes had fallen upon this place and she'd said, "Look—that's where we're meant to be. Daddy will approve. He'll watch over us."

Once Rhi got an idea in her head, it was hard to argue. And we didn't have time to reconsider. We needed to get out of England, post haste.

Out of England, and away from the devil who wanted us dead.

Three years before, back when we were doing a lot of drugs—speed, mostly, but also a ton of acid—Rhi met a demon in the ladies' toilets at a nightclub in Liverpool. He introduced himself as Frank (his actual demon name was, he said, unpronounceable) and told her that, in return for a favor, he would make us stinking rich. She agreed on the spot, without even waiting to find out what the favor was, and Frank handed her a Lottery ticket.

"I'll call with full details," he said, disappearing in, she said, a puff of smoke that smelled like sulphur.

The next morning, Rhi woke up in a puddle of puke, the screwed-up lottery ticket in her hand. She took it to the supermarket where the woman behind the counter shrieked and told her she'd won three hundred thousand quid.

Now, Rhi could have run off at that point and kept all the money for herself. I wouldn't have known anything about it. But she loved me. She even fancied me back then and would happily entertain my kinks (dressing up as Princess Di, mostly, when we weren't too stoned to shag). She came bouncing in to our crappy bedsit screaming, "We're rich!"

For the next two years, we lived like kings. We burned through that money. A swanky new pad. The finest coke, the fanciest linen, the foxiest call girls. We had a threesome in a helicopter over Liverpool with the ex-wife of an Everton player. We partied hard. We partied till we couldn't party any more.

And then Frank called.

"I hope you're enjoying that cash," he said. "Because

now it's time to keep your end of the bargain. And I'm talking about both of you. When Ed accepted a share of the money, he bought in to the deal too. Capeesh?"

I'd never heard anyone say *capeesh* before.

When he told us what he wanted us to do, we told him to take a running jump.

He said we were making a big mistake. Because if we didn't do what he asked, he would curse us. "Fire. Pestilence. Flood. And when you die, your souls will be mine."

Rhi was scared—she was still doing a lot of acid and believed Frank actually was a demon—but I was convinced he was a lunatic who, for some nutty reason, had decided to part with a winning lottery ticket. I told him to do one and Rhi and I went back to our life of fun and debauchery.

A month later, we got home from a weekend living it large in Blackpool to find our flat dark and filled with a terrible buzzing. I turned on the lights and it barely got any lighter—because the bulbs were covered with flies. Big, fat bluebottles. Millions of them. Possibly billions. They swarmed through our flat, crawling on the windows, creating a second carpet. I crunched across them, batting them away from my face, and threw open all the windows. They didn't leave. Then a couple flew into Rhi's mouth and she started screaming, "Pestilence!"

But after pest control had been—their faces were a picture—and all the flies were dead and gone, I persuaded Rhi the insects must have been drawn in by some rotten meat we'd left in the bin when we went away. Plus it was an unusually hot summer. She wasn't convinced.

She was even less convinced when we both got sick. It happened suddenly. We both woke up one morning with fevers, liquid bursting out of us at both ends, one of us yelping on the loo while the other barfed into the bathtub. Worse, we were both covered with boils—big shiny throbbing boils that burned. I wanted to die but lacked the strength to jump out the window.

"It was the flies," Rhi said. "They made us sick. *Frank* made us sick."

I laughed this off. As if he could actually curse us. It was crazy talk.

You can probably guess what happened next. We woke in the middle of the night, a few weeks later, feeling like we were going to melt. The flat was full of smoke. Yep, it was on fire.

We managed to get out—just—but as we sat trembling on the pavement below, while firefighters battled the flames that had already destroyed all our possessions, Rhi whispered, "Fire."

Now, I was scared. And as I watched our flat burn above our heads, coughing from smoke inhalation, Rhi convinced me. Frank really was a demon. We really were cursed.


"This is it," Rhi says now, pacing around the bedroom. "He's found us. We're going to die. Oh God oh God oh God."

She explains that she went down to the 7-Eleven to buy cigarettes and everyone was running around panicking, going on about how the whole town was going to be underwater by morning.

It's dark in the room so I try to turn the lamp on, but it doesn't work.

"The TV's dead too," she says.

I look outside. The streetlights are out and the surrounding houses are dark, except for candlelight that flickers behind the windows of a couple of neighboring homes. There's no sign of any flood water though. Not yet. I grab my phone and turn on the torch app, doing the same with Rhi's phone so we can, at least, see.

"We need to get out," I say.

But Rhi is hysterical, sitting on the bed and hugging herself, rocking back and forth, muttering about how it's too late, this is the final part of the curse, that we need to break it now, it's the only way to save our souls.

She looks up at me. Mascara streaks her cheeks. "We have to do it, Ed. We have to do what he wants."

"No. I'm not killing anyone."

"Even to save yourself? To save me?"

"I can't, Rhi." We've had this conversation so many times.

"But I don't want to die, Ed. Not yet."

"I don't either. But I can't do it."

"You're a coward," she spits. "A fucking coward. If you can't do it, I will."

She opens the cabinet next to the bed. One of the great things about America is that guns are piss-easy to get hold of. We got this one for protection. The guy in the shop said it was perfect for home defense, but thankfully we haven't had to use it yet.

"I'm going to find a kid, like Frank instructed us to do, and I'm going to save us."

A kid. If Frank had instructed us to murder an adult,

maybe I could have done it. There are plenty of assholes in the world, people who deserve to die. Rapists and bigots. That guy who cut me up in traffic last week. But not a child. No way I could murder a child.

"There's that little girl next door. The one who stuck her tongue out at me. Remember we saw her that time being cruel to her cat."

"She was dressing it up as a fairy," I say. "It's not like she was kicking it."

"She's a nasty little bitch," Rhi says. "And she'll grow up to be the kind of woman who looks at us like we're dirt. She deserves to die."

I've never seen Rhi like this before. I've seen her with wild eyes and skin pale with fear before. But now she's desperate. I try to plead with her, to tell her to put the gun away. We can get out of town, escape the flood.

"No," she says. "I'm tired, Ed. I can't run anymore."

She gets up and moves towards the door. When I try to stop her she points the gun at me and says, "I'm doing this."

She leaves.


Five minutes later, I'm lying on the bed, wishing I wasn't such a coward, when there's a banging noise from downstairs. It sounds like someone just came into the house. Rhi? But then I hear a cough. A man's cough.

Oh fuck.

I creep out into the hallway and strain to hear. There's definitely someone downstairs. It sounds like he's opening drawers, rifling through our possessions. I tread softly down the stairs. And there he is—standing with his back to me, by the door that leads down to the basement. I'm peeking over the banister when he turns for a moment and I almost crap myself.

It's Frank. Except he's taken demon form. He has a red, rubbery face and a black beard and horns. He's got a cardboard box in his hands which is full of stuff. He's got the PlayStation in there and a load of games, along with the Bluetooth speaker and several other gadgets. I can't believe it. Not only does the fucker want us dead, he's going to steal our shit too!

Then he does something unexpected. Probably thinking there's some valuable stuff downstairs—maybe he's heard about my vintage *Playboy* collection on the demonic grapevine—he sets down the box and enters the basement, standing at the top of the steps and looking down.

This is my chance. I rush down the stairs and before he has a chance to turn around, I shove him in the back. He tumbles down the steps. There's a crack as he hits the concrete floor at the bottom. I slam the basement door shut and lock it. As I retreat across the room, he yells up the steps.

"Hey. Let me out."

"Fuck you," I shout. It's weird. He sounds like he's from round here, but maybe that's what demons do. They're like chameleons, changing their accents instead of their colors. Anyway, I'm exultant. I've got him trapped. This is my chance. Kill him and we'll be free.

Except Rhi's got the gun. And she's on her way to murder the little girl next door.

Shit shit shit. What to do? I flap around for a minute then head out the front door, into the darkness. There's still no sign of the flood water. Not for the first time, I thank the Lord that we didn't have time to burn through all our money and could afford to rent somewhere in the nicer part of town, up on higher ground. But I can hear mayhem in the distance. Gun shots, the buzz of a heli-copter—the happy memory of our airborne threesome flits through my head—and dogs barking.

I approach the house. Please don't let Rhi have killed her yet. She's actually a sweet little girl. She loves her cat, even if she does sometimes dress him up. Last year she came to our door selling cookies and they tasted pretty good. Also, her mum's hot. I can't bear the idea of that sexy mum crying at her daughter's funeral.

There's a ladder propped against the house. The girl's bedroom window is open. Mouthing a prayer, I climb the ladder until I reach the open window and look in.

Rhi is sitting on the end of the girl's bed. The girl is asleep, cuddling a stuffed bear, and Rhi's face glistens with tears. She has the gun pointed at the girl's head. That's when I remember her name. Lucy.

Rhi lifts the gun and her finger flexes on the trigger.

There's a cactus in a little pot on the windowsill. I snatch it up and fling it at Rhi. It strikes her on the chest. She cries out, and Lucy sits up, clocks the woman at the end of her bed and starts screaming.

"Come on!" I yell.

There's shouting from outside the room, thundering footsteps. Rhi looks at the girl, at the door, at me.

"I've got Frank," I shout. "I've got him locked up."

With a gasp of surprise, Rhi scrambles over the bed. I slide down the ladder and she follows, just as Lucy's dad reaches the window. "What the hell?" he shouts, but we're running, across the road and into our house. I double-lock the door.

Panting, I explain what happened while Rhi was out.

"You were really going to do it, weren't you?" I say. When she nods, I decide. I can't be with her anymore. After this is over, whatever happens, it's the end of the road for us.

But first, we need to deal with Frank and break this fucking curse. And we need to do that before Lucy's dad and the cops turn up.

I unlock the basement door and, using my phone for light, go down the steps. Frank is lying on the floor, looking like he's asleep. As soon as he hears us coming, he pushes himself up on his elbows and I realize, by the way he drags himself backwards, he's broken his leg.

Rhi gawps at him, at the red face, the horns, and shines her phone torch at him.

"It's a mask," she says.

"What?" But of course it is. A joke shop devil mask. I grab hold of the horns and pull it off to reveal a young face, coated with sweat. He's got a pathetic little moustache and his eyes are wide with fear and pain.

"My leg," he says. "You need to get me to a hospital."

"What the hell were you doing?" I ask.

I think he's going to cry, but he swallows and holds the tears back. "I didn't realize anyone was here. I just..." He breaks off, in too much pain to speak.

"You're a looter," I say. It makes sense. I guess all the cops are busy. I imagine there's looting going on all over the city. Opportunists, making the most of the darkness and chaos.

"How old are you?" Rhi asks.

"Fifteen."

There's a long pause, and then Rhi looks at me.

Immediately, I understand what she's thinking. Upstairs, I can hear someone banging on our front door. Lucy's dad, I guess. But I can't worry about that right now. Because Rhi is pointing the gun at the looter's face.

"This is it," she says. "Our chance to break the curse. To save ourselves."

"He's only a kid," I say.

"Exactly."

I'm not sure if the looter knows what's going on but he understands enough. There's a gun in his face, after all.

"If we do this," Rhi says, "it will stop the flood. Frank will be happy and we'll be safe."

Above us, Lucy's dad is trying to break the front door down. I need to make a decision, quickly. I think about the last few years, hiding away, unable to live our lives, stuck in this shithole, looking over our shoulders. How blissful it would feel to be free of all that. I can start again, a new life in a new place with a Princess Diana lookalike.

"Please," the looter says.

I don't know his name. He's a bad kid. He was going to steal my PlayStation.

"Ed?" Rhi asks. The gun trembles in her hand and I know she's not going to be able to do it. The gun's wobbling around so much she'd be more likely to hit me. I take it from her and point it at the boy.

"Please," he says again in a desperate voice.

I pull the mask back over his head so I don't have to look at his face. I can hear Lucy's dad upstairs, yelling, telling us to show ourselves.

"Sorry," I say to the looter, just as he tells me his name—Frank, of course, it had to be—and with Rhi crying beside me, and the boy begging for his life, for mercy, I do what I have to do.

One, I shoot my girlfriend in the head.

Two, I blast Lucy's dad as he runs down the stairs.

Three, I shoot the boy through the demon mask. I wipe down the gun, place it in his hand and wait. Will flood water suddenly come crashing through the basement door? Will I drown down here? Will the universe get the last laugh, Frank appearing in a puff of that sulphurous smoke to tell me I'm still cursed, that he'll see me in Hell?

Nothing happens. So with a last look at Rhi—less attractive with half her head missing—I climb the steps and go out. Out into the Everton night.

Free at last.

# AND THE WATER KEPT RISING

Alan Orloff

The water rose.

Torrential flooding in some places. Seeping and oozing in others.

Destroying homes, lives, dreams.

And evidence.

## Lionel

Lionel Westchurch, Manager of PennWest's Everton Branch, sat on the floor of his bank's vault, crisscross applesauce, with a loaded shotgun in his lap. Two battery-powered camp lanterns threw enough light for him to see the fruits of his labor. He'd been staring at the neat stacks of money three feet in front of him for twenty minutes, since just after ten o'clock. Ninety-seven thousand, four hundred and twelve dollars. He hadn't bothered to count the loose change.

He'd tallied it twice, same result. If there was one crucial skill for his job, it was how to count money accurately. Now the question was what to do about it.

The vault door was open, and a few random gun shots and explosions sounded in the distance. Looters. Trouble-makers. Rabble rousers. He clutched his weapon a little tighter. If someone came to rob the bank amid this chaos, he'd be ready.

He didn't blame the Daughters for their outrage. He was pissed, too. Seemed that Wilbourne woman was protecting herself. Seemed those assholes got what they deserved. But blowing up the dam? A lot of innocent people got hurt. People who called Everton home.

He pushed the destruction out of his head and wondered what the higher-ups at corporate would think if he'd told them he was going to camp out in the vault and protect the bank's assets. Probably think he was an idiot. Especially after they'd turned him down—twice—for a promotion to the Tower of Power in the big city.

An idiot, for sure.

He and DeeAnne had been counting on that promotion, big time. They needed the extra income. But those muckity-mucks on the forty-fifth floor in Pittsburgh didn't care about him or his family. Just kept promoting cookie-cutter Ivy Leaguers to play squash with, instead of those who actually did the work in the branch offices.

Asswipes.

Ever since the metal works plant closed and DeeAnne lost her job as a clerk in accounts receivable, they'd had to scratch to make ends meet. And those ends weren't anywhere close to coming together. Now, with the latest troubles his twins were having in public school, he had no idea where they could get the money to send them to a private one. For the last five months, DeeAnne had gone to bed sobbing every night, convinced the kids were going to wind up juvenile delinquents. His life was turning to shit, and he blamed his greedy corporate overlords. Those smug bastards.

He stared at the money again. Everything from the vault and from the tellers' drawers. Ninety-seven thousand, four hundred and twelve dollars.

It would be a start. A pretty damn good one.

## Jackson

Jackson Tate was a proud product of Everton. Born there, some forty-two years ago. Busted his hump at the metal works since he dropped out of high school the day he turned seventeen. His father had worked at the plant for forty-three years, and his grandpa had been there from day one, a total of twenty-eight years before he died one night in the plant parking lot after a double shift.

Time, poverty, and now, a flood, had a way of mellowing one's perspective. Jackson was still an Everton man, but after giving to the town for so long, he figured he was owed a little something back. Maybe a *lot* of something.

Because of the flooded roads, he'd tried half a dozen routes to get to his destination, avoiding the submerged central business district altogether. He felt as if he was in a life-size maze, bumping into one dead end after another. Finally, after some off-roading onto a sidewalk or two, he rolled up to the curb in front of the PennWest bank. One of the plate glass windows out front had been busted, but it appeared that whoever had done it was long gone.

No lights were on inside the bank. Electricity in the whole area seemed to be out, and the streets were deserted. Like an episode of one of them post-apocalyptic TV shows, where only a few humans had survived the nuclear holocaust and had to use their wits to stay alive.

Jackson had plenty of wits.

The bank was situated on a small rise, and water had gathered around it, the way a moat surrounds a castle. Pretty soon, though, Jackson figured the whole place would be knee deep.

He had to hand it to those angry women who'd demolished the dam. They had big-ass balls, all right. If he'd had half their conviction during the tougher parts of his life, he'd be living in style by now.

Time for that to change.

Jackson was prepared to encounter looters at the bank—hell, that's where they kept the money, after all—but he figured looters were amateurs, out for mayhem and looking for easy scores. TVs, microwaves, jumbo packages of Pampers. They might have broken into the bank *building*, but they'd never get into the bank *vault*. And being amateurs, they'd give up pretty quickly.

It was damn difficult to rob a bank without sufficient planning.

Good thing he'd been planning for months.

Now that opportunity had knocked on the front door with shiny brass knuckles, he'd be a fool not to at least answer it and see what opportunity had to say for itself.

This was about his family. *For* his family. Everton owed him and Kerrie for their hard work and unyielding dedication.

He parked his pickup a couple of blocks away from the bank and got out. Slid his Beretta into his hip holster. Took out a Maglite. Slung his backpack over a shoulder. Put on his black knit cap. Locked the doors.

And hustled to the bank using his flashlight only when necessary.

When he got there, he peeked through the broken window. A tire iron on the floor. A few chairs upended. Broken glass everywhere.

He paused. Six months ago, he'd come here looking for a loan so he could start his own contracting business. Since the plant had closed, almost seven years ago, he'd been doing odd jobs—landscaping, construction, custom carpentry—but he figured with sixty thousand bucks, he could buy another truck, hire a buddy, and start a re-modeling company the right way. He'd seen too many shoestring operations go belly-up, for want of just a modest amount of capital.

But they'd turned him down for the loan. They said, *No collateral.* But what they meant was, *We're not lending money to a loser redneck with no college degree and no chance in hell of success.*

To throw him a bone—Kerrie and the bank manager's wife sang together in the church choir—they'd hired him to renovate the customer lobby and teller area. The job wasn't a bad one; it brought in decent money. But two months' work hardly compensated for squashing his dream.

Fortunately, Jackson had taken advantage of his time in the bank.

He'd hidden a Wi-Fi enabled spycam—and a 4G hotspot—in the dropped ceiling, lens aimed through a diagonal slit in an acoustical tile, impossible to detect. Focused on the bank vault's lock.

Every morning, he could see the manager spin the dial and swung the heavy door open. Jackson had this week's combo memorized.

Technology rocked.

It paid to be prepared. Literally.

In case something went awry, Jackson also had some C-4 and blasting caps he'd bought from a friend of a friend. He knew he might not be able to blow open the vault, but it'd sure take care of a security drawer or the ATM, if it came to that. Something was better than nothing.

He'd done Internet research on how to disable the back-up generator, although it didn't seem to be working at the moment. But in case it popped on suddenly and the security cams came alive, he pulled the ski mask down over his head. Then he unsnapped the guard on his holster and stepped through the broken window, hand on his weapon.

## Lionel

Lionel stood and stretched his legs before cramps set in, thinking about the saying, *Money Talks*. Before him, the tidy sum of ninety-seven thousand, four hundred and twelve dollars was whispering in his ear, persuading him, cajoling him, soothing him with the promise of salvation.

In fact, the money was *begging* him to take it and put it to good use, for something worthwhile. His kids.

Stealing was a crime, Lionel knew that. But *borrowing* wasn't. Hell, borrowing was his business. He'd pay it all back when his mother-in-law died. Cheap bitch was loaded but wouldn't lend them the money—DeeAnne had broached the subject with her and had been shot down.

He thought of the corporate bigwigs sitting around their huge mahogany conference tables, smoking their fat cigars, deciding which impoverished customers to shaft. Didn't they appreciate a creative loan officer? The bank would get its money, with interest. Eventually. How much longer could an eighty-seven-year-old hag with a heart condition last, anyway?

He couldn't take his eyes off the prize. Now the whispers had grown into shouts. A chorus of Benjamins, Grants, Jacksons, and Hamiltons screaming, *Take Me Home*!

*Fuck it.* The flood would provide cover for the missing money, and he'd adjust the bank's books when he began paying back the loan. Because he *would* pay back the loan. And the account was insured, to boot. Everyone wins. At least that's what he was telling himself as he began stuffing the money into a duffel bag.

The bag was halfway full when he heard a noise. Faint. Crunching glass. He froze, perked his ears up. Another faint crackle. Coming from the lobby area.

Lionel picked up his shotgun and got ready to defend his treasure.

*Jackson*

Jackson pointed his Maglite at the carpet, and the glass shards twinkled. He'd tried to be as quiet as he could, but his hip had brushed a potted plant, and his weight shifted and, well, he hoped no one heard him.

A small glow shone from the back of the bank where the vault was located. He drew his weapon, shoved the Maglite into his pocket, and carefully—very carefully—made his way deeper into the bank, senses on alert.

Every few steps he'd pause to listen. All quiet, except for the thunderous pounding of his pulse in his ears.

Illicit activities were foreign to him, and even though he'd been planning to rob this bank, there was a mile of difference between *planning* and *doing*.

A mile over rough terrain.

At any time, he knew he could turn tail and run—like he had when he'd found himself in other tight spots. He'd be just another miscreant taking to the streets to wreak havoc during the flood.

Jackson passed through the space he'd renovated, a small part of him registering the fact that the vandals had left his work intact.

When he got within view of the vault, he paused. Crouched. His heart, already racing, shifted into a higher gear.

The vault door was open, and the glow came from within.

Someone had already been here.

A wave of emotion threatened to drown him, just like the rising waters outside. Was it relief, knowing that someone had beaten him to the punch, and he wouldn't have to commit a felony? Or was it disappointment? He'd finally screwed up his courage enough to do something to change his life, and now he was being denied.

He called out. "Everton Police. You, in the vault, come out with your hands up."

No one answered. No one came out with their hands up.

Most likely, the thieves had already gone.

Jackson crept closer. Called out again. Still no answer.

He reached the vault's entrance and grabbed the door handle, slowly pushed it open a little wider. Perspiration soaked his cap, and he struggled to keep his gun hand from shaking.

Two lanterns on the floor. Stacks of money. In plain sight. Just sitting there.

But no one would just leave—

Something hard poked into his side, followed by a deep voice. "Drop your gun. Nice and slow."

*Lionel*

"You heard me. Drop it. I don't want to kill anyone tonight, but I will. I sure as shit will."

The intruder bent over slowly and dropped his gun. Lionel picked it up, then shoved him farther into the vault and spun him around. Solid, compact. Dressed like some kind of neo-ninja. "Go ahead, take off the mask."

The man hesitated, then slowly pulled his hat off and tossed it on the ground.

*Shit.* Under all that black terrorist clothing, Jackson Goddamn Tate.

"What the hell?" Lionel's voice rose. "What are you doing here?"

Tate cleared his throat. "I saw the busted window and I came in, just to see if everything was all right."

"You just happened to be driving around here, in the middle of a town-wide emergency, and you wanted to make sure the bank was okay?" Lionel choked back a laugh. "You expect me to believe that?"

Tate nodded, spoke a little faster. "I done a lot of work in this bank. Don't want some meth-head to come around and destroy it."

"Pride in one's handiwork. I like that. But we both know you're full of shit."

"Believe what you want." Tate shrugged. "I'll ask you the same question: what are *you* doing here?"

"This is my bank. I'm protecting it. It's my job, you know."

"Making sure nobody steals the money, right?" Tate asked.

"Now you're catching on."

"So if you're trying to protect the money, why isn't the vault locked?" Tate nodded to the money on the floor. "And why is there a duffel bag full of cash sitting there, next to all the other neatly stacked piles of bills?"

Lionel blew out a breath. Tate might have tilted toward country rube, but he wasn't a dummy. "Someone busted the window and broke into the vault. I interrupted them."

"Yeah? So where are the cops?"

"You know, I'm the one holding the gun. Maybe I should be asking the questions." Things had gone off the rails. Lionel's idea about getting away cleanly with the money had just evaporated. The shotgun weighed heavily in his hands. Dead men tell no tales. But killing a guy? Let alone one he knew? People got killed for a lot less than a hundred large, but that's not how this was supposed to go down.

Another idea sprang to mind. What if he let Tate go, as long as he promised not to say anything? He stewed on that for a moment, but as he played out the scenario, all he saw was Tate blackmailing him at a future date.

Rock, meet hard place.

"Seems we got ourselves a *sit-you-ay-shun*," Tate said, sides of his mouth curling.

No. He wasn't a dummy. At all.

*Jackson*

"Did you really think you were going to get away with it?" Jackson asked. "You think the police will figure the generator just went out on its own? And that someone managed to get the vault open without any inside help? I mean, the water can only cover so much."

Lionel seemed to be calculating something. "So how were *you* planning to get into the vault? That's where all the money is." He pointed with the barrel of his shotgun. "Take off your backpack and slide it over here. Gently."

Jackson did as he was told and watched in silence as Lionel bent down, unzipped the pack, and unloaded the items inside.

"Blasting caps. Explosives? They would hardly put a dent in the vault." Lionel stood. "You'd be an idiot to risk everything over what's in the security drawers."

Jackson ignored Lionel's questions. "The water's rising. Pretty soon, it'll be in here. We'd better figure out what we're going to do."

"I should turn you in for trying to rob the bank," Lionel said.

"I was thinking the same thing."

"On the other hand…" The timbre of Lionel's voice softened. "Hypothetically speaking, if we each wanted to borrow some money—as a loan, an off-the-books loan— might we be copacetic with that?"

"Huh?"

Lionel shifted the shotgun in his hands, and it no longer pointed at Jackson. "Copacetic. Means 'okay with.'"

"Yeah, I know what copacetic means. I was questioning your idea. Like what, exactly, you mean."

"I *mean*, if we each took some money, say half of that pile there," Lionel said, pointing to the money with his toe, "with the intention of repaying every last cent, we'd both be okay with that? Hypothetically, of course."

"Of course." Jackson nodded at the money himself. "How much is it?"

"Ninety-seven thousand, four hundred and twelve dollars."

Jackson arched an eyebrow. "Pretty exact."

"I'm a banker." Lionel gave Jackson a full-fledged wink. "Look at it this way. I'm going to use the money for the benefit of my kids. To help my family. And I'm assuming you'll use yours to start up your contracting business." Lionel smiled apologetically. "By the way, sorry about turning you down. We've got certain corporate earnings projections and performance benchmarks we have to adhere to when it comes to loan approval, and…" He shook his head. "Anyway, both of us will be using the money for the betterment of our families. Strong families are the bedrock of our community, after all. This will help Everton."

"Families. They're important. And you're right, that's what I'd use the money for. My family." Jackson felt a little like he did after listening to a Sunday sermon. Inspired, but with a sense that he'd just been told a good story. *Kumbaya, fool.*

"So what do you think?"

Jackson considered Lionel's offer. His half would be a little shy of fifty grand. He'd be short of his ideal seed money goal, but he could work with that. Definitely. "How do I know you won't turn me in?"

"Same reason I know you won't turn me in. We're co-conspirators. Whatever happens to one, happens to both. Hypothetically speaking."

"I don't think it will make me feel any better if we both go to prison."

Lionel donned his smarmy bank manager smile, just like when he'd turned Jackson down for the loan. "Prison? We're not stealing this money. These are *loans*, Jackson. And as such, here are the terms. We borrow this money and agree to pay it back with interest, maybe prime minus one. Which is a reasonable rate, commensurate with any other loan possessing community development impact."

"Community development?"

The smarmy smile brightened. "Absolutely. Your business will hire workers, and the private school needs to pay their teachers, and the town will reap tax revenue along the way. Our families will be stronger, and our communities will be, too." He nodded, mostly to himself. "Repayment will begin, say, three years from now. No, make it five years. One tenth of principal and accrued interest per year until it's paid off."

"Seems fair to me."

"And let's add a clause. 'Terms of the loan are subject to change only by agreement of the two parties'—us. So if we needed to adjust the repayment terms..." Lionel said this without a hint of humor.

Jackson knew a sweetheart deal when he heard it, and it was nice to be on the right side of it, for once. "I'm in. Thanks for finally approving my loan."

*Lionel*

The knot in Lionel's stomach loosened. They had an arrangement, a mutually beneficial, mutually destructive one. Something could go wrong, sure, but life wasn't a toaster—no guarantees. Since he'd counted the money, he'd been planning on ninety-some thousand dollars. Now his cut would be half that. He shrugged it off. Sometimes you just had to deal.

"Come on, let's get out of here before we drown." Lionel returned Tate's gun to him, and they got busy, each stuffing money into a duffel bag.

Tate stopped stuffing. "How do you figure to get away with this, anyhow?"

"I'm the manager. I know how to take care of everything—alarms, cameras, generator, and whatnot. The flood will wash away any forensic evidence. As for the cover story, a looter broke the window. I came to investigate. He jumped me, forced me to open the vault. He'd already knocked out the backup generator so the cameras were down. No video record. Unfortunately."

"You think they'll buy that?"

"More likely now."

"How's that?"

"'Cause I got an eyewitness. See, I figured it was just a vandal when I saw the window had been smashed in. So I called a buddy of mine, one of the contractors who worked on the renovation, in fact." Lionel smiled to himself, as he improvised his story on the fly.

"You called me, rather than the cops?"

"On a night like this, I didn't want to bother the cops, at least until I knew for sure there was a burglary. My buddy was happy to lend a hand and he rushed over.

Unfortunately, he was just a little late. Saw the fuckers getting away though. Two of them. Tall, skinny guys in a van with New York plates."

"That's exactly what I saw." Tate grinned, nodded. "It's all insured, anyway, right?"

"Yep. No victims here." They continued bagging the money.

A sound from the lobby—crunching glass—reached the vault. Both men stopped, lifted their heads. Listened. Lionel put a finger to his lips, and motioned Tate to a dark corner of the vault. Tate bent to turn off a lantern, but Lionel touched his shoulder and shook his head. Jackson retreated to his corner.

The light in the vault attracted burglars, moths to a flame.

Lionel picked up his shotgun, slipped out of the vault, and hid, just as he'd done when Tate came in.

Where Tate had been cautious and had taken his time, this intruder wasn't concerned about making noise. As he approached, Lionel heard sloshing. A few seconds later, the intruder came striding through the shadows, coming to an abrupt stop at the vault's entrance. "Water's rising fast. Already in the lobby. Everybody okay in here?"

As before, Lionel stuck his shotgun in the man's back. "If you want to live, don't move a muscle."

Five minutes later, Lionel and Tate had tied up the burglar, using duct tape from Lionel's desk. They huddled by the vault's entrance, while the intruder scowled at them from the back corner, trying to say something through his taped mouth.

"Any idea who that guy is?" Lionel whispered.

*Archie*
"Mfsfnmx!" *Goddamn shitheads! Let me go before I cut out your fucking spleens!* "Fmtsthp!"

*Jackson*
"I've seen him around. Hanging out with Vic the Orphan. Name's Artie or Arnie or..." He snapped his fingers. "Archie, that's it. Don't think he's from around here."
Lionel nodded. "What do you suggest?"
Jackson just shrugged.

*Lionel*
"Let me think a minute." Archie's arrival complicated things. Lionel considered the options. They were same as before, when he'd nabbed Jackson, only this time there'd be less money to go around. Thirty-one thousand dollars was a far cry from ninety-three. Thirty-one thousand wouldn't help very much at all. He pictured yet another guy waltzing in, then another, until an army of intruders each got a measly thousand bucks.
Lionel knew he could take this in an entirely different direction. If he killed Archie, would it really be so much worse killing Tate, too? He could blame his death on the confusion caused when Tate came by to help and the crooks started shooting and the darkness and...*Shit.* Too many crazy ideas.
And the water was rising.

*Jackson*
They'd almost gotten away with it. Now this clown had come sniffing around. They couldn't leave him here.

116

Archie had seen their faces and Jackson had no doubt this little turd would finger them in a second. If they cut him in on the take, they'd be down to about thirty large each. And that was only about half of what he really needed. Worse, they didn't even know this guy. They couldn't trust him to keep his mouth shut.

Could they kill him?

Men did terrible things when confronted with terrible circumstances. But murder? And if they killed this guy, why not go all the way and take out Lionel, too?

He stepped back, regarded Lionel. Had he come to the same conclusion? Jackson put his hand on the weapon in his holster.

*Archie*

Archie stopped squirming. They ignored him, involved in their little-girl talk. He turned his back to them and managed to free the KA-BAR tactical knife hidden in his sock. He quietly unfolded it, turned it around in his fingers, and sliced through the duct tape on his wrists. Fuckers might just get their spleens taken out yet.

*Lionel*

Lionel hadn't come to a conclusion, but he knew one thing. They couldn't stay there. Not with the water getting higher. "Okay. Let's go. We'll take him and the money, head up into the hills a ways. Decide what to do there."

He started toward Archie, but spun around when Tate started talking.

"What about the cops and our cover story? If we

hightail it away now without calling them, they'll know something's up."

Lionel opened his mouth to answer when two hands gripped the shotgun and yanked it right from his grasp. As he turned after it, Archie hip-checked him to the floor. *Shit.*

Archie aimed the shotgun halfway between where Lionel sprawled and where Tate stood. With one hand, he peeled the tape from his mouth. "Okay, fuckers." He jerked his chin at Tate. "You. Take your piece out of the holster and slide it over here. Now!"

Tate slid his weapon across the floor, and Archie scooped it up, jamming it into his waistband.

"Take off your clothes. All of them. And your shoes." He glared at Lionel. "You too. Both of you. Hurry the fuck up!"

Lionel joined Tate as they stripped in silence.

Archie leveled the shotgun at Tate. "Put the clothes in one of the empty duffel bags, and toss it out of the vault. But don't try anything slick."

Tate found an empty duffel. Stuffed the clothes in and tossed the bag through the open door.

"Good. Now get in the corner." As they moved, Archie circled toward the door. He drew Tate's handgun and held it on them as he tossed the shotgun out of the vault, followed by one of the lanterns. Then he grabbed the three bags of money, and tossed them out, too, one at a time, keeping his eyes—and the pistol—trained on him and Tate.

Lionel could kick himself in the head for not dealing with Archie when he had the chance.

*Fuck.*

After everything had been thrown from the vault, Archie broke into a big grin. "Well, gents," he said, picking up the remaining lantern. "It's been nice doing business with you. This is a mighty friendly bank, all right. Just like the ads say."

He darted out of the vault and pushed the door shut, plunging them into complete darkness.

"We'll drown in here." Tate's voice sounded wobbly.

"Relax, these vaults are made to withstand natural disasters. Even woman-made natural disasters." Lionel started laughing, slowly at first, but it built up steam and he kept laughing until his sides hurt.

"What's so funny?"

"I was worried I wouldn't be able to lie about getting robbed. Now I won't have to. Don't worry, Jackson. Something good may come of this after all. Maybe those chuckleheads at corporate will pay me some respect— and give me the promotion I deserve—when they hear how I risked my life confronting bank robbers. And the first deed in my new position just might be taking another look at your updated loan application."

*Archie*

As soon as Archie sloshed out of the bank, he tossed the gun aside, where it disappeared under six inches of water. He splashed down the block as fast as he could, threw the bags of money in the back seat of his Charger, and took off.

*Ohio, here I come.*

Archie took to the hills along wooded back roads, in case the cops somehow had gotten wind of his heist. But he only got about three miles closer to Ohio before he turned a corner and almost plowed into a woman standing in the middle of the road flapping her arms like she'd seen the Devil.

He blew his horn and waved her aside. Didn't have time for any bullshit. Not with three bags of money in the back seat.

He hit the horn again, then turned to his left to see another woman, not ten feet away, holding a gun aimed at his head. Archie slowly put his hands up, then—even more slowly—reached for the window button and rolled it down.

"Can I help you?" He tried to sound pleasant and perky, choosing to ignore the gun entirely.

"We need your vehicle. Turn off your car and hand me the keys." She smiled and held her palm out. "Please."

Hard to ignore the gun when she moved it four inches from Archie's ear.

Archie turned off the motor, gave the lady his keys. He was aware of a few more women emerging from the woods lining the road. Each brandished a handgun. All of a sudden, his mouth felt like it had filled with cotton. "I can, uh, give you a ride, if you want. I'll make some room in the back seat, and we can get going."

"I don't think you understand. We're taking your car." The lady with the gun stepped back. "Okay. Get out."

Archie figured he might be able to overpower one broad with a gun, but four? Not bloody likely. Movement from the other side of the car caught his attention, and Archie watched in the rearview mirror as a middle-aged woman opened the back door and grabbed one of the bags. Opened it. "Oh, ladies. Ladies!" She practically sang the words. "We've hit the jackpot!"

The biddy with the gun aimed at his head didn't seem impressed, still focused on Archie. "Did you know those monsters, James Manning and Trevor Daw?"

"How would I know—"

"Don't shine me on, boy. You all know each other." The lady jabbed her gun at Archie. "Give me your wallet."

Archie reached into his back pocket and handed it over.

She opened it, read his name off the license. "Archibald Keener. Well, *Archibald*, I'm a Daughter." She pointed at another woman, then gestured vaguely at the others with her pistol. "And she's a Daughter. And her too. And her and her and her. We're *all* Daughters."

*Bitches be crazy.*

"I've just got one question for you. Do you think Maggie Wilbourne got a fair trial?"

"I honestly don't know what kind of trial Wilbourne got." Archie licked his lips. "But at least she got a trial, unlike those boys."

The lady cocked her head at Archie, then a cold smile grew on her lips. She called out to the tallest and meanest-looking Daughter. "Roe, take *Archibald* into the woods and show him exactly what kind of trial Maggie got."

Archie's insides melted into a hot mess, and the last thing he remembered was the insane laughter of those crazy bitches.

And the water kept rising.

# BAD DAY TO BE THE BAD GUY

### Angel Luis Colón

Days, maybe even weeks later, the bartender could only remember the man who shattered three pint glasses against the left side of his face, broke his legs, and provided him with permanent sight loss in his right eye, as a "skinny, Irish monster" a "psychopath with no remorse." The description would come in a whisper. Never to the law and never to anyone who knew him well. The words would go to those who needed warning—to understand the severity of the man who did those things to him.

Blacky Jaguar would never in a million years disagree with that assessment.

The beating had a purpose. Blacky needed to know where Nora Wheelhouse lived. The bartender, in a fit of rebellion, skipped the niceties and played hard to get. Being as the town was in the throes of disaster and Blacky was very much uninterested in the more than likely arrival of local, state, and/or federal law enforcement, a proper beating seemed the best path to proper answers.

"Few things on God's green earth really sink my heart into the depths of my gut like the sound of a perfectly good pint glass shattering," Blacky said as he hefted the bartender to his feet. "I'm wagering you're about a glass off from a righteous concussion and then I'm stuck asking you the fucking ABCs and what day it is. I'd rather we focus on the now." He smiled. "Wheelhouse, where's her roost?"

The bartender snorted. His breath rattled. His eyes were wide. "Can't you speak fucking regular English? You sound like you're the one with a concussion." His voice was a little slurred.

Blacky sighed and drove a fist between the bartender's eyes as he maintained his grip on the man's collar—easy as Sunday morning. It was a short, sharp blow meant to stun more than damage. "Last chance before you're learning to read again with a fucking Speak and Spell, my friend. Wheelhouse, her address or current location, if you will."

The bartender blinked, clearly deep in thought over his options. "I need a pen and paper."

"I look like your fucking secretary?"

The bartender motioned over his shoulder. "There's a mug next to the cash register."

Blacky looked over to where the man was pointing. "I shoulda laid lower. Apologies in advance. I'll try to make it so you're not using a cane the rest of your life."

"What? What does that...?"

The bartender was interrupted by Blacky jamming the heel of his boot just under the outside of his left knee. The snap was loud and the pain was immediate. The bartender fell over and grabbed at his leg like a lost lover. He let out a scream that sustained.

Blacky swaggered behind the bar. "You've got a voice for opera, lad." He fetched a pen and a piece of paper.

Gave the cash register a jostling and it opened easily. Blacky collected various bills and the loose change—he never knew when he'd be at a toll. "Now, if your pride is as ludicrous as I'm imagining given the state of this town and this bar, I'd recommend telling the law you were overwhelmed by looters taking advantage of the situation. Savvy?" He walked back to the other side of the bar and crouched next to the bartender. "Dot and cross—big letters. Ain't as young as I used to be." He held out the pen and paper.

The bartender, wet with sweat, stared at Blacky before snatching the stationery. He laid on his back, broken leg elevated, as he wrote down an address. "I doubt she's home." He held out the paper for Blacky.

Blacky took the paper and read it. "Any idea why? You know what this Wheelhouse woman was playing at?"

"It's a small town, man; you hear plenty of shit if you keep your head down."

"And you didn't do shit, eh?"

"Least I didn't profit off it."

Blacky choked back a laugh. "Oh lad," he said as he walked to the exit, "I've yet to begin profiting."


The drive wasn't as bad as Blacky expected. The bartender's car was certainly helpful. All-wheel drive or whatever that was, didn't matter, all Blacky knew was the car handled the wet roads well. The driving went easier as he drove toward higher elevation—of course the rich lived above everyone else. It seemed the power outage hit area-wide. People out and about; all dressed a little out of character for such a nice neighborhood.

Blacky spit out his window. "Looters," he said. With the presence of these geniuses, he wondered if his bartending friend was accurate in his assessment that Wheelhouse was scarce. A person with that kind of money and that kind of heat had more to gain on a private jet than sitting pretty in a master bedroom. Still, Blacky's experience with first-time criminals always proved unpredictable. He was banking on Wheelhouse being dumb or cocky enough to take her time fleeing the area. His experience with people of privilege taught him to never be surprised by their idiocy. Money ate away at an IQ like a termite in an oak tree.

Blacky found the address, turned his car around, and parked down the road from the house in front of another residence with all of its lights on courtesy of an emergency generator—something everyone on the block seemed to have. The positioning gave him a chance to approach the house from a less obvious vantage point. The houses had plenty of space between them and Blacky was certain he could sneak around the back. He eyed the other houses, noted they probably had motion-activated lights. He'd have to stick near the trees to avoid the spotlight or at least leave people assuming deer were being frisky. Blacky wished he had a gun but realized that amount of noise would do more harm to him than any target.

The walk was bumpy, the path annoying to navigate. It was dark as a Goth kid's poetry but Blacky was used to sneaking around at night and the pitch was nothing like he'd experienced in Ireland or other places. Something about America, he reckoned; the level of light pollution was so pervasive at times that even in a small town, the dark wasn't as dark as he knew it could be. He wondered about the need for all this wasted land. If the paths and trees were so unkempt, why pay the premium for it? Why not build more housing for other rich idiots?

All that thinking is what led Blacky to trip over a root on the path and face plant against a formidable tree. The sound and feeling of a broken nose was all too familiar to the Irishman and he groaned more out of frustration than pain.

"Of fucking course we go this route." Blacky grabbed the bridge of his nose and twisted the cartilage until another snap pierced the space between his eyes and he saw more stars at eye level than he'd seen in the sky above. Blacky blinked and sat up. He shot out a bloodied snot rocket from each nostril and shook his head. "We're starting off on a shit foot, aren't we? Even fucking talking to myself like a goddamn maniac."

It took longer than Blacky wanted to get back to walking toward the Wheelhouse residence. His face hurt and he was feeling particularly ornery—not that he wasn't feeling that way earlier but a broken nose had a habit of turning him a little more sour than usual—this did not bode well for his initial plan of subtle extortion. No, Blacky was pretty certain the extortion was going to be a little louder and filled to the brim with smashed valuables. Blacky swore he'd lose his mind if he couldn't throw at least two vases against the wall. Vases were fun to break.

A low brick wall separated the path from Wheel-house's property. Blacky took care to scale it without another pratfall and approached the rear of the house in a crouch, like a roadie approaching a toppled mic stand at a gig. The house was large and lights were on in multiple rooms above the ground floor. A gas generator hummed nearby. Blacky paced back and forth as he scanned the windows. This neighborhood was for certain patrolled by the law and the time spent harassing Wheelhouse for his extra payment would need to be both quick and quiet. Still, it didn't seem as if there were people at home. Maybe this was a bust. The bartender led him on a wild goose chase—something to warrant another broken limb.

Blacky stopped in his tracks as he heard a voice. He edged closer to the house and pressed against a slatted fence lining the property on its east side. Definitely a voice—more like voices—a group stationed outside on the opposite side of the fence. Blacky creeped alongside the fence and tried to get a view without exposing himself. He saw three men between the fence's slats—all dressed in dark blue; the goddamn law.

"Fuck me up the virgin arse with a sand paper dildo," Blacky muttered.

It was suicide to attempt any sort of direct approach. Wheelhouse was most certainly not present and Blacky had the distinct feeling his bartender friend was responsible for the police presence. That was a shame; Blacky hadn't had a real bloodthirst in ages and that bastard bartender brought it back with a vengeance. Turning around and going back where he came from was an option. Though, this meant no chance at collecting the extra cash Wheelhouse conned him out of. Blacky could take a chance and see if the door leading inside the house was open, but for all he knew there were more cops inside waiting for him.

Option three presented itself as Blacky leaned against the fence: a gorgeous brick BBQ pit with three large propane tanks beneath the grill. Not far away from that humming generator too.

"Ah, well," Blacky said with a smile, "that'll fucking do."

The explosion was larger than Blacky expected. Large enough to feel the heat against his face from at least a hundred yards away. Large enough to send a rolling fireball across the west side of the house that took out all the windows facing the BBQ pit—with scorched grass, scattered bricks, and the odd flaming lawn gnome included. Blacky kept low to the ground even if he suspected he was a little too close to a patch of poison oak as the police shouted in the distance. Would this cause the police to focus their search on the surrounding woodlands? Sure. Would the fire department show up as well? Most certainly.

Not a damn one of them would expect Blacky to be inside the house. It was a reckless plan and would cost him some arm hair—in the best-case scenario—but Blacky opted for a quick search of the property. He imagined there had to be jewelry or a vase of some value inside. If he couldn't get the satisfaction of personally fucking over Nora Wheelhouse, he could at least cause pain down the line when she realized something she cared about was missing.

Blacky rushed through what was a sliding glass door and into the house. He was in a kitchen, dimly lit and mostly covered in debris and shattered glass. "Upstairs," he muttered. All the good things were upstairs when it came to big houses. Rich people never kept valuables on the ground floor. Too easy for the help to slink off with the shiniest stuff, he assumed.

Blacky purposely dragged his dirty boots along the floors and carpets as he walked around in search of valuables on the second floor of the house. Most rooms were sparsely decorated and a few were completely empty—the floors covered in painter's tarp. That didn't feel right to Blacky. He thought Wheelhouse was a local fixture, not some nouveau riche idiot with an Amazonian mythology fetish and a hard-on for extreme domestic terrorism.

A bedroom provided some extra context. A family photo on a nightstand. Three kids, a father and another father. This wasn't the right house. Blacky hurried from the room and the trap was confirmed—four men with a baseball bat each and smiles for miles. None of them were in the picture Blacky found, so at least he didn't have to ruin a family's month. They weren't dressed to the nines like the law outside either.

"Well, shit," the smallest of the men said, "Looks like we got ourselves an awkward situation here."

Blacky narrowed his eyes. "If this is about the bar tab, the service was fucking rubbish, if I'm going to be honest."

The men looked at other with bemusement. Another stepped forward. "No idea what that means, all I know is I see another looter dead set on getting his ass beat."

Blacky took a step back. He noticed the men were wearing the same white tee shirt. There was a little logo on the left side of the tee; an eye with words too small to read. Still, it wasn't hard to read the situation. "Fucking neighborhood watch."

"He's a smart one. Smarter than the goddamn keystone cops running around out there." The leader spun his bat in an attempt to impress—it was not impressive. "At least we got ourselves someone that could use a lesson in civics."

Blacky rolled his eyes. He wondered what he'd have to do now. The idea that five witnesses could ID him was a bother but he knew better than to follow instinct in unfamiliar territory—no matter how much it helped him avoid using his brain. He eyed the landing. A small table to Blacky's left appeared to be made of a decent wood—this probably gave it a little heft—and its legs were narrow enough to grab with one hand. Civics lessons be damned, he thought to himself as he ducked and stepped to the table. Blacky grabbed it and used his momentum to bring the table up in a wide arc as he sprinted to the closest neighborhood vigilante.

The table was made of sterner stuff than the right cheek bone of the man unfortunate enough to be closer to Blacky than the rest. The snap was so loud, Blacky thought the table broke, but he was mistaken—it was the man's face that broke. The victim collapsed onto the shag carpet with little complaint. Blacky didn't hesitate to come in at the next neighborhood watchman with a burst of violent energy. He hefted the table over his head and brought it down as hard as he could, connecting with the second man's chest. No snap this time but the man expelled a sudden burst of air that sounded like a violent hiccup before falling face first onto the carpet and turning onto his back, struggling to find his breath.

"Whoa, whoa, whoa. Fuck, man." The leader of the group held his only standing companion back and edged away from Blacky. "Jesus fucking Christ. It ain't like that."

Blacky stopped mid-stride and placed the table down. He cackled and stared at the surprisingly ornate decorations on the table's legs. "This is a sturdy piece of fucking furniture," he said. Blacky looked up at the men. "To your statement, though, having a particularly hard time understanding how the baseball bats don't make you a liar." He pinched a nostril closed and expelled a big honking wad of bloodied snot on the wall.

The leader of the group motioned to the men sprawled out on the carpet. "Let me get them out of here." He moved—stupidly—into a position that left him conveniently facing away from the guardrail protecting the homeowners from falling down onto the marble tiles in the foyer below them.

Blacky heard boots downstairs and shook his head. "Ain't any timeouts in being a man—even if you're playacting, boyo." He flipped the table so the legs were facing outward and pressed its surface against his chest before charging the neighborhood watch leader and leaping off the landing. The landing came quick. Both men yelped but Blacky was better off than his cushion. The force of the fall sent all four table legs flying off. They rattled on the floor.

"Jesus," said a voice from the landing above.

Blacky scrambled to his feet, seeing blurs in blue at his periphery. He charged through a sitting room and past a few doors, positing another exit further down the hallway—these big houses were odd like that. Taking the only door left to use, Blacky found himself stumbling down a flight of stairs and landing ass-first in an underground garage. He stood up, turned around, and nearly fell back down.

A minimum of six incredible machines in front of him. Enough to leave Blacky in sloppy, sloppy tears, but with an arrest imminent, he reckoned crying would be more suitable for when he made an escape.

Blacky went for the first car in front of him, a Chevy Nova with an incredible mother of pearl paint job. He slipped into the driver's seat and pulled open the compartment beneath the steering column to unleash a jumbled mess of wires.

"Like when you was younger, yah daft bastard," Blacky said as he worked to hotwire the engine to life but he got no result. Confused, he popped the hood of the car and frantically ran out to see what the issue was.

There was no engine. No goddamn anything. It was a fancy chassis—a trick to get his hopes up.

"Fuck me." Blacky went down the row. All the cars were in a state of reconstruction. Another missing engine, not enough tires, no seats. No luck until he found a car beneath an old painter's tarp, a 1959 Plymouth Fury in absolute dismal condition. The damn thing did start, which made it a better machine than any of the wastes of metal surrounding him. The next problem: getting the hell off this property without destroying the poor machine. Blacky revved the engine. It had strength despite its exterior—and interior.

"You'll have to do, girl." Blacky pulled the car out a few feet and the lights in the garage went on. A door a few feet ahead hummed as it lifted. "Let's hope that's all automated or this trip's the shortest you and I have ever had." He shifted the car into gear and powered out of the garage. It was dark outside. Police cars were in the distance but none close by.

Blacky didn't like the feel of this. Explosions usually provoked more activity. Where were the fire trucks and the EMTs?

That answer came as lights flared behind him—three trucks, all angry horsepower and overcompensating high beams. Another trap. The cops were gone and he was left here to what, be run down? That bartender certainly earned another visit. Blacky pressed his foot down and the Fury took off with power but little finesse. He fought with the steering wheel to keep from fishtailing.

The trucks gained ground, but Blacky had a shitty, no-good, terrible plan. He took a hard left and immediately turned his wheel right, the Fury lurching but performing like a goddamn rock star. Once off the property, Blacky spun the car around to position an empty cop car between him and his pursuers. He jumped out of the Fury and sprinted to the patrol car. "Be stupid, be stupid," he chanted as he held a hand out to grab at the passenger side door latch. The door lock was open and the latch gave to Blacky's pull. He swung the door open, dove headfirst into the car, and emerged with a police-issue shotgun in hand just in time to put a little fear of God into the first truck to pull up beside him.

"Right," Blacky spit, "State of that truck be a cold fucking day in hell if you're one of the standard good old boys."

The truck stayed parked. Nobody came out.

"This a standoff or do I have to start making noise

with this thing?" Blacky steadied his aim.

The truck's windows rolled down and a familiar head poked out with a wide smile. "Your reputation does not in any way, shape, or form speak to you in action Mr. Clarke."

Blacky grunted. He lowered his gun. "Fucking Wheelhouse." He pointed at her with his free hand. "We've got a matter of a light wallet, you and me."

"Must be very light to go through all the trouble of ruining that nice, liberal family's house."

Blacky held back a laugh. "Your natural charm ain't helping."

"How much?"

Blacky scratched his chin. There was a bubbling at the back of his head. He wanted answers. Where were the cops? Why did this woman seemingly have free reign to do as she wished in this town? "Yeh gave me what? Forty-five K? Gonna have to double that. Went and made me an active accomplice rather than a fart in the wind."

Wheelhouse threw a small canvas bag out of the window. "Part of my bugout haul. Enjoy." She leaned over and eyed Blacky. "Are we square?"

Blacky picked up the bag and unzipped it a bit. There was indeed money in there. "We are surely, but I take it that bartender called you?"

"He did."

"You attached to him?"

"Not entirely."

"Excellent." Blacky propped the shotgun on his shoulder, took the bag, and walked back to the Fury. "Let this be your last act of terrorism, lady, it's a shitty career path. Look at the state of me, for instance."

"You could have said no," Nora answered.

"And then I wouldn't be the fucking villain." Blacky slipped into the Fury. She seemed a good fit. Driving it felt right. Then he remembered why the car felt right. It only served to put him in a terrible state of dangerous anger.

Blacky parked the Fury off the shoulder of the road once he was ten miles out of town. The roads were awful and the police presence increased once he was down from the hills, but everything panned out. He lit a cigarette and took stock of his surroundings. No lights aside from his hazards, not a lot of traffic, and thick foliage over the guard rail. He walked around to the trunk and popped it open. He was greeted with a muffled scream; the bartender from earlier, pilfered from his hospital room— thankfully people who needed help distracted the staff.

Blacky motioned to his hostage. "Come on. We're almost done here." He helped the bartender to his feet and got him over the railing into the brush. He dragged the bartender along a few yards in until they found a decent patch of level dirt. "We're good." Blacky turned the bartender around.

The bartender shook his head. He lifted his leg—now in a cast—and struggled to maintain balance. The effort was too much and he fell backwards with a low moan.

Blacky scratched his forehead and stared ahead. "I can normally walk away from a lot. I figured you and I were a bit even. Broke yer leg, and you tried to get me broken back. I get it." He took a pull from his cigarette.

"This isn't even about you, to be honest. Been a long night. Got a lot on the brain. Found that car back there." Blacky pointed behind him. "Dredged a lot of old bullshit, you know? So I'm in a state." He cracked his knuckles. "So we're going to pick up where we left off. And the worst of it is I'll make sure you live, because I'm doing this for my own pleasure, not business." He put out his cigarette underfoot. "For that, boyo, you have my apologies."

# MARTA

## Gwen Florio

Marta Hernandez sat in the dark with her employer, watching Everton go to hell.

High View, the turreted stone pile that Nora Wheelhouse called home, dominated Everton's highest point. The Monongahela flowed far below, on most days a sedate curl around a horseshoe bend, tonight a furious torrent. They couldn't see the river but could hear it, a full-throated growl punctuated by an occasional crash as volume and velocity tore loose another boulder from the bluff.

"Sit with me," Nora said when Marta crept from her room at the rear of the house, jolted awake by a faraway crash followed by absolute stillness, the absence of the hum of the various electrical appliances standard to a well-appointed home. Marta felt her way through the long blackness of the hall to the living room. Moonlight silhouetted her employer, ensconced in a wing chair pulled close to the bay window.

"*Señora?*"

"It's happening. Just as the Daughters said it would, if they dared to execute Maggie Wilbourne. Bring the other chair."

Marta dragged the chair—it was very heavy, and surely would leave marks across the rug—toward the window, and perched upon its edge, making sure as little of her body as possible came in contact with the antique damask that covered it. Even so, her feet barely touched the floor.

"I presume the noise woke you. It was the dam. It's gone now," Nora said. "The electricity's out, gas lines broken. Look. Downtown is flooded and burning at the same time."

Fires daubed the night. Lights spun toward the orange smears. Police. Fire trucks.

Nora stood and unlocked the window. It slid open easily, silently. Cold blasted in, carrying the whine of sirens and, unexpectedly close at hand, a scream. "They're looting," Nora murmured. Marta couldn't see her smile, but heard the satisfaction in her voice, followed by the jingle of gold bangles and the rustle of silk as Nora wrapped a shawl around the age-ravaged body whose increasing fragility Nora took as a personal affront. "Light a fire, please, Marta. *El fuego, por favor.* And candles, too. *Los...candelos?*"

Marta knelt before the fireplace and selected sticks of Georgia fatwood from the kindling basket. She made a pyramid of the sap-sweating pine, lit it, then layered it with pieces of cedar, chosen for their fragrance and cut to precise lengths. She waited for her employer to point to the candles, *las velas*, before touching a match to them. Marta understood English, and spoke it nearly as well, but it was to her advantage to pretend only a rudimentary comprehension. She carried a three-branched candelabrum to the end table next to Nora's chair.

"Thank you. *Gracias.*" Nora used Spanish, or an approximation thereof, with Marta whenever possible, a nod to her notion that despite their difference in social status—along with ethnicity, age, nearly everything else, in fact—they shared the solidarity of gender, which trumped all the rest. Nora picked up her needlepoint and resumed her work, the needle flashing in the wavering light. The pop of steel pushing through stretched canvas heralded each stitch, followed by a long hiss as Nora drew the thread taut.

*El patrón*, his face rendered in sepia-hued oils, gazed down with benevolent approval on his daughter's well-bred calm. Dead for decades, Nora had said when Marta asked if he ever visited. "A fall."

Which, Marta guessed from the vagueness as Nora averted her gaze, meant suicide. A luxury—the how and where of death—afforded only to the rich. She stirred the fire with a poker. The flames leapt high, a tamed version of the blazes below. They reminded her of the fires that burned day and night in the sprawling dump that bordered Marta's neighborhood in Ciudad Juarez. As a girl, she and her playmates sifted through its stinking heaps in search of treasures that could be sold for a few pesos. They were all dead now, her friends, just like this woman, this Maggie Wilbourne. She searched the flames for their faces. "Alma," she whispered. "Paloma. Nita."

They left Alma's body in the back of one of the old school buses that shuttled shift workers to the *maquiladoras*, stuffed beneath the seat as though she were a piece of clothing or a lunch that someone left behind. You had to wonder about the people in the front of the bus, eyes trained ahead, brains denying what their ears unmistakably heard as the ones in the back did those things to her.

Paloma lay in the open, probably tossed from a car after they'd finished their business. Her body was found by the people Marta thought of as *turistas de asasinatas*, the murder tourists, the ones who drove into the desert on weekends to see if it was indeed true that the bodies of the slain women of Ciudad Juarez lay like *basura*, trash, among the chaparral. It was.

And Nita? Her death—she was only thirteen, and oh, they had used their knives on her with great inventiveness before the merciful final cut—was the one that caused Marta's parents to gather all the money they'd saved toward a real house. Her mother insisted she leave Ciudad Juarez, where the numbers of murdered women climbed into the hundreds. Better a live daughter, she said, than an empty house. "Alma," she said in a half-sob when Marta protested that they might never see her again. "Paloma. Nita." Their mothers would never see them again, either. So which way did Marta want it?

As Marta understood it, Maggie Wilbourne had wreaked her revenge on her assailant, a final satisfaction not accorded the dead women of Ciudad Juarez; and that the death prescribed as Maggie's punishment involved a clean bright room, a sterilized needle in the arm, oblivion. Not darkness. Violation. Terror.

\* \* \*

The sounds from below grew louder. Shouts, the faint tin-kle of shattering glass, even an occasional jarring gunshot. Enough to mask the crunch of tires on the pea-gravel driveway, the slam of a car door, footsteps.

The doorbell buzzed. The women jumped. Marta peered through the narrow window beside the arched doorway.

"*Policía*," she whispered.

"Oh, dear," said Nora.

"Upstairs," Marta hissed, heedless now of revealing her competent English. "Into your nightgown. Take your hair down. Wash your face. Act your age." And then, through the door, "*Momentito*." She waited until she heard Nora's bedroom door close behind her.

The cop's hair gleamed silver beneath his cap. Marta would have preferred young, inexperienced. She glanced at his nametag. "Wheelhouse." Just like her employer.

Good. Maybe.

"Just checking on Nora," he said by way of introduc-tion.

"You mean Mrs. Wheelhouse?" She drew herself up as though offended, and broadened her accent. *Ju meen Mee-sus Wheel-hous-ay?* The slightly stupid servant.

"My aunt," he said. And, almost below his breath, "Not that she'd ever let anyone know it."

"She ees sleep."

He stepped into the house without asking, brushing so close that Marta stepped back. "Can't remember the last time I was in this place. Candles. Nice."

The bedroom door opened. Her employer's voice, thin, querulous, floated down the stairs.

"Marta? Why are the police here? Is everything all right?"

The cop moved to the bottom of the stairs and shined his flashlight high.

"Just checking to make sure you're all right, Nor—Mrs. Wheelhouse."

"Oh. Bobby." Her usual queenly tone. Behind the cop, Marta moved into the light, gave a single shake of her head, and mimed fragility. A hunch, a palsied shake.

Nora bent, her hair wild, a nimbus in the flashlight's glare. She clutched a bathrobe closed at her throat. "Why do you ask if I'm all right? What's wrong?" A convincing quaver returned to her tone.

"She go to bed *muy* early," Marta said. "Maybe she no know."

"Those crazy women made good on their promise. They blew up the dam. It's a mess in town. And we've gotten reports of looters up here. Just be sure you keep the place locked." He swiveled and shone the light in Marta's eyes. "Don't open the door to anyone." Then, calling up the stairs again, "Does your girl understand?"

"I'll make sure she does." Nora put a hand on the wall as though for support and tottered back to her room.

"Good night, ma'am."

Marta moved toward the front door. But instead of following her, Bobby Wheelhouse ambled in his heavy shoes across the rug to the fireplace. Marta detected no urgency on his part to return to the roiling streets below. Saving his own skin, she thought. Wasn't that what they were all doing? He held his hands above the flames. "Warm-o up-o," he said.

Marta bobbed and smiled. "*Sí, señor.*"

He sighed. "Well. Back to it." He stopped beside Nora's chair and picked up her needlepoint. "My mom used to do this." He bent toward the light and examined the piece. Nora had been working the flowers around the border, had already filled in the full moon with long stitches in metallic silver thread. He ran his fingers over the letters below the moon.

The Daughters.

"What the..."

The fireplace poker caught him behind the ear.

"So long-o," said Marta.


"Marta? Marta? What was that?"

Fragility fled Nora's voice. She came down the stairs so fast that Marta feared a fall, a broken hip. She ran to catch her. But Nora arrived intact. She stood with Marta beside the cop's body. "Oh, dear."

The poker hung damning in Marta's hand. No way to pretend Bobby had fallen, cracked his head on the stone hearth. In Mexico, police officers ended up dead as a matter of routine, but Marta had come to understand that *los Estados Unidos* took a more severe view of cop killers.

Which she was, now. A cop killer with a witness—the latter considered expendable by criminals in every country. Her fingers tightened around the iron shaft. Blood leaked from Bobby's head and flowed in lazy curlicues across the floor.

"Oh, dear," Nora said again, sounding truly rattled this time. She put her foot to the body, more kick than nudge, moving it closer to the fireplace. "The Aubusson. Let's clean this up before it reaches the rug. Paper towels, please," she called.

Marta opened her hand. Let the poker fall. It rang against the hearthstones, its echo following her as she headed for the kitchen. She returned with an entire roll of towels. She tore off a few and blotted up the blood, then tucked the roll against the cop's ear. Nora took the soaked pieces and threw them into the fire.

It blazed high, but Marta's teeth chattered. Until this moment, deportation had haunted her nightmares. Now, new words stabbed at her. *Arrest. Trial. Execution.* Just like Maggie Wilbourne, whose gentle death was no longer a comfort.

She tried to collect herself, to say something to somehow mitigate the disaster at their feet. "I'm sorry. He was your nephew."

"He was a shit," said Nora. "He has a stack of complaints against him a mile high. I don't know how much he's cost this family, what with all the lawsuits we had to settle out of court."

Marta's head reeled, both from the onslaught of information and the fact that her employer had just said "shit," a word she couldn't associate with Nora Wheelhouse in any form. Surely the food her employer ate merely wafted, perfumed, from her microscopic pores, rather than being eliminated in the usual way.

Nora stooped and examined the roll of paper towels. The bottom was crimson, but the stain shaded toward white at the top of the roll. "Good. With luck, the bleeding will stop soon. The less we have to clean up, the better. We don't have much time."

Marta forgot she was showing off her facility in English, forgot she spoke English at all. *"Señora?"*

Nora lofted the candelabrum and strode down the long hallway that led to the garage. Marta trotted to keep up, struggling to take in the brisk flow of words. "He'll have radioed in his location before he stopped here. When they don't hear from him for a while, they'll start looking. They'll come here. Ask questions. We can't be here when that happens. And neither can he."

She swung the candelabrum toward Marta. Long shadows crawled up the walls. She fixed Marta with a calculating eye. "You know something about getting away, don't you?"

The trick the *coyote* had told her as he lay atop her, was to keep moving.

At first, Marta thought he meant the sex he had imposed upon her. Try as she might, though, she couldn't force her unwilling body into any approximation of acceptance, let alone enjoyment. But, no, he was doing her the favor—and of course he expected still more physical gratitude in return—of giving her pointers on how to avoid the officers of *La Migra*. Stay only a few months, tops, at each job. Preferably a new state each time. And, always, new papers. The best you can afford. Otherwise—he grinned, and flipped her over—you'll end up with me again.

And so, stoop work at a tree nursery in Oklahoma; then on to Colorado's eastern plains, snapping milkers onto the rubbery teats of cows at a stinking factory dairy, always wary of the lash of a cowshit-laden tail.

She dismembered chicken carcasses in Arkansas, knife flashing as she turned a perfectly good chicken into the pieces that would look more palatable when arrayed on Styrofoam, her legacy the scars that crisscrossed her hands like silver threads. She washed dishes in a restaurant in Kentucky, changed unspeakably soiled sheets in a rooms-by-the-hour motel in Ohio, then on to a better motel (although with little improvement in the sheets) in West Virginia. Which led, improbably, to the offer of a babysitting job from a grateful guest in Maryland; then, in Delaware, a nanny's position—squalling brats, and hours that made the *maquiladoras* look benevolent—and finally, *qué milagro*! A miracle, this job as a live-in housekeeper to a wealthy woman. Her own room, the smallest in High View, yet still larger than the shipping container that had housed her whole family. A salary that allowed her, on her days off, to take the bus into Everton's tiny barrio to shop for familiar foods at the bodega, to laugh and gossip in Spanish with other maids and housekeepers, to wire money home. She stashed the *coyote's* advice away in the secret place that housed the things he and far too many others had demanded of her.

This was her fifth year with Nora Wheelhouse. She'd thought the safest thing was to pretend she knew nothing about Nora's...interests. Now, she wondered: What if she'd left the minute she realized what was going on? Before things got out of hand?


Nora Wheelhouse's cell phone chimed its musical signal.

She turned away from her nephew's body. "Yes?" A genteel gasp. Nora was too much the lady to scream.

"No. Betty and Megan? Both of them? Oh, no."

A pause. "Lisa, where are you? Can you come he—"

Marta crossed the room quickly and took the phone from Nora. "No. Not here," she mouthed at Nora, and handed the phone back. "Say it," she hissed as Nora stared at the phone, which emitted the panicked sound of Lisa's voice.

"You should—" Nora's voice quavered. She looked again at Marta, who nodded. "You should stay where you are. The water's coming up? Oh, dear."

"Someone will come," Marta mouthed.

"We'll send someone for you. Just stay."

More squawks from the phone. Marta took it, clicked it off, and handed it back to Nora. Her employer's face had gone as white as her hair. When she spoke, her voice trembled. "She'll drown."

"Then she won't be able to tell."

Nora caught her breath as the implication of those words sank in. The uncertain light erased the wrinkles and threw the cheekbones, the imperious arch of nose, the patrician forehead into prominence.

"You speak English."

"*Sí, señora. Algunos*. Some."

Nora's lips twitched toward a smile at the broad sarcasm in Marta's voice.

"So you understand, too."

"*Sí*."

"How much?"

Marta opened her hands, spread the fingers wide, no words needed.

She understood everything.

\* \* \*

The Daughters met at Nora's house for months before the execution.

"It's perfect," Nora said when they objected. "I'm the only one of us beyond suspicion."

Because she was old, and therefore deemed incapable. And because she was rich, and therefore unapproachable. The Wheelhouse family was among the first to settle Everton, old Zacariah Wheelhouse a blacksmith who soon realized there was more money to be made in hammering out tools for steelworkers in nearby Pittsburgh than nailing shoes onto thousand-pound creatures who took every opportunity to bite and kick him. The blacksmith shop morphed over the years into a tool-and-die plant, and in addition to running the factory, the smarter Wheelhouses found their way onto the city council or landed in the district attorney's office, while those less adept, like Bobby, populated the police department and any agency tasked with issuing permits.

The line ran heavily to males. Nora's birth and her status as an only child caused consternation that lasted nearly thirty years, until a suitably wealthy man was found for her, one with whom she'd presumably produce the sons capable of taking over the business. But she inexplicably broke off the engagement after her father's untimely death and, despite the vigorous efforts of various uncles and cousins, ended up at the helm of Wheelhouse Metal Works after all. In a single nod to propriety, she also did good works around the town, including hosting teas at High View for women less fortunate.

Marta moved silently through the rooms on those

days, pouring from the heavy silver service, serving tiny crustless sandwiches smeared with odd fishy pastes. She always suspected Nora's guests of making a beeline to McDonald's—as she herself longed to do—upon leaving.

After the first few months, Marta thought maybe Nora had run out of poor people. The guests were down to the same handful of women, so identically thick of body and coarse of skin that Marta wondered if they were related. They wrapped work-reddened fingers with broken nails around the silver flask that Nora produced, liberally dosing their tea. The conversation grew animated. A single name echoed. Maggie Wilbourne.

The women talked and talked and talked. And Marta listened.

On one of her days off, instead of taking the bus into town, she walked past the estates scattered along the bluff, and entered the forest. The ground was soft and black and fragrant. High shrubs brushed her arms. Leafy trees leaned over her, their emerald canopy pierced by shafts of gold that reminded her of the rays that surrounded the Virgin of Guadalupe on the votive candle in her room. She knew people feared the woods, the wild animals that lurked there, but she marveled at her surroundings, so clean, so quiet. As for the animals, a laugh escaped her. The only animal she feared was man. *Men.*

She arrived at the dam sooner than expected, found a large sun-warmed rock, and sat. She ate her lunch of tortillas folded around refritos, chewing slowly, thoughtfully, as she studied the wall of concrete, the lake that spread like a black mirror behind it, the town below.

Yes, she thought. It could work.

Nora took something from a shelf. "I've got a tarp," she said. "You bring the car around to the front door. *Por favor.*"

The candlelight receded down the hall. Marta felt her way through the garage to the boxy 1972 Mercedes. Nora had been delighted to find that Marta could drive, and fired her chauffeur immediately upon the discovery.

"One less man about the house," she'd said gaily. Now, as of a few minutes ago, there was another less man in Nora's life.

Safely alone in the car, Marta rolled her eyes. A dead man in the living room, and all Nora worried about was that his blood not mar the rug. She hit the remote that lifted the door, turned the key in the ignition, and checked the gas gauge. It was full. She pulled out of the garage and paused, gazing yet again over the town. The number of whirling lights seemed to have quadrupled. Every cop in Everton, and the surrounding towns, must be on duty.

Marta pressed the accelerator. The car responded with a surge of power. She could drive as fast and far as she wanted on this night without pursuit. Because what was Nora going to do if she fled? Call the police?

She was ten minutes in, headlights off, driving by the full-moon's light, when sense returned. The farther she got from Everton, the more attention would be paid a mestizo in a housedress at the wheel of a classic Mercedes. The police could add car theft to the murder charge.

Besides, there was Nora, so ridiculous with her bad Spanish and her insistence upon a fake egalitarianism. But still. Marta thought of all those other jobs. The indignity of long hours and low pay and bosses whose hot breath and filthy hands were just like those of the *coyote*.

She pictured Nora, frail and frightened, beside the body of her nephew, the man that Marta herself had killed. Of Alma, Paloma, Nita. Wondered if anyone had been close when they needed help the most. Had instead driven away.

She eased up on the accelerator. The car slowed. Came to a stop in the middle of the road. And turned around.

She parked under the porte-cochere and used her key to enter through the front door. She had pictured Nora distraught, maybe cowering in the kitchen or her bedroom, far from the sprawled body.

Instead, she was back in the wing chair with her needlepoint, the tarp folded neat as a tortilla around the cop. She'd dressed in slim dark slacks and her customary white silk shirt. Pinned her hair back into its chignon. Fastened pearls around her neck. Even by the uncertain light of the candles and the fireplace, she looked remarkably serene, greeting Marta with a wordless smile.

"How did you—?" Marta looked toward the body. The cop had to outweigh Nora by close to a hundred pounds.

"I used the poker as a fulcrum and rolled him. It's simple physics. And, practice."

"Practice?"

Nora pointed with her needle at the portrait of *el patrón*.

"But *Señor* Wheelhouse killed himself."

Nora gave what Marta thought of as her company smile, pleasant, practiced. Marta herself had tried it, standing before her mirror, stretching the corners of her lips, making sure not to show any teeth. An inoffensive smile, she'd thought at the time. Useful to a servant. Now, it terrified.

"We were walking along the edge of the bluff. He was a birdwatcher, and one of the neighbors had spotted a rare bird up there. He had just started using a cane. He handed it to me so that he could look through the binoculars. He...slipped," Nora said. Her hand jabbed the air. Marta pictured the cane punching *el patrón* in the small of the back, adding force to Nora's shove. Physics.

Oh, Nora. Beautiful, rich Nora, made impervious by the Wheelhouse name. Marta began to question her decision to return. Nora didn't need her help. Nora didn't need anybody's help.

But she did.

"I was younger then. Stronger. But now I can barely drag myself around, let alone him. Can you please—?"

Marta moved automatically toward the cop.

"There's just one thing," Nora said. "I think he's still alive."

Marta peeled back the tarp's top flaps. The poker had caught Bobby across the back of the head. Blood pooled dark beneath the skin around his eyes. Marta touched her hand to his face. He didn't move.

Dead, she thought with relief.

Just in case, she held a finger under his nose. It warmed.

*Mierda*. She hastily closed the tarp and stood. Now what?

She became conscious of Nora beside her. Handing her the poker. Stepping away. No words needed. Maggie Wilbourne had taught them what happened to women who got caught.

Marta swung, a word escaping through gritted teeth. *Alma*.

And again. *Paloma*.

A third time. *Nita*. The final crunch less distinct, mushier than the other two.

She handed the poker back to Nora, who this time showed her teeth in a real smile. She touched the poker to the spot Marta had struck. Added names to the list.

*Marta*. Tap.

*Nora*. Tap.

"There," she said. "Now we're truly in it together."


Being in it together was easy. Getting out?

"To the river?" Marta asked as she rewrapped Bobby Wheelhouse.

Nora shook her head. "One fall, they believed. But not two, even twenty years apart."

Help came in the form of a sound wholly unfamiliar on the bluff, the rumble of a motorcycle. Marta rushed to the window and watched the lights disappear toward town.

"Looters," said Nora. "Perfect. Did you see where they came from?"

"Next door." As in, a quarter-mile away.

"Better yet. Then we don't have far to take him. Quick, let's get him into the car."

Quick being a relative term. But somehow, with Marta pulling from within the car, and Nora shoving from without—so much for physics, Marta thought—they got him into the backseat. Nora sat at the wheel and steered while Marta put her shoulder to the bumper and pushed, both of them fearful of engine noise. High View's position at the top of the bluff made for the slightest downhill incline to the neighbors' house. Marta gave thanks to the Virgin and all the saints as the car rolled silently with minimal effort.

When they reached the neighbor's driveway, Nora killed the overhead lights before Marta opened the back door and took hold of Bobby Wheelhouse's big feet and hauled him from the car.

"The tarp!" Nora reminded her. "Bring it with us. It has to look as though he ran across the looters."

Marta gave a sharp yank, much as she had those motel room sheets of old, whipping it from beneath his body, stepping back to avoid any droplets of blood. She folded it in a few practiced motions. Nora climbed into the passenger seat. Marta got behind the wheel and released the emergency brake, a laugh bubbling up in her chest as the car coasted faster and faster down the hill. She had just killed a man. Was fleeing the police. And yet, for the first time since arriving in *Los Estados Unidos*, she felt free.

\* \* \*

The Mercedes hummed through the night at exactly the speed limit, Marta decorously switching to low beams on the rare appearance of another car.

Nora fiddled with the radio, an old style, with dials instead of buttons, snatches of news emerging from the speakers.

"A state of emergency has been imposed upon the city of Everton…"

"…the downtown business district nearly destroyed…"

"…a dragnet for the members of the shadowy group. The Daughters…"

"Oh, dear," said Nora. "We'll have to find you a good lawyer. After tonight, you're going to need one."

Marta stiffened. Her hands went sweaty, slipping on the wheel. So much for being in it together. She should have run when she had the chance.

"Let's see." Nora, who in most things hewed strictly to an era bygone by decades, had made an enthusiastic exception for smartphones. She tapped at hers, the screen bright within the darkness. "Lillian Halsey. She's the best, I think."

The road rose before them. The unmistakable hump of a bridge. Low concrete walls along the sides. Marta accelerated. Steeled herself for the hard turn that would send the Mercedes into the impervious barrier. A car this old, no airbags. It would be quick. Death preferable to whatever awaited her in America's legal system. If Maggie Wilbourne, white, middle class, with her own high-priced lawyer, had been put to death, what hope was there for her?

"Lillian's in Philadelphia," Nora said. "But it'll be worth the drive. She's the best in the state for immigration. Marta, shouldn't you slow down a little? The last thing we need is to be stopped by the police. Are you all right?"

Marta gasped for air. How many shocks could she withstand in one night?

"Immigration?" she said finally.

"Of course. You'll need citizenship. You can't imagine that I fell for those papers you showed me back when I hired you."

"*Claro que no.*"

"And English lessons. You're very good. Far better than I knew. But you'll need to be better still for college."

"College?"

"Surely you don't want to wait on an old lady for the rest of your life? And what happens when I die? Back on your own, vulnerable to men again? Do you want to end up like Maggie Wilbourne?"

"No, *señora.*"

"You'll maintain a three-point-oh average, of course. That will be the condition. I can't just give you something for nothing. You understand that, don't you?"

Oh, yes, Marta understood. You want freedom, you pay—the coyote with her body, and now Nora, apparently with her mind.

"*Si, señora,*" Still the obedient servant. For now.

Nora tapped a manicured nail against her teeth. "Wait. Stop the car. Back up, back to the bridge, please."

Marta, whipsawed by extremes of panic and relief, of

hope and the inevitable kick in the ass of cynicism, followed directions in a daze. She stopped the car in the middle of the bridge. "This is good?"

"This is perfect. Here." Nora handed her the tarp. Pointed to the barrier.

Marta got out of the car and held the tarp far over the edge. Not the flood-maddened Monongahela, but still, a healthy creek, running high. Plenty of water to wash all traces of blood from the tarp before anyone found it. If anyone ever did.

She let it go. The tarp opened as it fell, waving a farewell to her old life. She turned back to the car, where Nora sat smiling, queenly, no doubt satisfied with the generosity she'd bestowed upon her servant. Marta opened the door with a smile of her own, one that carried the remembrance of the feel of the poker in her hand, its weight arcing high, gaining velocity on the downward swing, the surprising strength of the blow, a knowledge that would stand her in far, far greater stead in her new life than Nora's predictable plans.

# CARTER HANK MCKATER TAKES A SEDATIVE AT ONE IN THE A.M.

Shannon Kirk

Here I am, one in the a.m., floating in flood water, on *my* yellow raft. Got the pop-up seats and table flat, so I can lay with my hands clasped on my belly and my *tool* at the ready, lengthwise by my side. I'm tempering my breathin' and watchin' the galaxy while I wait to spring my trap. That pearly princess of a fat-ass moon, she's plopped like a push-pin in the black, starless sky, showing nothing but calm, her gray splotches on creamy white, like come-hither freckles on a woman's titties. Like that militant Betty's titties, and her mama's too, the ones I had my face in all week in this here Everton, Pennsylvania stink-bottom town. Daughter a clone of her mother, both of 'em gave me good lovin', and both of 'em liked to talk when I licked their necks. Talked too much about their separate secrets. I do like my women big, round, moony, and militant, yet calm and talkative. The moon and Betty and her mama, all three in control and straddling my lay-down hips. They're like me once I purge my rages: calm. I need to be calm so I can write my thriller.

People say people don't tie their rafts up no more, and

it's true. Had my eye on this yellow one all week. The molded plastic kind for dumb-nuts to jump off. This one high-end too, with pop-up blue seats in the center, a pop-up blue table between. How sweet. A yellow and blue raft in a river for kids to laze away on, put they sodas in sunken can holders, and then body slam some doosh-goon pimply friend with a cannonball. This here raft is a factory: an asshole-maker. I ain't never going to have no kids. But I will use them for information. I ain't above using kids to get the dirt needed to tag my, well, *targets*, like I did this week.

People also say it's premeditation if you watch residents along a river, clocking which owners have rafts, spying for families packin' for vacation, and the one that do, well their raft becomes your raft. Means, this here yellow raft, out of all the river rafts, is yours. Yours to use as a, well, let's say, getaway vehicle, and also perhaps, your dismembering floor. People say that's "pre-med-i-ta-tion," and they right.

But who gives a shit what people say. We got ourselves a right flood, and I aim to sedate my rage. Been needin' a fix all damn week. Too much work. Editor says I got a deadline for my next thriller, and he ain't know I got to really gut someone to get the story. He thinks this shit is fiction. I needed a target to kill and then to write about and pass off as literature. Seemed to me, all that junk in the papers about some lady named Maggie getting raped and killin' her rapists, and yet she was the one tagged with the death P, well, made me want to live in the stew of her town the week of her execution. I smelled a stench of corruption so thick, wafted to me in my apartment in Chelsea, New York City. I could almost visualize a target or two materializing in a stink vapor, floating and taunting me to leave my comfy, puffy armchair, like some Dickens ghost of the future.

Yeah, jerk, I talk like a country hick, but I read me the Dickens.

Right now, my eyes are twitchin' and my mind is flashin', watchin' memories of Daddy's beatings like they're movies on the screen of the black sky. Rushing water bubbles whoosh around me, and my raft scrapes underwater metal objects as I glide along with the current. My nose drains liquids and chills the space above my lips; my 'stache stubble is wetted, so the hair buds freeze in the cold air. I didn't have time to shave today. I smell smoke, nothing but smoke, all around me smoke. This liquid comin' out my nose could be brain blood, feels like the drainin' that came the ten times Daddy broke my face, with his hands, with a rusty shovel, a concrete owl we had in our shit garden to keep them crows off, whatever his scarred hands could grab. Now comes the movie in the sky of the time Daddy forced me to burn my own mama's body in our compost pit, 'cuz he'd got too drunk and caved her skull in with his boots. I hate to think of me as a child. I hate children. I am no child no more.

It's always like this when the rages come on strong, and it's been too long. I need relief. Twitchin' and flashin' got so bad tonight, I was blinded. Almost choked the boy who gave me the intel on my target when we met for the payoff behind the Laundromat. The flood was already ragin' from The Daughters who blew the Big Dam. But what that sad, pathetic boy said, stopped my clenching fists from choking my rage on him, righted me back on track with my original premeditation.

Coming to be close to the time for my trap, so I sit up, stretch my twitchin' lids to stay open, pupils focused. Right level with me on the "river" banks, both sides, fires, yelling, shadows of people scurrying black tree to black tree with other people's TVs, picture frames, and other shit they don't need. Flood water is navy in the skunk-stripe center, where my pearl moon princess paints a line of lovely light; the margins of the water are black under the rows of trees on both banks. This here what I'm floating on is normally a valley road. So we got submerged cars below my yellow boat, floating bicycles beside me, plastic pails, several shit-crap, cheap-ass solar lights from Home Depot, Rubbermaid garbage cans, soda cans, soda bottles, soda cups from McDonald's— lots of soda in this rot-teeth, rural town.

I got my rages high tonight, so things ain't so settled here on my yellow raft, none. I pop to an agitated standing, shaking my restless legs, pounding my fists up and down like I'm curling the prison weights. I look to my moon to keep my eyes from twitchin' until my sedative arrives.

A week ago, I followed the stench vapor of Everton and exited a bus I'd hopped in New York City. Had to walk a couple of towns to get here, but I like to arrive in my killin' places analog. No cell ping. No credit card tracer for the bus. No nothing but my boot prints on the gravel roadsides from town to town. Wore my label-free gray coat, 'cuz it's November, and also this here southwest Pennsylvania is gray everywhere, in the stiff air, in the cold clouds, in the leafless trees, in the coal miners' black lungs, in the soulless dead stares from the down and out. So I blend in just fine.

I started right away in trying to find a target, the one who'd be the sedative to my rage and the "motivation" for my next thriller. Now, hear this, I don't need to have no reason to sate my rage, no moral high ground, but, according to my bitch-ass editor, I do need some motivation to drive the plot. So findin' a deserving victim with a dark backstory helps my writing. It's that simple. I'm no punk Dexter now, ya hear. I'm not working to rid the world of bad guys to generate some "conscience"—nah, I just like my royalty checks with lots of commas is all.

First place I went is the first place you go for the best intel in these types of towns. And it ain't no bar neither. It's the Laundromat. Found Everton's in a single second, off Main Street, about a block from the Big Dam. Name is Suds O' Tons O' Funs, annoying for the grammatical bullshit and the suggestion that laundry is funny and fun. But fuck it, you find the most vulnerable, love-starved, puffy, moon-round women in the laundry. The kind who like to talk when you lick they necks.

I felt depressed to look at the one-floor, square building made of cinder blocks, drafty glass doors to enter dead center on the front, no windows on none of the walls. Doors didn't seal tight when shut, so a November wind bit my butt when I entered. I hurried to the back wall where they hung the predictable bulletin board. A circa-1990, faded-red Coke machine stood like a bug-eyed, blockish robot to the side of the board, along with his shorter and fatter friend, a scratched and mangled vending machine with two bags of Fritos and one roll of mouth mints. Below the bulletin board was a folding table, a high one, came to my ribs, and I'm a tall man.

They say I'm good-lookin', a "rough and tumble temptation," I've heard tittered behind my back. I'm always listening, always lookin' for marks and targets.

Two rows of dated washing machines marked the middle of the square interior like a giant yellow equal sign. Clottish dust and rolled sheets of dryer lint lived in the middle of the washing machines, bulging over electrical cords and thrown trash, forming a layer of gray to separate the yellow lines of the equal sign. Dryer units taller than me filled the two side walls, except for one notch on one of the walls. In the notch was the manager's office for the Suds O' Tons O' Rank Depression.

A black-haired boy, 'bout ten, sat in a green chair in the Suds' office. Kid stared at me, burrowing his beady, black eyes into my back, as I pretended to read the tacked flyers on the board. I blew hot breath into my chilly hands, turned and looked at the kid. He trembled his lips a bit, like he might wince at the sight of *all* men. And I know that wince, I know no boy don't wince like that at a man he don't know unless he's learnt to be afraid of men. I guessed on the spot, what with his scrawny arms, and his Mama's boy pout, he learnt that from his daddy's belt.

I should be a fucking psychiatrist, 'cuz I was bull's-eye right.

A short-haired, short woman with wide hips and double Ds waddle-walked around the washers, unjamming coin trays by slamming them out and in, out and in. Tag on her olive T-shirt said, "Betty." I winked at Betty, called her "ma'am," and pantomimed the tipping of a phantom hat. When she lifted her brows and side-smiled at me, I knew I had my mark. And ain't nobody got more dirt than the woman who runs the town's Laundromat. Betty, mid-twenties, still got all her teeth, but they're stained bad of coffee. Given the locked gun case in her office, above the boy's head, the stuffed raccoon on her desk, and the way she waddled with authority, I guessed she'd seen her time huntin' like a tom boy.

Boy ran from his chair in the office to Betty's strong, thick leg, hugged it. I hid a scowl for him. Betty told the boy to go on back to the office and finish his school work. He obliged, slinking back with his shoulders high, his squint eye of suspicion on me with a growin' confidence. I considered whether I could do my work with him around. To now, I've stayed out of the law's crosshairs by avoiding complications and witnesses. As a published author with triple layers of pseudonyms, a new chin, different hair, and how my author photo is nothing but a black box on my books' jackets, I hide in plain sight.

"Where you from, mystery man? You look like you need some gin," Betty said and winked, stepping closer and into my space. She smelled like a mixture of patchouli and musk, so her stench was dense like a man's, which fit her style of dress, but didn't fit her push-up bra and done-up eyelashes. What did I give a shit though, she was practically givin' it to me within the first minute.

"Don't drink, ma'am, but I sure do like the taste a' liquor on a woman's lips," I whispered in her ear, slathering on my Southern drawl like a tangible spread of aphrodisiac. Sometimes your first mark is the easiest mark, so you stick with her, even if she does have to feed some kid fish sticks before you can get down to business.

That night, after I thought her beady, black-eyed boy

was in bed asleep, I shoved my face so far into Betty's breasts, I nearly suffocated myself. And when I licked her neck, I asked, "Why was you whispering on the phone earlier, like three times. You got an old man gonna come and try to give me trouble?"

And she say, "Oh no, nothing like that. I got something big I'm preparing to go down. This week."

And I say, "Yeah, what is that, baby?" Betty, she liked it when I called her baby, plus my fat fingers were down her fat pants and between her fat thighs.

"Oooh oooh, now, I've got to right some wrongs. It's wrong how the law is planning to kill my girl, Maggie. Others involved should get the death penalty, not her."

Bingo. I am good at executing the death penalty. And this here, what Betty revealed, this exactly why I came to Everton. My senses have always been like this, like I got a bat's sonar and my sonar detects mines of malevolents prime for killin'. I'm like the better Batman, the bad one.

"You mean, Maggie, the one got raped? In the papers?" I asked. At this point, Betty was naked, so I flipped her over to scan her big white moon. I slapped her cheeks, they jiggled. That's when I saw her tattoo, *The Daughters* in a navy-blue script.

"Oooo oooh," she said again, 'cuz she liked when I slapped her. "Yeah her. Maggie never should have gotten the death penalty."

"What's this here *The Daughters* on your ass?" I asked, reading her tat.

"The name of our group, big boy. It's a nod to Diana, daughters of Diana. We're the ones who are going to right things. Now come on and show me what you got."

So I showed her what I got.

Afterwards, when we lay in her double bed, watchin'
candlelight dance shadows on her wooden walls, she
told me about The Daughters and how they was a band
of girls going to blow up the Big Dam and flood the
town, all in retribution for old Maggie.

"So you're into Greek mythology then?" I said.

Diana is a virgin goddess of hunting. She wears short
tunics and carries a bow, usually emblems of the moon
about her, so she is right hot. I assumed this Daughters
thing was a nod to their mythical leader, Diana, even
though Betty's skin weren't the lovely honey of a Greek
or Italian. Her white-on-white-on-transparent color had
to be from a place where it's normal to drive on ice.

"Greek wha'?" She said.

"Diana, the Greek goddess, she's the nominal figure-
head of your group there?"

"Nominal what? Fool, Diana's my mother."

So Betty meant the name literally, and I should have
known. I was back in the deplorable backwaters of the
country. Made me miss my adopted home, Chelsea, and
all my books there.

"My sisters and me are the original Daughters. All the
other members are just hangers on. All this blowing up a
dam thing, all my mama's idea. She's angry about who's
really to blame, got us all spun up over Maggie. She
won't say who's to blame. But when Mama says it isn't
right to punish Maggie, I believe her."

"Why your Mama so mad about Maggie? Who do
you think is really to blame, if not the rapists, who
else?"

"You'd have to ask Mama that."

Betty thought she was just talkin' in bed. Like some

throwaway statement, assuming I wouldn't be literal too, and go on and ask Diana why she so mad about Maggie. But I couldn't come right out and ask Betty where her mama live. I was playing the part of some irrelevant wanderer, some mystery man passin' through town, lookin' for nothin' but simple lovin'. I had to find Diana another, more inconspicuous, way. I convinced Betty to open her mouth wide, the sheets over her splayed legs, her sitting up against the pillows and headboard. Down the hatch I poured more gin and licked the trickles off her chin, and she liked that. She passed out alright. With Betty snoring open-mouthed, I sprung to rummage for her mama's address.

I creeped my way out of Betty's bedroom, and as I was about to open the frig to cast light in her brown kitchen, her black-eyed boy steps out of a corner shadow and stares at me. His bare toes looked cold on the orange and brown linoleum. He held a rifle to my face. And I have to admit, I had a minor twitch of respect for the boy.

I didn't jump. I didn't yell. I hang-dogged my eyes at him and shut the fridge. Then we was both in the dark.

"Give me the gun, boy. You ain't gonna shoot."

"How do you know?" He whispered, in a perfect diction and high voice.

"'Cuz you want to join me, right? You want to be on my team."

"And what team is that?" He said, no longer the boy who winced at me in the Laundromat. *Is he playin' me?*

"The winning team, boy."

He handed me the gun.

"Now make me a salami sandwich," I said and sat in

a tiny metal chair, man-spreadin' my long legs, taking up the whole middle of the kitchen.

"I don't know what salami is," he said, his voice revealing a little crack. Not so tough without his gun, I guessed.

"What the fuck good are you then?"

"I'm no good," he said, and he whimpered.

*Fuck.*

"Look here, boy. You want to help me?"

"I don't know." But the way he said it, I know he wanted to help me. He wanted a male protector in his life and on his side. I know how it is.

"Well, I need information, boy. And you can't go tellin' your mama, ya hear?"

He opened the fridge, cast a wedge of light on me. He stood in the open door, his beady, black eyes wider than they was at the Suds O' Fun, like he might actually have a soul. But I kept talking, 'cuz he said nothing, like a creeper. Again, I had a flash of maybe liking the little shit.

"So, where's your grandmamma Diana live?"

He pointed out the window. "Next door," he said.

*Well Holy Hell that was easy.*

"Don't go tellin' your mama I asked."

"Then give me back my gun," he said. He stepped into my space and held out both his hands. No shakin' in his fingers, no doubt in his voice. So I gave him his gun back, and he nodded, which was as much of a contract as two grown men shakin' hands. He went to bed, and I plotted my plan.

Next morning, Betty got the boy off to school and said I could enjoy my coffee in her messy bed, if I wanted, 'til she came back after noon. She had errands to do in the next town, needed another pack of ammunition as part of her Big Dam mission. Blew me a kiss on her way out the door, and when she did, she didn't see Devil Boy under her arm, staring at me with his black eyes. When I looked back, he didn't blink, but he winced. I think the boy might be mentally conflicted, one side of him dark and evil, one side of him scared. I know how this always turns out. If you made up of nothin' but fear and dark, dark gonna win. Eventually. I noted to keep an eye on him, watch my back, until I was able to tag my target, slay my target, sate my rage, plot my thriller, and get on out of town.

'Twas easy to woo Betty's mama, the grand Diana. And oh boy, she grand. I waited about twenty minutes after Betty and the boy rolled out of her driveway. I showered in Betty's one bathroom. And I did think it sad that that boy had no boy stuff of his own in the bathroom. The sink and shower were cluttered with all of Betty's incongruous shit: pink lipstick and mascara on one side, and musk spray and a black comb on the other. Scrapin' in her cabinet, I saw one crusty bottle of Johnson & Johnson No Tears shampoo, which I presume was for the boy when he was a baby. Little Devil probably used a bar of soap on his hairs now, like I used to at his age. This week though, I used Betty's Pantene— when I wasn't showerin' at her mama's. I guess I thought Betty's bathroom was sad regarding the boy 'cuz that's how it was for me. And I only know the difference 'cuz one time, and only one time, I spent the night at another boy's house, and I saw he had all kinds of toys in his bathroom, tub crayons, kid toothpaste, kid toothbrush, some cartoon character on his own washcloths. Betty's boy, like me, used the grown-up toothpaste and a store-brand, thin-bristle adult toothbrush. Shit was sad.

After my sad shower, and don't worry, I didn't wallow in no pity or nothin', I waltzed on over to Diana's. Diana herself answered the door, and as with her daughter, I greeted her by saying "ma'am," and tipping a phantom hat as a gentleman's honor. She blushed. Big red blotches on her big round cheeks. She too was about five-foot-two, same wide hips, same big titties. Did I say big enough? She big. Got about twenty years on her daughter, so she mid-forties. Just right. They just right and ripe when they in their mid-forties.

I think the only thing keepin' my rages intact for one full week was going back and forth between mother and daughter, Diana keeping the ruse up for us and the secret from Betty. She cloaked me in the shadows of her home when Betty was off workin' at the Suds O' Fun. Oh boy did Diana spill the beans, talked even more than Betty when we were hanging in her sheets.

I solved the whole damn corruption web just by sleepin' in their beds. Why all these detectives don't get it? Why they work so hard? Why they go sleuthin' about, doing stupid interviews in their suits in rooms with blinding lights? Trollin' about for witnesses who ain't want to talk, beggin' dumb judges for subpoenas, reading emails, looking for murder weapons, and all the missing body parts. Blah, blah, blah. Too much work. You follow the Carter Hank McKater method of detecting, and you be done with that shit fast:

Step 1: Go to the Laundromat.
Step 2: Find the one who wants your jock.

Step 3: Trick her to talk.

Step 4: Follow leads from there.

Step 5: Repeat steps two through five until done.

Simple.

One night, Betty and the boy were at the Laundromat, which meant I was face-deep in Diana.

"You're a quiet man," Diana said, pulling my head away from her body by yanking hard on my hair. I liked how she was rough with me.

"'Cuz I like when you talkin', honey," I said. "Tell me what's got you so hot and bothered about this Maggie girl." I'd waited a couple of days to ask, until she was comfortable with me. Diana had already figured on Betty telling me about the dam plan and all, but I hadn't yet pushed Diana for the reason why and the who. Diana dropped my face back into her chest. My legs sprawled long across the rest of her king bed. The amber lights of her room were dimmed and they flickered like candle light with every whir of the ceiling fan. Diana liked the air in her home to be moving all the time, in every room, "like we're floating on sea breezes," she said.

She remained quiet, exhaled hard into my scalp a couple of times. I figured she was wondering whether she could tell me what had her so spun up, what would compel her to compel a group of women to blow up a dam in her name, even though none of them, even her closest daughter, knew why.

"Quiet man, you're quiet, but you've got the tough questions, alright."

I looked up and stared into her eyes. But know this. I

don't never go lookin' into no one's eyes, unless I'm about to slice them up right quick and I'm looking for the moment when they realize they dying and their soul floats to the surface for some final plea. But I know a lady. And I know ladies are susceptible to men like me, staring in their eyes, two inches away, and especially if the man got sapphire eyes and a Southern drawl, like I do. These are my natural weapons. So I used them.

Diana's eyelids flashed, slow closed and slow opened, and her pupils got all whoozy and wide, like she drugged. I laid it on thicker, by staring longer and saying, "Now, hold on, darling, I just like to hear you talk. And I'd love to relieve what's weighin' on your mind, by you talking 'bout it, and me listening. Your secret's safe with me," I said, in the most sickeningly slow Southern charm you ever did hear.

"Oh boy, you're good," she said. I bounced my head, still staring, showing I was a good listener. "Alright then, I don't mind telling you, but you can't go and tell Betty."

I smiled is all, indicating it was funny to suggest I'd hold a secret with Betty over Diana. Truth is, I would have. But Betty didn't know nothing. Just a cog in a wheel meant to blow up a dam for her mama.

"Thing is," Diana said. "Maggie's father's to blame."

I furrowed my brow. "Hmm," I said.

"That's right. The newspaper's say the police questioned him, and then he ran off and run away he's so distraught. But that's not the truth. There are some good cops, a couple, and they know there's more to tell. But they can't do anything, they have nothing to go on, and then the bad cops, and the damn DA, they're holding everyone's tongues. Maggie's father is the one who holds the pin. I think in part, if I flush this town, I'll flush him out. Otherwise, I need to flush this town anyway. Too dirty and corrupt." Diana pressed my body to her side. I'm taller than her, and still, I was lower on her shoulder in the way she positioned me. I let her think she was in control of the situation. This is how I trick most of my killin' victims too. Serial Killer 101.

"Truth is," she said. "And I know this because I heard it with my own ears. I work at the strip club one night a week, out on the highway. Thursday is the night they headline big girls, so that's my night. It was late on the night Maggie got raped. It was after two a.m., I know, because that's when I finished my shift. I went to my car and realized I forgot my body glitter in the bathroom, and I didn't want any of the skinny skanks who work the morning shift shaking my glitter on their rib cages and scarecrow legs." Diana paused to laugh, so I smiled and waited on why whatever made her laugh at her own story. "Imagine how pathetic you have to be to work the morning shift at a highway strip club outside Everton, Pennsylvania!"

I laughed along to play polite.

"Well, I guess I got no room to talk. Whatever, whatever," she said, waving the moving air of her bedroom.

I burrowed in the crook of her arm like I was her baby boyfriend. "Go on," I said.

"I go back in the club to grab my glitter. Nobody heard me come back in, I guess. Everyone else was gone, even the bartender. Except, Big Mike, the owner, was there, also Maggie's father, the two assholes who would end up being Maggie's two rapists, and here's the fucking kicker of the century, who would end up being Maggie's state-provided defense attorney. Mutherfucker."

I didn't move a single inch. Diana was off on a roll, in her own mind, reciting some awful monologue she lived with. Sounded like guilt on her tongue. I couldn't imagine what was comin' next.

"Oh boy," she said, her voice crackin' a little before she exhaled hard and long. "Here it is. I heard them whispering loud, like fighting. Those jackasses run a poker ring in the back room. The DA, he's all in on it. That's why that piddly-dick government worker drives a new Saab. Otherwise, asshole makes less money than me. Ha. So I waited in the hall and listened. And I didn't have to wait long. DA says to Maggie's father, 'It's too late now. We've waited six months. You owe twenty grand. Pay up or I'll exercise the liens on your house. You know I can.'"

Diana popped her lips loud, shook her head in a way to indicate shame at what she heard next. "So Maggie's father says, 'No, Joe, no. You can't. Look. Look. You two,' here I believe he was talking to the two who ended up raping Maggie. 'You two. I know you got eyes on my Maggie. She's home alone tonight. Go on over there. She's a fun girl. Likes to drink. I'll stay away. Have a party with Maggie. And give me another week, come on, fellas, we've know each other since grade school.' Mutherfucker sold his daughter out to buy more time is what." Diana took a short pause to inhale. "Now I don't think the man meant for them to rape her. I think he was only insinuating his own daughter Maggie might be loose, an easy time. And I don't know what all was said or happened or why the DA and Big Mike went along with it. All I know is I had to scoot out because Mike suddenly said he needed something from the back room. And after that, I woke up the next morning, in this here bed, and the news was reporting Maggie had been raped, hard, violent like, by those two assholes. Same ones as was at the club. Same ones Maggie's father sent on over to Maggie. Same ones Maggie killed."

"Shit," I said.

"Shit's right," Diana said. "Now don't go believing we're the only ones working to blow the Big Dam, okay. There may be some other interests, perhaps I got us a backer. Oh there's all kinds of corruption in this town, quiet man. But *my* reason is I need to fix my guilt for not doing more that night, and I've got to make the strongest point, even ruin a whole town, that the corruption in this town is so bad, that's what caused Maggie's rapes. Her jerk father, not brave enough to stay out in the open during his own daughter's trial. Of course it was right that she shot her rapists! She shouldn't die for it! Her father should! Maggie had every right to kill those boys."

"Of course," I said. "Where you think Maggie's daddy hide off to?" I asked, for he became my primary target of Diana's story.

"Funny thing," Diana said. "I don't know where specifically, but I do know it's somewhere in this town. That's why the flood is going to flush him out. Betty's boy, my grandbaby next door, he said something peculiar to me. He said he saw Maggie's father in disguise, but he won't say where. He clammed up good and tight because I reacted so hot when he told me. He thought I was mad at him. Now he won't tell me anything about whatever it was he saw." Diana pulled my face out of her arm crook so she could look at me. "*I* can't hunt around for Maggie's father, waste of time. I'll just flush him and the town out. Best I can do. I have to focus on the Big Dam. *I* don't have time to hunt," she said, stressin' the word *I* while winking. Or maybe it's more true that I'm choosing to remember her as stressin' the word *I*, while staring me down and winking.

Although I didn't need the permission or to be asked, I chose to interpret Diana as asking me to hunt out Maggie's daddy. It would help the plot of my thriller too, had a character unwittingly asked a serial killer to off a man.


The Suds O' Fun interior was mostly the same this morning, the day of Maggie's execution. But there was one thing different when I entered at nine a.m. with crullers and coffee for me and Betty and her boy. She managed the Suds in the morning today, given her plan to blow a dam tonight. The boy was with her, not in school. I had to make the boy talk and tell me where Maggie's daddy was ASAP. I was running out of time. The day before, the day after I'd figured out Maggie's daddy was my target, the boy wasted all day at school and fell asleep like a lazy-ass goodfornothin' as soon as he got home from doing homework and helping his mother at the Suds O' Fun. Little shit thwarted me.

What was different this morning in the Suds O' Fun was how in the middle of the washing machines there was no more of the clotted dust or sheets of dryer lint. The space had been picked clean, and I noted how the boy kept rooting through the dryer grills to capture more sheets of lint.

"What you doing?" I asked him, as I set the crullers and the coffee on the high folding table under the bulletin board.

"Oh, he's been picking up all the dust balls and lint rolls for two days now. I'm not complaining. My little helper," Betty said.

But I knew Devil Boy was up to something, and this thought solidified when he stared at me under low lids and snarled, all behind his mama's back.

"Hey Betty, I got a favor to ask, baby," I said, and I did my blue-eyed stare and Southern swang.

"What do you need?" She said all sweet, but in her mismatched way, spread her legs in A-frame and crossed her arms like an Army sergeant mistrusting her whole troop.

"I was hoping you might go on to the pharmacy and pick me out a cold medicine. I'm not good at medicine stuff, and I sure could use a woman to take care of me."

Betty jumped in her car at the chance of treating me, promising to cloth me up "snug and well" in a hotel bed she had rented one town higher, because her flood was coming. And she promised to "check in on" me between blowing the dam and dealing with some other stuff on her agenda tonight. I didn't care about her other stuff. I planned to be long gone by then.

Moment I had Devil Boy to myself, I said, "Boy, what are you doing with all this lint? What you up to?"

He tilted his face and studied me. His black eyes and black hair clashed with the whitest of his white skin. He knew I had him cornered, so he puckered his lips in defeat. "The man out back pays me for it. Pays me a dime for each armload. So I can buy the Fritos." He nodded toward the squat vending machine, which when I came on Monday was sparse, only two bags of Fritos, but now was empty.

"This man, he Maggie's father?" I asked.

Kid stared, which told me, yes.

"Show me," I said. I didn't know what the fool would need all this dryer lint for.

"You going to tell on me?" The boy asked.

"Boy, we got a deal. Remember? We're on the same team," I said.

He fought a tremble in his chin and also fought a smile.

I confess. I was fully playing the kid. I don't have no team. Nobody is on my team.

We traipsed on out behind the Suds O' Fun, and sure enough, tucked beside a dumpster and directly under a dryer vent was Mr. Daddy Maggie, seller of daughter. Under him was a gray bed, made up of matted dryer lint. Of course he was sleepin' under the dryer vents in November, and of course he made a ground bed out of gray matter.

The man scurried into himself, a human ball pressed against the dumpster when I appeared.

"Why you out here? Why you ain't skipped town, fool?" I asked.

"I can't leave before visiting my baby girl's grave," he cried. "And they're killing her tonight. Wouldn't be right with my faith if I left before praying at her plot. But I can't have nobody see me. I don't know how I'm going to sneak out of town without being seen."

Fool needed to disappear but he stuck around for some bullshit, sentimental, superstitious reason. That was reason enough for me to kill him. People ain't got no sense.

"Yeah," I said, staring at him from my towering height, him there on the cowering ground.

"I got a solution for you, man. They gonna blow the Big Dam tonight. Whole town gonna flood. I got a way out. You meet me where Catbrier Valley Road meets the river, about one in the a.m., I'll be on a raft. You jump on my raft. We roll out of town. Hundred dollars."

"I ain't got a hundred dollars."

"You'll figure it out."

I know fools. That fool was going to spend the whole day scouring to find a hundred dollars, and he'd employ my little team member, Devil Boy, to help him. And anticipating all that, tonight, when my rages was high and I almost choked the boy out, after the DOD blew the Big Dam and the town was running in chaos, I gave the boy a hundred-dollar bill to give the fool, so as to trick him into swimming to my trap.

My hands were clenchin' when I handed the boy the hundred, told him to give the money to the fool and not tell him I did so. And the boy, he was sobbing, crying and snot flying out of his nose.

"What the hell is the matter with you, boy?" I said.

"A man. A man in the copy shop. He shot my mother. I saw the whole thing."

*Well holy rollin' hell. Poor Betty. I don't feel nothing for her, but I don't think she needed to be shot. Whatever.*

"You going to cry about all that, or are you going to

get mad?" I yelled, which was easy, because hell, I was angry and coiled up in my own chaos. Still am right now at one in the a.m. In fact, if that fool with my hundred doesn't appear and swim onto my raft in the next minute, I'm going to jump off this raft and fucking swing my *tool* at anyone, whatever living soul steps in my path.

Earlier this evening though, when I met up with the boy by the Laundromat, and he told me about someone shootin' his mama Betty, the boy trembled, and I don't know how to console no kid. So I screamed what seemed natural to me. "You can get mad, boy! You can get even. You're on my team, right?" And dammit if I didn't sound exactly like my own daddy. "Go on now, give that dryer vent fool the money and remind him where to meet me."

Boy ran off. I went to my yellow raft. And here we are. Right now. One in the a.m. If you're thinking it would have been easier for me to slay the fool where he lay on his gray matter, you may be right. But too dangerous in the middle of town, no poetry neither. Doesn't help the plot nor the prose I got to build. Diana wanted him flushed out, and I figured, she was going to flush him down to my sewer. I'm the only one who doles out justice in Sewer McKater. And, dammit, offing him in floodwater meant less mess. Actually, more I think on it, that's a stupid idea of yours, killin' him behind the Suds' O' Fun. Shut up.

Up ahead now, and it's my time, the time I've been waiting for all week. At the juncture where Catbrier Valley Road joins the roiling, rumbling, set-free river, on the bank in a tree shadow, black as black in that part of night, stands a man in hunch back, watching for me. My twitchin' legs can barely contain themselves, so I clench every muscle and now I'm stiff legged. I swing this yellow beast to the bank some, slow the glide as much as I can by dragging an oar I also stole. Maggie's father jumps in the river and wades toward me. He now up to his neck, his hands are on the sides of the raft, and he's starting to pull himself up.

"Where's my hundred?" I shout down.

He pulls my hundred out from under his dirty hat and hands it to me. I stuff it in my pocket. Next, I pick up my special favorite tool, a machete I brought with me from New York City. With a ting of metal meeting bone, I swing the blade hard and fast, severing the fool's head. It plops into the current like a dropped basketball, floats a bit, bobs along with the other debris of soda cans and solar lights, and eventually disappears in the shadows and the depths, along to where his body sank.

Ah, this release. My precious sedative immediately washes over me, and I smile at my pearl princess in the sky. My muscles ain't twitchin.' My muscles melt. I float to join the river, and just as I'm about to take the turn and flee on my stolen raft, a splash jostles me out of my gleeful release. Someone is swimming toward me. I grip the machete tighter.

Up onto the raft's sides, the boy's hands grip for life. He pulls himself up and on before I can stomp on his little fingers. He stands here now, drenching wet like the little shit rat he is, and challenges me with his stare down.

"I'm not leaving. I'm mad. I want revenge. I'm on your team," he says.

*Well, shit. I don't want no kids.*

But I suppose I could use an apprentice and maybe too a secretary for writin' notes of ideas that pop into my head for stories. And this boy is evil, you can read it in his eyes.

"You can read and write, boy?"

"You know I can," he says, dry as bone in his tone, yet still dripping like a squeezed sponge.

"Sit down," I say.

He don't sit. Just stands there, staring at me, challenging me to make him leave. This kid unnerves me with his black eyes. And truth be truth, I am respectin' this kid. Steel nerves to stand before a man holding a machete, on a raft, fires of chaos on both sides, on the night he see his mama shot.

This time, for the first time in forever, I was the one to wince. Only a smidge. "And don't mind the blood on the edge. It's nothing. I had a nose bleed," I rush out.

Kid doesn't even turn his head to look. Just stares at me. I feel like I'm looking in a time-warped mirror of myself.

I pace. A four-foot pace, back and forth. Kid has my rages up again, in a flare. My legs are twitchin' under my jeans.

"We're gonna need to make a stop along our way," I say.

He nods.

"And you can't come where I'm gonna go on this stop. So here," I hand him the hundred-dollar bill. "While I'm off, you go to a store and buy yourself some kid toothpaste and a kid toothbrush, and then you wait for me on this raft, and you don't say nothin' to no one, hear?"

He chin-ups his head as a way to acknowledge the command, and this act is as solid as a multilateral treaty signed in the UN. I don't know if this kid gonna go with the evil side in full or not, but I sure know he shook the fear side of himself, so things ain't lookin' so hot that evil didn't already win. And me telling him to buy the kid stuff, that sure is more about me, maybe getting a chance to vicariously have what I always should'a had growing up. I ain't got feelings of love or nothing, no way. It's my *projection* acting up. I really should have been a psychiatrist.

We join the flooded, rumbling river now, two of us lying flat, watching that pearl princess in the sky watchin' us, like we're some fucked-up version of Tom Sawyer and Huckleberry Finn.

That's right, stop insulting me. Of course I read me some Twain.

And p.s.—throat clear—you really have been bamboozled, simpletons, if you believe I maintain triple layers of pseudonyms, but talk in such a pedestrian way. Perhaps I'm also a conduit of poetry and sonnets, but you'll never be wise to my ways. You'll never know who I really am.

Love, not,

*Carter Hank McKater*

# BALES

## Rob Brunet

Axel Baarde woke to the sound of too much snoring for one motel room. Before he could sit up, he shifted a fleshy thigh from his chest and rolled the woman who'd said her name was Penny onto her back. She half-swallowed a snort and rumbled something about "getting home" before picking up her throaty song louder than before.

Different snores echoed from the double bed across the room. Axel couldn't decide which was worse: that he recognized Ted's distinctive gasp-and-whistle or that it was hard to hear it from under the hoarse and labored respiratory efforts of Penny's friend Trish or Trixie or Tess—he could neither remember her name nor care what it was, and he doubted Ted would do any better.

He flicked the bedside light switch on, off, and on again. Nothing. The room stank of sweat, dirty socks, Doritos, and overflowing ashtrays. The lack of air circulation had done nothing to make the place feel like home. A panel of still-dark sky hung between the blackout curtains on the other side of Ted and Tracy's bed. He had no idea how long he'd been asleep, but the power had been out for at least five hours when the couples had

piled onto their respective beds and made entirely different noises before the snoring started.

Yesterday evening, the two men had barely arrived at
the Sleepy Time Motel with armloads of snacks and beer
when the sirens started blaring and fire trucks followed
cop cars up the road in front of their second-floor digs.

Ted had argued nonstop they ought to go looking for
stuff to break. "What good's a disaster if ya don't get in
on the mayhem?" But Axel told him there was no way
he was leaving the truck unattended, flood or not.

A half dozen motel guests, one in curlers and a house-
coat, had huddled outside on the balcony, jabbering
about an explosion at some dam north of town.

"It's 'cause a that whack-job killer Maggie Stillborn
they fried this afternoon," a toothless neighbor said.
"You watch. We're gonna pay." He flashed a gummy
grin, seemingly excited by the prospect.

"Wilbourne. And they didn't electrocute her,"
shouted the curler lady. "We're a lethal injection state."

Gumnuts didn't care. "She's a witch, anyhow.
Shoulda burned her, I say." He stomped his rubber boot-
clad feet and pumped both fists in the air, as if it called
for a celebratory jig. Green and orange paisley shorts bil-
lowed around his chicken legs the color of mayonnaise.

Curler Lady chewed a cheese string she pulled from
her pocket. "I don't much care how they do 'em. Just
think they oughta put it on TV."

"Better yet, Facebook." Gumnuts did a pirouette.

Hours later, lying in bed in the dark surrounded by
the esophageal symphony of Ted and the girls, Axel
figured Maggie Wilbourne got a better ticket out than
he'd enjoy if he couldn't get the truck moving next

morning. The Milwaukee buyer might not give a shit the eight bales of skunk weed were stolen, but he was sure to make calls if they didn't arrive on time. And if he found out *who* the pot was stolen *from*, it'd be a different story.

This kind of pay check only came once in a lifetime for a guy like Axel. Enough money a man of simple tastes could leave the game once and for all. He'd been counting the hours to his exit when the pickup struck a pothole outside of Everton late yesterday afternoon. The AAA guy charged an extra hundred to tow them to Woods Automotive because Axel said he wanted a garage with a motel nearby. The owner-mechanic did little to inspire confidence until Axel offered to pay triple rate for a spindle rod, whatever the hell that was. At least he could keep an eye on the load from across the street.

Hanging on the motel balcony after the dam blast, he and Ted watched some guy in a Penguins sweater and a seventies haircut offer fifty-dollar rides out of town in a rusted-out Aerostar. He'd been and gone twice. The third time he pulled into the parking lot is when Axel and Ted first caught sight of the girls from downstairs. They wobbled out of their first-floor room on four-inch heels, dressed for a night in the sleaziest dive bar Everton could offer. First one then the other propositioned the bushy-haired Aerostar driver, but he wasn't buying.

Axel kept eying the F150, fighting the urge to cross the street and wait things out in the cab. He would have done it, too, had the meat mountain of a mechanic not shown up with a kid and a shotgun soon after the dam broke. Last thing Axel wanted to do was draw that giant's attention to the burlap bungie-corded across its bed.

Ted tried again. "Least we could pretend to buy rides from that jackass. Roll him five miles up the road. Ransom the other riders, I dunno. Chance like this...we could be back in an hour."

Axel grabbed his sweatshirt, pulled him in close, and hissed in his ear. "I'm not going anywhere and neither are you. Showing up late is gonna cost me enough. Losing the freight isn't what I hired you for." Ted tried to wriggle out of his grasp, but Axel twisted the shirt tighter. "There's six hundred pounds of don't-fuck-with-me in that pickup says we sit tight until that fat-ass mechanic gets us back on the road to Milwaukee."

"I told ya we shoulda stole a better truck."

"And draw heat we don't need? Brilliant." Axel let go of Ted's shirt. "You should plan *everything*."

In the parking lot below, the party girls were trying their magic on a flabby-looking guy hanging a suit-bag in a Volvo. He said he could only fit one of them, what with the child seats in the back, and seemed to be considering which one to take when Ted called down with an offer they couldn't refuse. He made chips, beer, and skunk weed sound like a buffet in paradise. "Plus we're on the second floor. Can't beat that."

The water crested the bridge across the river as the Aerostar pulled out. Ted helped the girls trundle their suitcases to the room while Axel nibbled the nails on his left hand and scowled at the garage.

"I'm Penny," said the taller one.

Ted said, "And this here's Tammy."

"I got candles," she said, waving a pair of amber hurricane jars she must've stolen from a restaurant.

Penny said Tammy knew the words to more than a hundred songs, and they piled into the room for a party.

After maybe half an hour of massacred Beatles tunes, a shot rang out from across the street. Axel peered out the window, but there didn't seem to be any movement at the garage. He ripped open another bag of Cheetos to keep from biting his nails.

Twenty minutes after that, another squad car rolled down the street, spreading a wake through water more than six inches deep. The car broadcast an evacuation order most people had already followed. Apart from Ted and the girls—who had declared life more fun without TV and telephones—the only other person fool enough to have remained at the motel was the toothless bugger in rain boots.

Perched next door on a gray plastic chair, Gumnuts assured Axel the water could only rise so far. "Lived here back before the dam, when they were still running logs on the river. It's a shit-ton of water but it's gotta fill the valley south of here before we got anything to worry 'bout."

"You sure about that, are you?"

"Matter of physics." The man got up and clomped down the stairs. He sloshed over 'til he stood directly below Axel. "See? My boots are under water." He raised and lowered his right foot for emphasis. "But my foot's all dry inside."

"So?"

"That's how the dam works."

"Worked." Axel wasn't sure winning an argument with Gumnuts was worth the effort, but Ted had started singing lead on "Yellow Submarine" and he wasn't overly keen on joining in on the choruses.

Gumnuts said, "And when the water gets high enough, it'll pour in, right?"

Axel just stared.

"But my knees will still be dry." The old man touched them and turned his palms toward Axel, brushing his fingertips with his thumbs. Satisfied he'd made his point, he came back to the balcony. "You can swim, right?"

"Why?"

Gumnuts shrugged. "In case I'm wrong." He wandered down the balcony trying doors.

It had appeared the guy was right. By the time Ted and Axel and Penny and Whatshername stopped singing and blew out the candles, the water had only half covered the truck's hubcaps. Axel doubted they'd be going anywhere in the morning, but at least his cargo would stay dry.


Listening now to the other three snoring, Axel decided no amount of candlelit entertainment was worth the price of this midnight cacophony. Worse, he realized lying there in the dark, it hadn't been a dream when he heard Ted whispering how Tabitha could fit in the truck no matter how big her makeup bag. He swung his feet to the floor and cried out when they splashed into ice-cold water. A vision of Gumnuts's rubbers flashed through his mind and he swore at the man under his breath.

Penny sat up and grabbed his elbow, tugging him back to bed. He yanked himself away and used his feet to splash the bed next to theirs. "Wake up."

"What the hell?" said Ted.

"Where's the smokes?" Axel asked.

"How do I know? What'd you do here?"

Axel fumbled on the nightstand between the two beds, found a pack of cigarettes and lit one. He flipped the pack at Ted but lit a candle before giving him the lighter. He slapped a bare foot in the water. "We're swamped."

Ted took a drag and considered that a moment. "Holy shit. The water's all the way up here?"

Penny told them to shut up and go back to sleep. She scissored Axel with her legs and drew him onto her. He pushed himself off, stood, and grabbed a shoe floating by the bed.

"For shit's sake, put on some underwear at least," Ted said.

Axel ignored him and looked around for the other shoe. The candle reflected off the water sending shimmering orange streaks across the ceiling but doing little to light more than the strip of water between the beds. He lit another candle and held it in his hand like a torch. The girl with no name moaned and rolled over. She opened one eye and studied him standing there naked with a shoe in one hand and a hurricane candle in the other. "Man, that's good weed," she said and went back to sleep.

He sloshed across the room to the bureau and sat on it to pull on his jeans. Rolling his pant legs past his knees, he put on a T-shirt that wasn't his. He slipped on his one wet shoe and scooped the other as it floated into the bathroom. He stood on one leg to tug it on and told Ted to get dressed.

"Screw that. I'm warm and dry and that water's a

good foot and a half from the top of the mattress." He made a show of pulling the covers out of harm's way and wrapped one arm around his partner.

Vaulting across his bed—and Penny in it—Axel landed with a cannon ball splash in front of the night table. Ted swore. Trina sputtered. Penny got up and went to pee, making Axel realize all the toilets on the first floor and up and down the street were already part of the water he was standing in. He opened the door and a gust of wind pushed a wave through the motel room.

From the walkway, he glared at the sign advertising gas that was way too expensive across the street. That was all he could see of the service station. Beyond it, Everton's rolling skyscape was lit by stars and scattered fires. Downright peaceful, were it not for the echoing gunfire and sirens.

"Helluva mess," said a voice over his shoulder.

He turned to look up at a pair of pink rubber soles— the bottom of Gumnuts's boots. The man sat on the motel roof, swinging his dangling feet like a kid at the circus.

"Guess the valley on the wet side of the dam was a damn sight bigger than the one downstream." The man sounded positively gleeful. "Shoulda guessed it. Used to deep dive ten miles north a here. Jumpin' off the top of Dead Man's Cliff. They called it that before the dam. After, when the ledge was maybe fifteen feet from the surface of the water? The name stuck, but it was kinda a joke. Some folks was pissed. Them that needed to look for a new place to die. Popped all hell outta your ears, I'm telling ya, goin' down like that."

"Did it come up fast or slow?"

"Did what?"

"The water."

"Depends how you looked at it. Like I said, it was only fifteen feet. Doesn't take long to fall that—"

"Tonight. The flood. Did it rush in or just keep rising bit by bit?"

Gumnuts grabbed hold of a drainpipe and shimmied down next to Axel. "Slow and steady," he said. "Been up watching it all night."

Axel asked, "See anything float away?"

"Like what?"

"Like a truck. Full of bales."

"Shit no. Trucks don't float."

"They can. For a bit."

"In a torrent, maybe. This one's more of a creeper. Your truck's safe." He looked over at the sign, thought about that a moment. "Maybe not."

Ted joined them on the balcony. "Holy fuck."

"Yeah," said Axel.

"Where's the truck?"

"Where do you think?" Axel rubbed his index fingernail against the worn cuticle on his thumb.

"Think it's dry? The weed, I mean."

Axel shot him a dark look and bent his gaze toward Gumnuts. He said, "Triple wrapped. Tighter than a nun's panties. Can you imagine the reek if it weren't?"

Ted looked at the old man's green and orange shorts. "Dressed for a party?"

Gumnuts gave him two thumbs up and a raspy cough.

Ted said, "So what do we do?"

"Sit tight and wait for the water to go down then steal another truck."

"And if the water goes up instead?"

"We drown waiting."

Gumnuts looked from Axel to Ted and hissed.

Ted said, "What are you still doing here?"

"Where else would I go?" The guy pointed at the roof. "I'm pretty sure the water can't get higher'n that."

Axel said, "Like you were sure it wouldn't fill the valley?"

Gumnuts shrugged. "Never was good at math."

Axel alternately rubbed chilled ankles with his feet, wishing he had the old guy's boots. A burst of giggles erupted from the motel room and Penny stumbled out wearing a bra and a pair of Axel's boxers. "What's with the shamrocks?" she asked. "These your get lucky pair?"

Gumnuts gave her a once over and she wrapped her arms around herself.

She said, "Sure is quiet." For a moment, the sirens fell silent and the only sound was water lapping against the motel brick. "C'mon out, Trix. You can see the moon reflecting on the water."

Axel made a mental note of Penny's friend's name and promptly wondered why. Ted glared at the old man who was more than a little appreciative of the way Trix looked—wrapped in a bed sheet, wet from the knees down, leaning over the railing, looking stunned.

"Where is everybody?" asked Trix.

"Split, long gone." Gumnuts cracked a red-mouthed smile. "Them that didn't go under."

"People drowned?"

"Saw a couple floaters an hour ago." Gumnuts gestured southward. "Moving at a good clip."

Trix whimpered and disappeared back into the room.

Axel walked to the end of the balcony and craned his neck around the corner. Though the river itself was no longer discernible, the path it cut through the half-submerged buildings on either bank was clear. The distant horizon glowed creamy gray, bathed in reflected electric light from some other dam in some drier place.

Some city full of easy targets. That's what Axel went for. Nothing too rich, nothing too complicated. For a couple of years now, his specialty had been wine. He had a regular route of less-than-reputable restaurants and roadhouses who weren't fussy about his labeling efforts. He copied fancy script from French bottles for sale on Amazon and pasted them on hooch he picked up from mom-and-pop wineries with excess production—barrels that didn't quite make the grade, anything he could score cheap. It was a back-door-to-back-door operation—more work than it was worth, but it didn't involve a ton of risk, and that suited him fine. Until yesterday.

He considered it fate. A simple screw-up involving a load of passable chardonnay and a mistaken calendar entry that had him show up a day early. He knew some of his vintners grew pot on the side but he'd never expected to walk in on a pair of young fieldworkers bagging marijuana by the half-ton. When he saw they were more scared than he was, he swaggered a bit and threatened a call to INS if they didn't toss a few bags in his van. It wasn't until he passed a half-dozen bearded men on Harleys in the vineyard parking lot that he realized exactly who he'd ripped off.

In a rest area five miles down the road, he drove the van a few hundred feet down a bike trail. He phoned Ted and told him he'd give him three thousand bucks if he could steal a truck—something cheap and dirty—and take a ride with him. Then he called a guy who'd once turned down his offer of counterfeit wine but told him to get in touch if ever he had something more significant to sell.

Within an hour, he and Ted had transferred the load, abandoned his van, and were en route to Milwaukee. Along the way, every radio station was bleating something about some woman about to be executed for taking revenge on a couple of low-life rapists. No one was reporting a half million-dollar heist of marijuana from Pearling Estates Winery.

Ted wouldn't have been Axel's first choice of partner for anything as serious as this, but you could choose a worse pal for a road trip, and he knew he wouldn't ask a lot of questions. Besides, Ted had always told him he could hook him up with fake ID—a passport even—if he ever needed one. Something about a guy who owed him a favor for a one-of-a-kind Ironman tattoo. They were on their way to Everton to make the connection when they busted the damn spindle rod.

And now here they were, paying for some woman's sins, stuck at the Sleepy Time Motel, next to sunken treasure.

Penny appeared beside him. She climbed onto the railing so her feet hung above the water and said, "It's like being at the lake."

"More like being *in* the lake," Axel said.

"Trix and me used to go to summer camp."

Axel wasn't in the mood to feign interest.

"Y'know. Horses, sailboats," she said.

"I'm happy for you."

"We learned all kinds of stuff."

He grunted.

"Plus boys." She waited for a reaction, sighed, and said, "Maybe we shoulda gone with that guy in the van."

"You'd be somewhere dry by now."

"Why'd you wanna stay?" She shot him a flirty glance. "Was it so we could party?"

"Yeah, that must've been it," he said, "because this is exactly how I wanna die. Drowned in a strange town after a night in a budget motel room with Ted and the two hottest women we could find in the parking lot."

"Really?" It took a moment before the look of hurt crept across her face. Axel could see it in spite of the dark. As he fumbled to say something less caustic, Penny wiped a smile back on and said, "Every time Trix and me take a trip, you never know what's gonna happen."

"Must be exciting for you."

Axel wondered what it would be like to take a trip—travel for pleasure. With someone like Penny, with Ted, alone even. He figured he'd find out soon enough. If the bales were dry and he could somehow swing his delivery—late or not—he planned to head someplace cheap and warm. Guatemala, maybe, or Belize. Somewhere a few hundred thousand could stretch to a lifetime, if you played your cards right.

If the bales were soaked, any trip he'd take would be different. He'd be on the run with empty pockets. There was no going home. The people he'd ripped the load from didn't look like the forgiving kind and his Milwaukee buyer would have no use for a guy who wasn't smart enough to steal a truck that could drive eight hundred miles without breaking down.

Either way, he needed to know.

He left Penny staring at the water, imagining herself at a beach in a bikini instead of on a rusted railing wearing someone else's underwear.

Ted and the old man were sharing a beer, arguing about whether this would be about the best or absolutely the worst time to go fishing. Axel listened to them for a moment and lit a smoke before asking Gumnuts how long it'd been since he'd last dived.

"August," said the geezer, "and it was fulla fish in the lagoon the other side of the dam. I coulda caught 'em with my bare hands. That's what I'm trying to tell—"

"Got a job for you," Axel said.

Gumnuts tilted his head and listened, looking every bit a dog eager to please his master.

"Think you could go down about twelve feet and loosen a few bungie cords?"

"This got something to do with whatever it is you're hauling in that beat-up truck you got towed in with?"

"It's worth a thousand bucks."

Ted said, "A thousand? You're only giving me three to make the haul with you."

"You much of a swimmer?" Axel asked Ted. When he didn't answer, he said, "Then shut up." He explained to Gumnuts exactly where the pickup full of marijuana lay submerged. "You gotta watch the bales don't float away when you free them. The way they're tied down, they should come up in pairs."

"I'm thinking four."

"Right. Four pairs."

"Four thousand." The old man drew his shoulders

back and jutted his chin a little.

Axel said, "That's a thousand a dive."

"All kinds a crap in that water." He flashed a mouthful of pink.

Axel looked at the man's rubbers. "Three thousand, and I get your boots."

Ted started to say something, but a glance from Axel shut him up.

Gumnuts took off his rubbers and handed them over with a polite nod. Axel slipped off his sopping wet shoes and offered them in return, but the old man had already scampered onto the railing, peeled off his shirt, and tossed it to Ted for safekeeping. Axel slipped on the still-warm boots, thinking the guy had surprisingly large feet for such a scrawny bastard.

The old man carved a perfect arc into the water and popped up thirty feet away a few seconds later. His pencil-thin arms and big flapper feet made short work of the distance between the motel and the service station sign across the hidden road. He hauled himself out of the water, straddled the sign, and pointed just beyond it. "Over there, ya figure?"

"A bit back of that." Axel waved toward the left.

The man stood and dove in, his body scarcely throwing a splash.

When the first bale floated up, it was all Axel could do to keep from dancing a jig of his own. The three-by-two sausage popped out of the water with no more than a gentle sploosh. Were it not for the brilliant yellow plastic, he might not have spotted it at all on the ink-black water a hundred feet off the balcony. Immediately, it started to flow toward the river basin. He marched down the balcony to where he'd left Penny minutes earlier, prepared to dive in himself if Gumnuts didn't pop up.

But he did. Seconds later. Clinging to a second bale and letting out a whoop befitting a man half his age. He put a little weight on its back end and propelled his way across to the balcony with a splashless frog kick. Ted pulled the bale over the railing and Gumnuts climbed out. He ran the length of the walkway, and dove in to catch the first bale as it approached the corner. After handing that one off to Axel, he walked back and swam over to retrieve two more.

"Put them on the bed," Axel told Ted, floating a bale into the room. "Stack the mattresses." The water had risen a good eight inches in the past half hour and he'd given himself a soaker when he'd moved too quickly chasing the first bale.

After delivering two more bales, Gumnuts took a beer break. Trix came out of the room and wrapped him in the spare blanket from the closet top shelf; that put a grin on his face. Ted passed around cigarettes, pointedly lighting everyone else's, leaving Penny to spark the old man's.

Penny said, "Told ya. Stuff happens to me and Trix. All the time. Ain't that right?"

Axel didn't know what surprised him more: how nonchalant the women were about a few hundred pounds of marijuana or that they didn't seem to care it was stacked on a double-height bed to keep it out of water that was lapping at their calves. Was that what it meant to be carefree? The very thought of it made his thumb's cuticle burn and he ripped it with his front teeth. Catching Penny watch him do it, he turned his head to spit skin at the water just in time to see a runabout round the corner of the motel at low throttle.

The driver gave a wave and navigated the sixteen-footer alongside the balcony. He cut the engine and tossed them a rope. Ted splashed over and looped it loosely over the railing.

"You still here?" the driver said. "Word is, there's at least three feet of water yet to come."

Axel said, "Nice boat." The rock-star hairdo made it hard to miss the guy as the Aerostar driver who'd been selling rides out of town a few hours earlier.

"Opportunity knocks." The driver patted the windscreen. "Amazing the stuff people will leave behind when they run for their lives."

"Found her floatin', didja?" Gumnuts gave the boat an appreciative look.

"I figured the marina would be one of the first places to go under. Need a water taxi?"

Axel scanned the bow-rider's front seating area, which was almost at eye level what with them standing in a foot of water. Ted looked at it, too, and they shared a discreet nod. Axel asked, "How much to take two guys and some cargo to dry land?"

"How much cargo?"

"Fill your boat."

The man said, "There's five of you."

"So make two trips. It's the cargo I care about."

The boat was drifting slowly from the balcony. Ted gave the rope a tug and Axel reached over and grabbed a cleat.

"Two hundred a person. Another five for the cargo."

The man squinted one eye. "Thousand bucks."

"Two twos and five is nine," Axel said.

"Expenses."

"What kind of expenses?"

"We gonna argue or load your cargo?"

Axel made like he was pulling his wallet from his jeans and he used his other hand to wave Ted into action. His partner yanked the rope tight and scrambled up onto the railing. Seeing the way Ted bared his teeth, the driver turned the key in the ignition, but the engine choked. He grabbed the boat hook pole from where it rested next to him and swung it round, catching the side of Ted's head. Ted went down swearing and the man slipped the rope loose and used the pole to shove the bow off the railing. He tried the ignition again. This time it caught. The engine roared and he shoved the throttle to forward. As the boat began to plough away from the balcony, Gumnuts folded himself over the railing and tumbled aboard.

Penny slipped under Axel's arm and lit a fresh smoke. They passed it back and forth while they watched the men fight. Mostly, it looked like Gumnuts trying to climb on the driver's back while the guy slapped at him with the pole. The confines of the cockpit being what they were, hardly any blows connected. Ted stood once and took a half step forward before being caught in the face with a flailing kick from Gumnuts's bare foot. From what Axel could see, Ted spent the rest of the fight on the bottom of the boat. The whole time, the vessel spun in a slow circle, jostling over and over on its own wake. The sound of its hull slapping the water was punctuated by grunts and squeals from the men fighting for control of the steering wheel.

The wave action sent water sloshing up Axel's legs and into both rubber boots. He held Penny snug for warmth.

She said, "Did I hear you say you'd leave us behind?"

Axel blew smoke over her head. "Did you hear me say the plan was to steal the boat?"

"No."

"Careful what you listen to."

"I could learn a lot from a guy like you." She pulled his arm tighter around her.

Eventually, Gumnuts managed to wrap his legs around the other guy's neck. He buried his fingers in the guy's hair and shook his head back and forth like his was trying to rip his head off. The driver shrieked in pain. Gumnuts boxed his ears and shouted at him to dock the boat against the balcony.

When the bow struck the railing, Ted drew himself up from the boat's carpeted floor and hauled himself out. He fussed with knots, bow and stern. Gumnuts looked at Axel expectantly, one hand buried in the boat driver's shaggy hair. "Whaddya want me to do with him?"

"Ted'll tie him up in the room," Axel said. "You got work to do." He nodded across the road.

"Aye-aye." Gumnuts punched the driver behind the ear and pushed him up and over. Ted half-dragged him into the motel room and Axel tossed a ski-rope in behind. Gumnuts hacked a couple times and dove back into the water.

Working their way down the balcony, Penny and Trix slid open what windows they could and smashed a couple they couldn't. They packed out bottles and food some guests had left behind and grabbed a half dozen dry blankets. Trix found a pair of battery-operated speakers. They made a few trips, stuffing every storage compartment on the boat, like they were packing for vacation.

They were still at it when all eight bales were free from the truck. Gumnuts stood in front of Axel, shivering. He asked to be paid.

"This oughta be good," Ted murmured.

Axel told the man he didn't travel with that kind of cash. "Money and dope in the same place, same time, is a recipe for long time if you get caught."

"That much p-p-pot," Gumnuts said, "you're not t-t-talking weekend jail."

"I get paid on delivery. So will you."

"Now I gotta help you move it? That wasn't the d-d-deal."

Axel shrugged. "I can mail you a check, if you'd rather."

Ted smiled for the first time since waking up.

"See if the girls can find him dry clothes." Axel splashed his way back to the corner, not caring any more how much water got in his boots.

He usually had a knack for turning crap luck to his advantage. He needed it, Axel knew, given how hard the universe liked to piss on his parade. Without ever acknowledging he had a hand in creating it, Axel embraced all of his misfortune, considering it a test. If he responded with resilience, he'd win. If he caved, someone else would get the prize. Things weren't so much zero-sum as winner-take-all, he figured.

This guy showing up with a boat threw him for a loop. He wasn't about to complain, but something felt too easy about it. Like the way he'd scored the truckload of pot in the first place. Like maybe he was getting karmic payback from someone else's account. He wanted his exit—craved it, in fact—and he could even convince himself he deserved it. But surely he'd have to have more of a hand in achieving it.

Ted showed up beside him and together they stared at Pittsburgh's halo in the distance.

"What's this river called?" Axel asked.

"The Monongahela."

"I'm trying to remember what towns it flows through on the way to Pittsburgh, or if it even goes there."

"Dunno," said Ted.

Axel waved at the debris floating past them, a couch jostling in the corner of the balcony where the railing stuck out. "We can probably go a fair distance before anyone pays attention to a couple guys in a boat, but I don't like our chances of going unnoticed once we hit the burbs north of town."

"And we're gonna need another truck."

"Exactly."

"What about the others?" Ted asked.

The bow-rider was likely rated for six adults, seven in a pinch. The weed weighed as much as three grown men, never mind how much space it'd take up.

"The old fart is probably right," Axel said. "The water's gotta stop some time. They should be safe on the roof."

A splash behind him was followed by Gumnuts's cackle and Penny's curse. The wannabe cabbie had wrangled a bale over the railing and was thrashing his way into the current.

"I thought you tied him up." Axel elbowed Ted in the ribs.

"Fucking knots." Ted started to climb on the rail as if to dive after the guy as he floated past them.

Axel held him back and pushed him toward where the boat rocked outside the room. "Load the rest," he said.

Gumnuts pitched in and the women wrestled a bale between them. By the time they clambered atop the bales, the gunwales were barely a foot above the water line. Axel's suggestion someone had to get off was met with a whimper from Penny and dead stares from the rest.

"Is there life jackets?" Trix wanted to know.

The shithead who'd stolen the eighth bale had a two-minute head start and even though Axel had no qualms about leaving people behind, he wasn't about to start tossing them overboard.

Ted fought with his creative ropework and Axel got the engine started on the third try. As the bow turned away from the balcony, he looked back. The trough behind the stern looked like it came from a boat twice this size. The bow lifted sharply. On instinct, Axel threw the throttle forward, realizing too late the propeller was trimmed up.

The boat tipped to near forty-five degrees and he watched Trix tumble past him and into the wake. For a split second, he expected to see her chopped apart by the propeller but she resurfaced twenty feet behind them, choking on water. He throttled back and began to turn the boat.

Ted put a hand on his arm and shook his head. He spoke softly. "We're overweight."

Axel looked in his eyes, could tell that he meant it. Penny was shrieking and Gumnuts was rolling a bale overboard. "This'll float. Grab it," he shouted.

Ted clapped his hands on Gumnuts shoulders and tried to strip him off the bale.

Axel grabbed the boat hook pole and clocked Ted better than the Aerostar guy had managed earlier. He watched him slump across the gunwale and resisted the urge to pull him back in the boat.

Even with two bodies overboard, the water poured in over the stern. The bow rose so high, Axel had to clutch the windshield to keep from falling backward. The engine whine became a gurgle, then choked and went silent as the stern slipped under water.

The last thing Axel heard before he went under was Penny scream, "I told you shit happens."

An oversized rubber boot got jammed between the driver's seat and steering wheel, pulling him down with the boat. He twisted his leg back and forth, wriggling his foot within it. As the boat settled on the pavement, it pitched forward and he worked himself free. His ears popping from the pressure, the dozen feet between him and the surface felt like a mile. Air blasted out his chest and he gasped, taking a throat full of water as his face broke through.

Something banged him across the shoulders, pushing him back under. He clutched and felt plastic wrap. His fingers slipped off and he grasped again, driving his nails through to gain purchase. His legs kicked someone else's and he heard a woman cough. Edging around the bale, he came face to face with Penny, her eyes wide and white-rimmed.

"I can't see her," she said. "TRIX."

"Got her here." Gumnuts's voice rang clear across the water. "She's breathing. Sorta."

Axel shouted, "Ted?"

Gumnuts said, "He's either a better diver than me or he's done for."

Penny slipped around the other side of the bale and got Axel to hold her forearms while she clutched his. "Don't let go," she said. "We can ride it like a canoe." They'd already floated to the motel's edge and were about to be pulled into the river's current. When that happened, she took a mouthful of water and he held tight while she choked it out.

"Kick for the shore," Gumnuts yelled, his voice further than before. "Hey look, I snagged another bag!" Then, after a pause, and from much farther back, they heard, "Watch out for the rapids."

Axel couldn't tell which shore was closer. The river had narrowed and they were jostling among branches and furniture and churning bits of crap he had no desire to identify. The water smelled of oil and felt gritty on his face. He told Penny to just hold on, not to kick, to save her strength and let him try to aim for the river's edge as they rounded a bend. A dull roar sounded downstream.

They got within yards when a paddle banged the bale from over his shoulder.

"Found ya!" It was the fucker from the Aerostar. In a canoe. He raised the paddle to take another whack.

Axel grabbed the paddle as it landed and held. The canoe tipped back and forth. The guy was sitting upright, and Axel could feel that one solid pull would land him in the water. Instead, he said, "Did you beach the bale you stole?"

"Did you sink my boat?"

"The boat you stole?"

Penny let go of Axel's arms and slipped under water. She came up almost instantly, clinging to the far side of the canoe. The dull roar had grown thunderous.

Axel yanked the paddle hard. Without him saying a word, Penny pulled hard on her side of the canoe and the guy rocked into the water. The canoe rolled over with him and Penny came up spouting water.

He reached across the canoe's hull and held Penny the way she'd shown him moments before with the bale. Together they watched the guy grapple with the plastic of their abandoned bale, clinging to its side as it got sucked toward the churning water.

It took both of them kicking together to reach the shore. The canoe jammed between picnic tables in what must have been a riverside park. They crawled up on one and lay staring at the sky, chests heaving.

After a couple minutes, when she had her wind back, Penny said, "I do it, too."

"Do what?"

"Bite my nails."

"I don't—"

"I seen ya."

"And this matters because...?"

"You seem pretty cool about everything," she said. "The water, losing your truck and everything. Even Ted."

"He had it coming."

"But you're nervous."

"I thought I caught a break. Figured I blew it." He rolled on his side and looked at her, saw the shape of her forehead, the ridge of her nose. He could feel her feeling him stare. "Wanna take a trip?"

"Where?"

"Doesn't matter."

"Shit'll happen," she said, turning her head toward him, her face in shadow.

Axel said, "I'm counting on it."

# THE DARKEST HOUR
### Hilary Davidson

"What if the water gets *this* high," Jackson said. "What would we do?"

"It's not going to get that high, baby, I promise." Miranda Reichert stroked her youngest son's hair. He was eight years old and his pale, silky hair was starting to darken. In the low light of the James Buchanan High School gym, he looked like a pint-sized replica of his older brother, who was sitting at the other end of the mat, stone-faced.

"But what if it does?" Jackson insisted. "It destroyed our house. It was on the *news,* Mama. Our street is *gone.* What if the water comes up here?"

"It won't," Miranda said. "It can't. That was the force of the dam breaking. The water's going down now."

"But what if…?"

"Stop it," Tyler barked at his brother, with all the snarling rage a thirteen-year-old can direct at a younger sibling. "Mom's only explained it to you a thousand times already. Shut up."

"Tyler, don't talk to your brother that way," Miranda said, as Jackson started to snuffle. "Look, I know you're both exhausted and you've been through the wringer tonight. You both need to sleep."

"In here?" Tyler surveyed the gym with contempt. Everton didn't have much in the way of disaster-preparedness training, and the James Buchanan High School, while high on a hill in an upper-class enclave, was ill-prepared for the motley crew who'd straggled in from the submerged streets closest to the central business district and the rougher areas near the old plant. Miranda and her sons were sitting on a pair of padded gymnastics mats. They'd been given bottled water and protein bars, but there wasn't a pillow or blanket in sight. The few possessions Miranda had grabbed before they'd run for their lives were in a plastic shopping bag.

"Why don't you try lying down?" Miranda said. "It's just for a night. Tomorrow, we'll figure out a plan."

"If you wanted us to sleep, you'd have taken us to Dad's house," Tyler snapped. "We have our rooms there. And you could've slept in one of the guestrooms, Mom. It's not like Dad doesn't have the space."

Miranda took a deep breath and counted to ten, a tactic she'd advised her sons to use when they were upset. "I know there's plenty of room at your father's house, but we're going to stay here tonight. We're not going to argue about it."

Tyler muttered something under his breath. Miranda let it go. She was too exhausted and stressed to discuss it properly with her sons at that moment. It was three in the morning, and they were all ragged and raw. No matter what, her rule was never to badmouth her ex to their sons, no matter how much he deserved it.

"It's time we all went to sleep," Miranda said.

"I can't sleep," Jackson announced. "I need to pee."

"But your brother took you to the bathroom half an hour ago," Miranda pointed out.

"But then I had another bottle of water. Ty got it for me."

Miranda sighed, glad that at least Tyler was doing something to take care of his brother.

"It's okay," Tyler said, standing. "I'll take him again."

"Should I come with you?" Miranda asked.

Tyler looked at her like she'd just suggested swimming in the water that had burst out of the dam. "You know we go to school here, right? We know where the bathroom is."

"Sure, but there are people here who've just lost everything..."

"And they'll steal our stuff if you leave it," Tyler said. "Come on, Jackson."

Jackson tumbled to his feet and padded after his big brother. When they got to the door of the gym, he turned and waved at Miranda. The hallway beyond was well lit, but once they turned that corner, they were out of view.

When they were gone, Miranda allowed her head to sink into her hands. She couldn't give into despair while her kids watched, but what they didn't know wouldn't scar their psyches. It had been a hell of a day, what with the threats made by the Daughters—whoever they were—then Maggie Wilbourne's execution and the explosion that destroyed the dam. Scary as the evacuation had been, she could at least talk about that with her kids, help them through it. What was harder were the things she couldn't talk about. The first was the phone call, the one that came in half an hour before the dam blew up: *Take your kids and run to higher ground* warned a whispery voice; before Miranda could ask who the hell was calling, the line had gone dead. It had left her shaken, and she'd taken it as a threat, as if her ex was coming after her. It had made her scramble, grabbing some documents and cash she had hidden in the house. That voice was the reason she was so ready to run when all hell broke loose.

But there was something far worse that she couldn't talk to her kids about: the torment she'd suffered at the hands of their father. What Tyler had said was entirely true: if they went to their father's house, her sons would be sleeping in their own beds; Miranda and her ex shared joint custody, so the boys were constantly shuttled back and forth between their houses. Tyler and Jackson would be far more comfortable there than in a chilly school gym. It wasn't even a question. Was it selfish of her to deny them that?

Miranda pulled her knees close to her chest, until she was curled up in a ball. The last time she'd been inside her ex's house—Conrad's house—he'd strangled her until she passed out. That wasn't even his worst attack on her, but it was his last. He'd never hit their sons, so she had no grounds to fight him on custody, even though she wanted to. She didn't have Conrad's deep pockets or connections, either, so her fantasy of hightailing it out of town remained just that, a cherished dream. She wouldn't be able to leave Everton until Jackson was eighteen and off to college. That was a long ways away.

Miranda always tried to put her kids first but, glancing around the huddled masses in the school gymnasium, she knew she'd let them down. They shouldn't have been there. Maybe she *should* call Conrad and ask him to come get them. She pulled out her phone and it hit her suddenly that she hadn't heard from her ex all night. There were texts and calls from Miranda's friends and coworkers, and even from Conrad's sister, Heidi, who'd always been kind to her. But there was nothing from the father of her children. Had something happened to Conrad? Miranda found that hard to believe, with his grand mansion on a hill. The flood wouldn't have touched it. Unless Conrad was in town when the water hit...

She was weighing the cost of calling him when she realized what time it was. Three-fifteen. The bathroom was just down the hall from the gym, so a trip there wouldn't take long. Not unless something bad happened.

Feeling panic starting to course through her veins for the third time that night, Miranda jumped to her feet and headed for the doorway. There were people everywhere, eyes wide and shaking, trying to contact their loved ones. The hallway was filled with unlucky souls who couldn't even score a gym mat; most of them were plopped on the tile floor, curling in on themselves like snails.

She knocked loudly on the bathroom door. "Tyler? Jackson? Are you in there?" When there was no answer, she stepped inside. The boys weren't there. But someone had written CHAOS on the wall in red.

* * *

Tyler's phone was off or the battery had died. Miranda couldn't tell which, because her calls went to voicemail. Her first instinct was to call nine-one-one, but that was a dead end. When she dialed the number, she got an angry beep, like the system had packed up and quit. It couldn't do that, could it? Weren't emergency calls supposed to be routed to nearby towns when the lines were over-loaded? But given the hellscape she'd seen in Everton, a part of her wasn't surprised. It *was* chaos.

That left the huddled people in the hallway. "Has anyone seen my boys?" Miranda called out. "Tyler's thirteen. Jackson's eight. They went to the bathroom and never came back."

A woman lifted her head. She was in her late thirties, but the shadows on her face made it look as if the night had already aged her a decade. "Is the younger one super chatty?"

"He never stops talking."

"They went down the hall," the woman said. "The little guy wanted to use the bathroom, but the older boy said they had to go."

Fear pricked the back of Miranda's neck. What was Tyler up to? "Go where?"

"He didn't explain. As least, I didn't hear him."

Miranda hurried down the hall. She passed classrooms, filled with more people seeking refuge from the disaster, but her sons weren't among them. At the end of the hall-way was an exit sign. Miranda went through the double set of doors, wondering what her boys could be doing outside. But they weren't there, either. She stood at the edge of the school's parking lot. She counted seven cars, all parked, all empty and silent. Where were her sons?

She smelled cigarette smoke and turned. There was a little knot of people outside for a smoke. "Excuse, me, have you seen two boys? My sons...I think they came out here but I don't know where they went?"

"Big kid and a little guy?" a man asked her.

"Yes."

"Could be them," the man said. "The little kid wasn't happy. He was saying they should go back and tell Mama."

"Tell Mama what?"

"I dunno. The big kid told him to shut up. He said Dad would take care of it."

The blood froze in Miranda's veins. "*Dad* would take care of it?" she repeated.

"Yeah. They got into an SUV and took off. I didn't think to get the plate. It looked like the kids knew where they were going."

Miranda's heart thudded in her chest. At that moment, she knew exactly where they had gone.


When she called Conrad, his deep voice was coy like a Cheshire cat's. "Of course the boys are here," he said, as if she'd asked the stupidest question in the world. "The town's gone to hell in a few hours. How can I keep my boys safe if they're not with me?"

"How dare you steal them in the middle of the night. I was out of my mind with worry."

"Well, so was I, worrying about my family." Conrad's voice was calm, but there was a peculiar emphasis on *my* family. When they'd been together, Miranda had often felt like a trophy, a shiny object that existed primarily for display purposes. Everything in Conrad's orbit belonged to him. "And I didn't steal them. I texted Tyler to see what was going on, and he told me you had them sleeping on the floor of the high school gym. I was worried."

"We were fine. The school is safe."

"I hate to break it to you, sweetheart, but nowhere is safe tonight. The power is out, police are stretched to the breaking point, and looters are everywhere."

"You knew this was going to happen, didn't you?" Miranda demanded.

For the first time, he seemed surprised. "Knew *this* shitshow was coming down the pike? Sweetheart, I'd have chartered a plane down to the Caribbean. I like control, not chaos."

She knew that was true. But if Conrad hadn't been behind that whispery voice, who was?

"Listen, Miranda, I know we've had our differences," Conrad went on. "But I think the best thing would be for you to come to my house. We've got a generator, so there's power, and it's warm and cozy here. I'll send a car for you."

"I don't want anything from you," Miranda said. "I'm on my way over, but only because I want to see that my sons are safe. Then I'm taking them somewhere else."

"In the middle of the night? Be reasonable, Miranda." Oddly, Conrad sounded more amused than angry. Either the court-ordered anger-management therapy had worked wonders on him, or something was up. Maybe he was counting on the fact that once she was inside a warm, cozy mansion, she wouldn't want to leave.

"I'll be there soon," she said, and hung up. *Soon* was a relative term. If she'd let her ex send a car, it wouldn't even have been a ten-minute drive on the swooping boulevards of Everton's most elegant neighborhood. But she was on foot. It was a cold night, so that made her hustle, and she was in sneakers, which allowed her to move fast. But she could feel the turmoil around her. Sometimes, the night seemed quiet, but it was punctuated with screams and car alarms and the distinctive peal of shattering glass. Three times, she had to change course or hide when she heard clattering footsteps coming toward her. Gangs roamed like centipedes, hugging the shadows. There were no streetlights, only moonlight to navigate by. Maggie Wilbourne came into her head suddenly, and not because her execution had been the fuse that blew up the town. No, it was simply because Maggie had been brutally raped by two men. And Miranda knew that night that anything could happen.

Weirdly, there were more stars in the sky than she'd ever seen before. Even inside this nightmare, there was something beautiful.

She was relieved when she finally made it to Conrad's street. The house was dark when she approached it, which surprised her because he'd said he had a generator. Maybe the lights were off because the boys were sleeping? She realized she would have to let them stay with their father that night; it was unreasonable of her to even think about taking them elsewhere. At least the boys were safe, and that was what mattered.

When she climbed the steps to the front door, her hand hesitated over the bell. Would that wake up Tyler and Jackson? She didn't want to risk it. Instead, she rapped on the big wooden door with her knuckles. There was a creak inside, and what she thought were footsteps, but the door stayed closed.

"Conrad? It's Miranda," she called out, realizing he wasn't going to magically open the door if he thought looters were outside.

She stepped to the side, thinking it might be easier to rap on the glass of the living rooms bay window, when a shotgun blast ripped through the front door.

Miranda screamed and ran past the bay window. Another blast shattered the glass, and she felt jagged shards dig into her scalp and exposed skin like claws. She ran for the side of the house and watched the remains of the door open and a tall, broad-shouldered man step outside.

She didn't hesitate. She ran around the side of the house and opened the gate, but instead of plunging through it, she darted into the hedge. The darkness worked both ways, after all. She watched the man walk past her and held her breath. There was something familiar about him. He seemed to be on his own, but there was no way to be sure. The one thing she *was* certain of was that he would kill her when he found her. She wasn't going to let that happen.

When he went through the gate, she doubled back to the front of the house. Without hesitating, she ran through the decimated front door. Inside was quiet. She took the steps of the grand staircase two at a time and rushed for the master bedroom. It was the walk-in closet she was after, the big walnut-paneled room where Conrad stored his bespoke suits and Italian shoes. It was also where he kept his gun safe.

She remembered the combination. Conrad had never worried about her getting a gun and shooting him; somehow, they'd both known that was beyond her. But she'd learned a lesson when she'd left him. She'd kept it from her boys, but she'd bought a gun and taught herself to shoot it at a range some forty minutes away from Everton, a place Conrad and his shooting buddies wouldn't be caught dead in.

Some of the guns were missing. Using the flashlight on her keychain, she loaded the .38. She was almost done when she heard a creak on the second-floor landing. Damn, Conrad would never get around to fixing that, would he? Then she positioned herself behind the closet door and waited. Under the door, she saw the hallway light come on. It didn't take long for the door to swing open.

She held her breath and fired.

Three times.

The man cried out and fell back against the doorframe. Miranda waited, thinking it could be a trap. What were the odds she'd hit him at all?

It was only when she heard him crying that she crept forward.

"Our Father..." he wheezed. "Who art...in heaven..."

Yes, the man who'd tried to murder her was trying to pray.

Even though he was clad in black from head to toe, she saw the dark, wet stain in his chest. He really was dying.

"I know you," she said. "You work for Conrad."

He glanced at her and winced. "Hallowed be...thy name."

"You tried to kill me!" she screamed. "Why?"

He ignored her. "Thy kingdom…"

She dropped to her knees so that they were face to face. "You just tried to murder an unarmed woman," she said. "Pray all you want, but if there's a hell, that's where you're going. Brimstone and pitchforks and the devil. That's where you'll call home for eternity."

The man closed his eyes and whimpered.

"Make this right. Tell me why?" she said.

"Conrad…asked me," he gasped. "He said…you're… bad mother." His eyes rolled back in his head.

"Don't you dare die on me. When did he plan this?"

"After…dam broke."

Those were the man's last words. Something gurgled in his throat and blood bubbled out of his mouth. He was gone.

Miranda stared at him for a long time. She reached out a hand to close his eyes. She thought his name was Jonas, but she wasn't sure. He was Conrad's assistant. She'd only seen him a handful of times in her life.

She was startled when his phone buzzed. She felt gross, reaching into a dead man's pocket, but that didn't stop her. He had two phones, a new iPhone and a cheapo burner that was buzzing.

*How goes it?* Read the new text on the screen. She didn't have to guess who sent it.

*Done,* she typed back.

*Damn. Good work.*

She thought for a moment. *It's messy,* she typed back.

*Don't worry. We'll clean up tomorrow.*

She wanted to ask Conrad where he was, and where the boys were, but that was impossible. *What now?*

*Come back when you can,* came the answer.

Miranda didn't think about where to go next. Moving on pure instinct, she headed for her former sister-in-law's house. It wasn't far, but that was only part of the reason. Heidi had never been close to Conrad, and she was the only member of the Reichert family who'd ever tried to help her out. Would Heidi believe her story? That felt like a reach, but Miranda was certain no one else would.

Heidi's place was modest for the neighborhood, a cottage oasis in a desert of McMansions. Miranda rapped on the door, wondering if she should be bracing for another shotgun blast. "Heidi? It's Miranda," she called. A moment later, the door opened.

"Am I ever glad to see you," Heidi said, pulling her into a hug. "Why is there glass in your hair? And where are the boys?"

"Conrad kidnapped them," Miranda blurted out. "And he just tried to kill me. He told me to come to his house and there was a man waiting for me..." She gasped and pressed her hand against her chest. She'd killed a man. She hadn't really processed it until that moment. It was kill or be killed, but it was something she'd never imagined doing.

"Come in, come in," Heidi said, pulling her over the threshold and into the house. There was a wood fire burning in the hearth. That and a few carefully positioned pillar candles lit up the living room. "I have a generator, but I'm using it to keep the fridge and some other stuff running," she added. "Plus, I don't really want to advertise that I have it."

"You're well-prepared."

"Well, unlike most people, I knew something was coming," Heidi said.

Miranda stared at her. "You were involved?"

"No, but my girlfriend is one of the Daughters," Heidi said. "She didn't give me much warning. That's why I was only able to call you a little before the dam blew up."

"That was you?" Miranda was shocked. "Did you warn Conrad?"

Heidi shook her head. "I know that makes me evil, but...I know the truth about my brother. You're not the only woman he's abused."

"I need your help," Miranda said. "He has Tyler and Jackson. I don't know where he'd take them."

"I'd bet anything they're at my parents' house," Heidi said. "Partly because they're out of town, and partly because Conrad is arrogant. He wouldn't hole up in somewhere small and quiet. He'd want another mansion."

"I have to get my kids out of there," Miranda said.

"I know. What do you need me to do?"


When they got to the house, Heidi walked up to the front door while Miranda slipped around the back. She heard Conrad say, "I'm surprised to see you, Heidi. See any marauders on the way over?"

She heard Heidi start to answer, but she didn't care about their conversation. She made for the back of the house and waited on the deck. Heidi was surprisingly efficient. Through the window, she heard Heidi say, "I need a glass of wine. You want one?" right before she unlocked the door. Miranda slipped inside.

"We should open a bottle of champagne," Conrad said. "I'm in a celebratory mood."

"With all the anarchy out there? Really?" Heidi said, pointing to the back stairway. Miranda headed upstairs while Heidi made a small ruckus, opening and closing cabinet doors.

She heard Conrad say, "Don't you know where the glasses are?" but that didn't matter because she was up the stairs and on the second story of the house. The lights were low, but she knew her way around. Tyler and Jackson had the same rooms they'd had since forever. Jackson's came up first. She eased the door open, wondering if he was asleep. Instead, she saw a tiny boy perched in the windowsill, peering outside.

"Mama?" he whispered.

Miranda stepped inside and shut the door behind her. "I'm here, baby."

Jackson jumped off the window and ran to her for a hug. "Dad said you were coming over, so I waited. I'm so glad you're here, Mama."

"Are you okay?"

"Sure," he said. "But I couldn't sleep with you not here. What if the water got you?"

"That's not going to happen, baby," she reassured him. "But we've got to get out of here. You have to be very quiet, okay?"

Jackson nodded seriously. "Okay," he whispered.

They crept down the hall to Tyler's room. He was in bed, but he wasn't asleep. The low light of the hallway caught the whites of his eyes. "Mom?" he said, sitting up. "What took you so long?"

Miranda took a deep breath. Even with the door of the room closed, she didn't want to have a conversation about this now. "I came here to get you. We need to leave."

"Leave for where? It's madness out there," Tyler said. "Dad said people are getting murdered all over the place. He said there were shootings on his street. But we're safe here."

"The only person who was shot at on his street was me," Miranda said. "And that was..." She wanted to say, *That was because your father arranged it,* but she couldn't, Instead she swallowed hard. "That was by a man who worked for your father.

"That's crazy," Tyler said. "He must've been part of the gangs out there. But it has nothing to do with Dad."

"Tyler, get up," Miranda said. "We're leaving now."

"No, we're not. It's safe here."

She reached for his shoulder. "Tyler..."

"WE'RE NOT GOING ANYWHERE!" Tyler shouted.

"Shhhh!" Jackson said, but it was too late. There were footsteps on the stairs.

"Tyler?" Conrad called. "What's going on?"

"Mom's trying to make me leave, but I don't want to."

Conrad swung the door open. "But your mom is..." He blinked at Miranda.

"Surprise," Miranda said. "I'm harder to kill than you thought, aren't I?"

Conrad stared at her for a moment. "Boys, go back to sleep. I need to talk with your mother."

"I wasn't asleep," Jackson said. "I was waiting for Mama."

"Go to your room, son," Conrad said. "Now."

Jackson frowned at him. Conrad put his hand on the boy's shoulder and gave him a shove.

"Ow," Jackson said.

"You'll do what you're told," Conrad said. "Now go to your room."

"It's okay, baby," Miranda said, not wanting her son to see what would happen next.

Disappointment was written over Jackson's face as he slowly walked backwards down the hall and went into his room.

"Come with me, Miranda."

"I'm not going anywhere with you."

"You're in my house, and you'll play by my rules," Conrad said.

"This isn't your house," Heidi called out. She was coming up the stairs. "It's Mom and Dad's house. And, if we're being honest, Mom and Dad gave you their company and bought you a house. It's not like you've ever done much of anything."

"Shut up, Heidi," Conrad said. "You should hear what Mom and Dad have to say about you and your *lifestyle.*"

"I'm sure you've got plenty to say at your evil capitalist society meetings," Heidi said. "But I really don't care."

"You conspired with my bitch of an ex-wife, didn't you?" Conrad said. "That's how she got into the house. It was you."

Before Heidi could answer, Conrad gave her a shove that sent her flying back down the stairs. Heidi screamed. There was a wail when she hit the landing.

"Heidi!" Miranda yelled, stepping into the hallway. "Are you okay?"

"My ankle's broken!" Heidi shouted. "He broke my ankle."

"Now where were we?" Conrad asked, shoving Miranda back into Tyler's room.

"You bastard," Miranda hissed. "You just tried to kill your own sister. Don't you think I know you're going to try to kill me as soon as we're out of Tyler's room?"

Conrad glanced at his son. "He's old enough for this." He pulled a handgun from the back waistband of his pants and pointed it at Miranda.

"You're going to kill me in cold blood?" Miranda asked. "After paying a man to try to kill me tonight."

"Dad," Tyler whispered. "Please put the gun down."

"It's high time you learned how to handle a woman who doesn't know her place, son," Conrad said.

"That's why you beat me when we were married, to teach me my place?" Miranda said. "Because I know the truth. You hit me because you were weak. You're a poor excuse for a man. And now I see that you're a poor excuse for a father."

Conrad struck Miranda in the face with the butt of the gun. She dropped to the floor, feeling hot blood fill her mouth.

"Dad!" Tyler shrieked. "Stop it!"

"Man up!" Conrad yelled back at him. "This is what you have to do with a bitch who doesn't know her place."

"You can't hurt Mom." Tyler was crying now, his face bright red. "Dad, you can't."

"This is your fault," Conrad sneered at Miranda. "Raising my sons to be useless sissies. I should've done this a long time ago. Those Daughter bitches might've screwed up the city for good, but they did me one favor. They gave me the opportunity to get rid of you."

"Dad!" Tyler leapt out of bed and grabbed his father's arm, pulling the gun out of his mother's face. "You can't do this."

Conrad smashed the butt of the gun against his son's head, and Tyler sank to the floor, next to his mother. "You ungrateful little…"

"Nobody hits my kids," Miranda said, pulling the .38 out from behind her back.

She fired at Conrad's chest and he flew back, out the door. His body hit the railing and he flipped over, crashing on the marble floor below.

Miranda touched Tyler's face. "Are you okay?"

He nodded quickly, tears pouring down his face and snot oozing out of his nose. "He really was going to kill you."

"He's been trying for years," Miranda said softly. "I thought I was protecting you by not telling you. I'm sorry. I should've told you, so you'd understand what was really going on."

"Is he gone?" That was Jackson from the doorway.

"I think so." Miranda got up and went to the hallway so she could peer over the railing.

"Believe me, he's gone," Heidi called up the stairs. "That bastard."

"I can help you, Aunt Heidi!" Jackson called.

"No, kiddo, you stay upstairs for now," Heidi called. "Your mom will help me."

Miranda rushed down the stairs. "I'm so sorry. I couldn't stop him."

"He only got what he deserved."

Miranda stared at Conrad's body. "I don't know how I'm going to explain this to the police. They're going to arrest me, aren't they?"

"Not if his body disappears. After a night like this, no one's going to be surprised when some people go missing," Heidi said quietly. "And I've got a few friends who can help out with that."

# A WATERY GRAVE
## Sarah M. Chen

When Loree Shipman walked inside the brightly-lit truck stop, it wasn't a *huge* deal that she was the only one there. Just figured there'd be more truckers inside, even if it was four a.m.

She went straight to the ladies' room to pee. Smelled like bleach and pine trees thanks to the cheap air freshener perched on the toilet. She glared at her reflection in the mirror as she washed her hands. Dark circles under her eyes, pale mottled skin, the ends of her greasy short blonde hair barely poking out from her beanie.

"Gross." Since she'd started working for Sinbad Trucking, she didn't pay much attention to her appearance anymore. It definitely showed.

"It's not gonna be forever," she told her reflection. "I'm gonna figure a way out." She blinked. "Yeah, I wouldn't believe me either."

Loree tried to pour herself a cup of coffee but the machine was empty. She scanned the quiet store, her eyes squinting in the harsh light. "Hello?"

Nothing. She was wasting time. Couldn't be late for her eleven a.m. delivery. But she really needed caffeine. She grabbed a Coke and a packaged cinnamon roll and headed out the door but then stopped and turned back.

Digging into her pockets, she threw down four bucks on the counter before running out into the chilly morning.

Kevin Chu didn't want to admit it—probably the first time he thought this actually—but Ricky Binkowski was right. He should have kept the pistol that Ricky thrust at him. At least a dozen people had tried to break into the flooded eye clinic since the looting started around nine p.m. Trying to steal sunglasses and frames. The cops had ordered everyone to evacuate earlier but no sign of them since, except for the intermittent wailing of sirens in the distance.

Kevin had assumed the people of Everton would respect his business, his livelihood. He'd been so naïve.

The baseball bat had been enough of a deterrent. If he could just stick it out until sunrise—another couple hours—he'd be okay. The looters would slink home and hopefully the National Guard would show up.

But undoubtedly someone will show up with a gun, then what? He'd already heard a gunshot over by Snyder's Copy Shop. An aluminum bat wouldn't scare anyone away. If anything, it would piss them off and then Kevin would be dead.

Kevin had closed his clinic early that day. He'd only had one appointment anyway, Mr. Wells, an elderly man who never seemed satisfied with his lenses. Always complaining the prescription wasn't right.

"I don't know," Mr. Wells said as he scowled at himself in front of the small mirror Kevin had placed in front of him. He turned his head back and forth, touching the glasses. "I guess I can try these for a while."

Kevin had finally ushered Mr. Wells out to prepare his clinic for the Big Dam blow-up. Locked up the few designer frames he had and put the money away in the safe. Stuffed a plastic tarp underneath the entrance doors. He thought of boarding up his windows with plywood but dismissed the thought. Made him look like a chicken-shit.

He also really didn't think the Daughters would go through with their threats. It was just for show. People wouldn't destroy their own town on purpose, would they? Now looking back on it, he realized he'd been a fool.

Something Ricky always warned him about. "People are only out for themselves. The sooner you figure that out, the better. Otherwise, they're gonna step all over you. Crush you like a cockroach."

Kevin reminded Ricky that cockroaches could live through anything. But Ricky told him to stop being a know-it-all.

There was shouting outside. Kevin hovered in the dark at the clinic entrance, the water past his knees. The silly plastic tarp had done nothing to stop the flooding. It was now buried underneath at least a foot of water. He stupidly assumed the flooding wouldn't be that bad since his clinic was up on higher ground, on the outskirts of downtown.

A figure leaped out of a boat, carrying a flashlight, and sloshed toward the clinic. Kevin's adrenaline spiked. He raised the bat, trying to look imposing but the harsh glare from the flashlight made him turn his head away.

A snort. "What, you think you're fuckin' scary with that thing, man?"

Kevin faced his friend, exhaling. He lowered the bat. "Jesus, Ricky. I didn't know it was you."

"What would you have done anyway, huh? You wouldn't have the balls to swing that thing at anyone."

Kevin stepped aside as Ricky came into the store with a sawed-off shotgun, kicking water as he went. "Did you find them?"

Ricky took his Steelers cap off his head, rubbed his dark brown hair. "Nah, not yet. But I'm gonna get them bitches, you just wait."

Ricky had been out looking for the Daughters, specifically Megan, the "real femi-Nazi" as Ricky put it. Wanted to punish them for what they did to Everton.

"They can't do this to our town," Ricky had insisted when the Big Dam blew earlier that night. "Hurt innocent folks."

But Kevin knew Ricky didn't care about protecting the innocent. All he cared about was how much pain he could inflict on people.

Kevin could hear his father now. *Do not remove a fly from your friend's forehead with a hatchet.*

Kevin never knew what that Chinese proverb meant until he met Ricky. If anyone took things to the extreme, it was his friend. Like the time he sodomized Darren Morris junior year with a wire coat hanger after Darren made the mistake of looking at Ricky "in a faggotty way."

Ricky had denied it, of course, and Darren moved away from Everton, never to be heard from again.

Ricky pulled two forty-ouncers out of his backpack. Handed one to Kevin who took it hesitantly.

"I need to stay sober. Alert."

"Psh, fuck that." Ricky cracked his open and thrust it in the air. "To our homies, Trevor Daw and James Manning. True God-fearin' brothers." He poured the malt liquor into the murky water blanketing the clinic's floor.

Kevin frowned and set his drink down on the counter near the cash register. He didn't want to drink to those assholes. He had no doubts they raped Maggie Wilbourne.

"Here, last chance."

Kevin turned to see Ricky holding the pistol toward him, butt out. He knew if he didn't take it, he'd kick himself for it later.

"Gimme that." Kevin grabbed the gun from Ricky.

Ricky grinned. "Atta boy."

Kevin weighed the gun in the palm of his hand. It felt strange and heavy. He thought he'd feel better holding it. A tough guy.

It made him feel weaker.


By the time Loree got the rig warmed up, it was already four-thirty. Terre Haute, Indiana was at least six hours away from the Flying T truck stop in whatever bumfuck town she was in and that was if she hauled ass. And even though Loree had only been driving for three months, one thing she knew was that big rigs don't haul ass. At least not safely. She figured that out the hard way.

Her dispatcher, Manny, reminded her to drive more carefully. She knew he was just looking out for her, but Loree wasn't exactly striving to be the model employee of Sinbad Trucking. It's not like she wanted this job, a nice little inheritance from her son of a bitch husband, Big Chris.

The thought of Big Chris made Loree's stomach curl and her teeth hurt. Fuckin' liar and thief. Okay, it's not like there weren't signs of his gambling that she ignored, like her Camaro getting repoed or their electricity shutting off. She was content to be the dumb blind little wifey, believing him when he said he'd get it handled.

Wasn't until she spotted him at the Surly Goat swapping spit with Reyna Cruz did she realize the only thing he was handling was Reyna's double D titties. Even worse, not just three hours before he'd called Loree to tell her he had to pick up another load for Sinbad in Ohio and wouldn't make it home for her birthday.

After the Surly Goat incident, Loree went to the bank to withdraw their entire savings, figuring it'd be enough to keep her afloat while she looked for her own place far far away from New Jersey and Reyna's double Ds. Only problem was Big Chris had already cleaned them out months ago.

Loree had nothing.

As if things couldn't possibly get worse, a couple days later she woke up to Ramon "Veto" Acevedo's hulking figure at the foot of her bed.

"Where's Big Chris, my angel?"

Loree blinked, terror temporarily paralyzing her. Finally, "On the road. Driving."

"Ah, but he's not. He's supposed to be but he's not."

"Then I don't know."

The next day, Big Chris was found washed up on the shore of the Delaware River. Shot in the face. His body bloated and rotting from soaking in all that sewage-infested water.

Everyone assumed it was the work of Veto and his gang. Turned out Big Chris owed the crime boss twenty grand.

Loree was ecstatic. Big Chris was dead and her life was whatever she wanted it to be.

That feeling didn't last long because the next morning, she woke up again to Veto in her bedroom. Only this time he wasn't so polite. Shoved a gun down her throat and told her she was now Big Chris and must work off the debt.

"Don't think I've forgotten about my twenty grand just because the cocksucker is dead. You now work for me, my angel, until I say you don't."

Which was how Loree ended up being a truck driver for Sinbad Trucking, a front for Veto's dirty money—drugs, gambling, extortion, you name it. Purchase orders for plushie toys, pooferballs, and troll dolls washed the money clean, leaving no traces. And drivers like Big Chris, and now Loree, hauled the toys all over the nation. Not a job so much as a fucking life sentence.

She'd stepped right in the asshole's shoes, like some sick twisted form of irony. Probably even parked in this exact space at the same Flying T truck stop.

As Loree turned out of the lot onto the main road, she noticed a voicemail from Manny but didn't feel like listening to it. Probably worried she overslept. If she was late, the customer would be pissed and it would get back to Veto. And you don't want things to get back to Veto.

Loree spotted the sign for 4th Street and turned right, the truck lurching as she cut too close, jumping a curb.

There was a slight uphill grade and the tractor whined and groaned as she shifted gears.

Loree had just put in her earbuds to rock out to *Jagged Little Pill* when she noticed how dark the street was. Yeah, it was only four-thirty so the sun wasn't up yet, but that wasn't the weird part. Not a single street-light was on.

The second thing she noticed was the giant fucking lake swallowing 4th Street. Her headlights glinted off the murky water about twenty feet ahead of her and she slammed on her brakes.

"What the hell?" She looked at her GPS in case it showed a huge blue circle where 4th Street should be. Nope. It was a road.

She glanced in her rearview but there was no one coming down the road. In either direction. Unless you count the poor folks whose cars were submerged in the water ahead of her. Like discarded children's toys. Some of them had their lights on, glowing eerily like demon eyes.

Loree didn't know any other route to Indiana. She *had* to take 4th Street to Route 136 to I-70. Unless she turned around and backtracked—going south to Route 88 to I-70, but that'd take forever. And she didn't have forever.

"Goddammit." Maybe there was a big storm she wasn't aware of. Why didn't she listen to weather reports more often?

She clicked on her radio and scanned the stations until she caught a news report.

"...National Guard troops have been mobilized and deployed to Everton. Authorities are on the lookout for anyone belonging to the Daughters."

The Daughters? What the hell was that? She scanned the channels until she found another news station.

"...fires are still out of control in some parts of Everton's south district."

It cut to a commercial. Loree looked at her GPS, wondering where the fuck Everton was and saw that, of course, she was in it. The Flying T truck stop where she spent the night in her sleeper cab was right on the border between Everton and Monongahela, the town to the east.

A Peterbilt pulling a loaded trailer could drive through six feet of water. Only problem was Loree had no idea how deep the water was. The road ahead was probably blocked off too.

"Fuck." She didn't know what to do and thought of calling Manny. Then remembered he'd left her a voicemail. She grabbed her cell phone and played the message.

"Loree, I hope you're nowhere near Everton. I know you don't watch the news or pay attention to anything important, but this is so big, I think even *you* would know about it. Unless you're a dumbass. Gimme a call, okay?"

Shit. Loree didn't want to call Manny for help because then what would she say? "Um yeah, I'm a dumbass."

Loree had no choice. She turned on the CB radio mounted on her dash. If anyone knew how to get to Indiana quickly, it'd be other truckers. The only problem was they were all sexist assholes.

She switched the channel to nineteen, the one truckers used. Hopefully they'd all be chatting about Everton and she could just listen in. At first all she heard was static and then there was a man's gruff voice.

"...got a lane lover in the hammer lane. Green Sentra. Late model. Dead pedalin' about thirty. Cars all going in the granny lane so watch out."

Loree heard laughter.

"Ten-four, Fuel Man." Twangy voice.

There was more random chatter about shit Loree didn't understand. Something about a meat wagon and gator guts. She took a deep breath.

"Hey...uh...breaker, breaker one nine." She knew that's what she needed to do to interrupt the conversation. "I'm on 4th Street, trying to get to Route 136 to I-70 but there's a giant lake in my way." She waited.

"Fuel Man here. You out in that Everton mess?" Gruff voice.

"Yeah, I'm in Everton, Fuel Man. Is there a way around? A shortcut to Indiana?"

"You need to turn around and go south on Route 88. Hits I-70 eventually."

Loree shook her head. "That'll take too long. I gotta get this load of toys to Indiana by eleven."

"No way that'll happen, little missy." It was twangy voice. "In fact, why don't you just turn around and go on home. Leave the driving to us men."

Asshole.

"Now Double E, quit your jaw jackin'. Listen, Santa Claus, there's one way you can go to deliver them toys. Bypasses 4th Street entirely and gets you on Route 136 to I-70. But you gotta go through Everton. And you don't want to do that."

Loree perked up. "Tell me."

Silence, then Fuel Man sighed. "Take Pine Road.

Follow that straight up through town, turn left on Chess Street, and you'll hit the Route 136 onramp."

Loree checked her GPS. Pine Road was behind her. No problem.

"Thanks, Fuel Man. Appreciate it."

"Be careful, Santa Claus. By the way, nobody says breaker, breaker, one nine, anymore."

Loree snorted. She shut her CB off and checked her rearview mirror. The road was clear behind her. Apparently, everyone got the memo not to be in Everton except her. It seemed easier to just back up the big rig rather than do an awkward three-point turn. She put the tractor-trailer in reverse, checked her mirrors, and started backing up until she reached the sign for Pine Road. It wasn't easy and her trailer kept wanting to turn left or right instead of straight but luckily nobody was coming behind her. Finally, she shifted into drive and turned onto Pine Road.

Loree checked the time. Quarter to five. She could still make it to Indiana if she hurried.


As Kevin watched Ricky stand outside his clinic, yelling at god knows what, he couldn't help wondering how they stayed friends all this time. Guess childhood bonds were hard to break.

When the Chus moved to Everton twenty-something years ago, they were the only Chinese family in the small town. Kevin's dad opened the Good Eye Clinic and his mom worked at the Sleepy Time Motel.

Kevin met Ricky Binkowski in the sixth grade when he rode his bike through the neighborhood one Saturday. As he passed James Whitlow's house, he spotted Ricky leaving what looked like a tire by his front door and stopped to see what he was up to. Whitlow was a fat drunk and adopted these weird kids who never smiled. Even though they were younger than Kevin, he stayed far away from them. They were total freaks.

Kevin had watched Ricky light a match, fling it onto the tire, and bolt down Whitlow's driveway. The tire exploded behind him, a fireball of burnt rubber and gasoline. It was the coolest thing Kevin had ever seen. They'd been friends ever since.

Kevin's dad didn't approve though. He said Ricky was "ruined in the head like soft melon." Kevin knew Ricky was a bad student, a bully, and a terror to all the stray cats in their neighborhood, but he chalked it up to an absentee father and a pill-popping mother. Besides, Kevin had no other friends.

When Kevin left for Carnegie Mellon to study optometry, he assumed he'd never see Ricky again, except for the occasional visit home or maybe someone's wedding. Then his dad passed and Kevin returned to Everton to take over the eye clinic. He wasn't surprised to find Ricky still there in his mother's house. He hadn't changed a bit; if anything, he'd gotten meaner.

Ricky was a supervisor at Wheelhouse Metal Works but when that shut down in 2007, he worked various odd jobs doing things Kevin never quite figured out. Probably best not to know. Ran around with those two assholes, James Manning and Trevor Daw, until Maggie blew their heads off.

Kevin couldn't help thinking that if Ricky were there with those two rapists, he wouldn't think nothing of joining in on the fun with Maggie. The thought sickened him.

Yet here he was listening to the guy whoop and holler outside his clinic, blasting his shotgun in the air like an idiot. He prayed the National Guard would get here soon.

Loree's GPS took her past chain-link fences, overgrown trees, and a rusted factory that looked like nobody had worked there in years. The road was submerged but the water wasn't too high. Only halfway up her tires. Maybe this wouldn't be so bad.

But as she continued further, the water rose higher and higher. Probably up to her lowest step by now right outside her driver's door. She followed the road around until she hit Chess Street, which luckily was on a slight uphill grade. She turned left and continued along until she gasped and slowed down.

"Fuck me."

It looked like any other small-town business district except for the murky water covering everything. Some buildings were halfway submerged, their cracked windows like soulless eyes staring out. Those on higher ground fared better with the water lapping at entrance doors. Sign posts stuck out of the water like white flags.

It was completely dark except for Loree's headlights and the five lights on the top of her cab. Several fires flickered in the distance. She crept forward, her headlights illuminating abandoned vehicles, furniture, and the occasional paddle or lantern bobbing in the water. She could see at least a couple hundred feet ahead of her.

Every now and then she'd hear a motor and then a

boat would whiz by with strobing lights. She heard shouts in the distance. Something was bubbling like a fountain in front of her on the right, maybe a clogged sewer.

As far as she could tell, if she continued straight, she'd eventually hit Route 136. As long as the water didn't rise any higher. Most likely, it was at her top step now. Sitting seven feet off the ground came in handy, although Loree never would have thought plowing through a river in her Peterbilt would be one of those times.

*Come on, come on. Don't crap out on me now.*

Loree hit the gas and passed liquor stores, fast food joints, and Woods Automotive. She weaved around a few submerged vehicles. Several shadows flitted in and out of buildings. Most likely looters. Every now and then something banged into her truck but she never let up on the gas.

A gunshot.

"Jesus." No idea where that came from. She floored it. The diesel engine roared and unfamiliar ticking noises made her nervous. The GPS flickered and sputtered. She was going to short circuit everything. The water had probably already seeped inside the engine.

But miraculously, her rig continued forward. Pushing water out of its way like a turbo-engine bulldozer. Waves churned and roiled in front of her hood. It was like the whole front end of her truck was engulfed in a frenzied whirlpool as she powered through the water as fast as the truck could go.

If she was religious, she'd be praying to whatever god was up there but since she wasn't, she prayed to the god of Peterbilt.

\* \* \*

Kevin heard it before he saw it. A loud diesel engine rumbling. Then he saw bright headlights moving toward them. At first, he thought the National Guard was here and relief washed over him.

It was about time. He didn't have to protect his store anymore, holding a pistol like he knew what the hell he was doing. He felt like a fraud.

Then he realized it was one of those big eighteen-wheelers. "Sinbad Trucking" printed on the side of the blue truck. Where did they think they were going? It was cruising at a pretty good speed, cutting through the water like an ocean liner. The truck was all lit up so Kevin could make out the surrounding people in boats and kayaks bobbing crazily in the water, arms waving.

"Hey, would you look at that asshole?" Ricky spun around, pointing his flashlight at the semi. "That truck is causing a fucking tsunami. Look!"

Kevin sloshed his way in the ice-cold water outside to get a better look, the smoke in the air from the fires stinging his nostrils. The semi passed right by his clinic, about a hundred feet away, and sure enough, fast-moving waves cut through the water in its wake. One kayaker had the misfortune of being too close to the truck and tipped right over into the dirty water.

The sound of waves crashing into sign posts, stores, and streetlights filled the early morning.

Ricky noticed it before Kevin did.

"Oh shit, here we go."

Kevin wasn't sure what Ricky was talking about until he saw what looked like two to three-foot waves churning toward them at a frantic pace.

They shouted and ran inside the clinic as fast as they could in knee-deep water, splashing their way to the cash register counter. They both ducked behind it just as Kevin saw the water *whoosh!* toward the building and *crash!* against the floor-to-ceiling glass storefront.

The sound of glass shattering was immediately followed by the alarm. *Wah-hoo, wah-hoo.*

Kevin looked over at Ricky who had the shotgun and flashlight tucked inside his windbreaker. The water lapped and swirled around them, but behind the counter, they were safe from getting completely drenched.

"You still got your pistol?" Ricky asked. He stood up from his crouch.

Kevin nodded and stood up, pulling it out from his jacket.

Ricky set the flashlight down on the counter, casting eerie shadows on the walls. He racked his shotgun. "We're gonna get that son of a bitch. He can't get away with this. Busted out all your windows. Cover your ears."

"What?"

"Cover your ears, man."

Kevin covered his ears with his hands. Ricky fired the gun in the air. *Boom!* Bits of ceiling fell around them. Kevin shook his head, trying to get the buzzing out of his ears.

"What the hell did you do that for?" Kevin yelled. His voice sounded muffled.

"Wanted to make sure it didn't get wet." Ricky grinned. He didn't seem as affected by the sound of the gunshot as Kevin. Probably fired the thing all day. "It still works." He gestured with the shotgun. "C'mon. Let's teach that asshole a lesson."

Kevin hesitated, then shook his head. "Nah, some-one's gotta guard the clinic."

Ricky smirked at him. "I knew you'd fuckin' chink out on me, man." He nodded to the flashlight. "I'll leave that with you so you don't get scared of the dark." He snorted.

Kevin said nothing. Watched Ricky slosh his way out through the broken glass and into the darkness. The screech of the alarm and the boom of the shotgun blast echoed in his head.


Loree was almost there. She could see the top of a sign sticking out of the water about thirty feet ahead. Instinc-tively, she knew it was Route 136.

In her sideview mirror, she saw a man in a boat zooming up, steadily gaining on her. Shouting.

What the fuck?

The boat was right alongside her now. She made the mistake of glancing to her left and they locked eyes. He was wearing a Steelers cap and a windbreaker. Standing up on the boat by the motor, one knee resting on a seat. Shouting something.

Curiosity got the best of her and Loree cracked her window open, cold air slapping her in the face. She yanked her beanie down further over her ears so she could barely see, trying to stay warm. Slowed the truck down.

"...buddy's store...busted..."

Loree shook her head, staring down at him. Brought the truck to a crawl. Noticed the water came up to her top step like she figured.

The guy reminded her of a pig. Small eyes and a wide turned-up nose. Ruddy skin. "What the hell you doing driving through here like Mario Andretti? You making all these big tidal waves. Busted all the windows out of my buddy's store." His boat rocked in the water. "Who's gonna pay for that?"

"What do you want me to do? I got a delivery to make, asshole."

The guy's eyes widened. "Holy shit. You're just a chick." He laughed. Even sounded like a pig snorting.

Loree glared at him. Started to roll her window back up.

*Klickt-klickt.* Loree recognized the rack of a shotgun and instinctively ducked down. *Boom!* Her driver's side window shattered. Loree screamed. Freezing cold air blasted into her cab and she felt a sharp pain to the back of her head. Her truck veered as she fought to regain control, striking sign posts and other debris.

The guy was fucking crazy.

She slammed hard into a streetlight. Her body jerked forward and back as the truck lurched to a stop.

*Klickt-klickt.* Pig Man racked the gun and Loree ducked down again. *Boom!* A blast through her windshield. Shards of glass showered her. Loree screamed but it was muted, like she'd stuffed cotton in her ears. She shook her head, trying to clear the ringing.

Before he could get another shot off, Loree scrambled over to the passenger side and flung the door open. Water gushed in, soaking her boots and the bottoms of her jeans. She jumped into the murky water below.

Luckily, it was deeper than she thought and the water swallowed her up. Her face and arms stung. She couldn't tell if it was because she was hurt or the water was that fucking cold. She awkwardly swam as fast as she could away from her truck, careful to remain completely submerged until she felt a safe enough distance away. Her clothes clung to her, weighing her down. She'd lost her beanie.

She maneuvered her way around what felt like metal street signs and other shit that she had no idea. Just kept surging ahead. She struck her ankle on something sharp, pain shooting up her right leg. No way was she opening her eyes to check what she hit.

Finally, when her lungs felt like they were going to burst, she surfaced, searching for Pig Man. She spotted her big rig, the truck's front end smashed against the streetlight, about twenty feet away.

Pig Man was now on the passenger side of her truck, standing up in his idling boat, the shotgun raised in the air. His head was bent down like he was searching the water. Looking for her.

Loree hunched down and scanned her surroundings. It was still dark but she could make out a few buildings in front of her, about fifteen feet away. An alarm was clanging, coming from one of the stores. The funk of the water and smell of acrid smoke coated the back of her throat, making her gag.

She searched for a boat, a piece of driftwood, anything to clutch on to. Her arms and legs felt like lead weights. She found a metal box thing sticking up out of the water and wrapped her arms around it, resting. Her teeth chattered and her face felt frozen.

The alarm stopped, the only sounds now were shouting and the distant roar of the river. Every now and then she'd hear the *vrrrrrrrrm* of a boat motor. She didn't want to wave her arms for fear of Pig Man spotting her so she remained still, her head barely poking up from the water. The sky was shifting from raven black to a dirty steel gray as morning approached. Loree guessed it to be about five-thirty, maybe six in the morning.

She needed to get out of the water before she died of hypothermia or a shotgun blast to the face. There had to be somewhere she could warm up. Loree pushed off the metal box and kicked her way through the water in search of somewhere warm and hopefully dry.

Kevin went in the back and managed to silence the alarm, although he swore he could hear ringing. His ears were probably still messed up from Ricky's shotgun blast. The clinic was arctic inside thanks to all the shattered windows.

He felt like he was going to puke. Watching Ricky shoot at that truck driver like some crazy vigilante was unreal. It happened at least half a block away, but the big rig's bright headlights spotlighted it for everyone to see. Kevin knew his friend had psychopathic tendencies, but this was the first time he'd seen it firsthand.

No way could that driver have escaped alive. Just thinking about it made the acid in his stomach bubble up to his chest.

The weight of the pistol inside his jacket suddenly felt ten times heavier. He pulled it out and set it on the counter next to the cash register. Wanted nothing to do with it.

Kevin heard movement outside. A person sloshing

through the water toward the clinic. Figured it was Ricky heading back in. Anger seethed inside him, thinking of what his friend did.

He grabbed the flashlight and pointed it outside. The person turned away, shielding their face with their hand.

"Can you get that light out of my eyes?"

Kevin lowered the flashlight, watched in silence as a young woman in her late twenties cautiously made her way into the clinic, limping slightly. She was soaked, her short blonde hair plastered to her bloody and bruised face. Jeans and a hoodie sticking to her like filthy wet cardboard. Her face expressionless.

"I saw your light on. Hoped you had something warm I could change into. Anything." Her voice shook but her eyes were hard, unflinching.

At first Kevin didn't move, just stared at her, then nodded. "Of course. I've got some lab coats in the back that are probably dry. Wait here."

She nodded.

He scurried to the back as fast as he could in knee-deep water. Luckily, he kept his lab coats up on the top shelf in the supply closet so the water didn't get to them. He grabbed a bunch, figuring she could use one to dry herself off.

"You can go in the back to change. There's a restroom. Not sure how dry it is but—" Kevin stopped.

The woman was gone. Kevin looked around, confused. "Miss?"

Movement outside. Ricky tied the boat to a tree and walked into the clinic, water swirling around his thighs. He held the shotgun in one hand and looked extremely pissed.

"Man, can you believe that truck driver was a chick? Son of a bitch. Shot that truck up good though. Hopefully I fucked her up enough that she drowned out there." Ricky frowned. "What the hell's wrong with you?"

Kevin looked around the clinic, then back at Ricky. He opened his mouth. Closed it.

"And what you got all them lab coats for?"

"I—I was bringing these for the woman..." Kevin trailed off. Realization hit him.

"Woman? What woman?"

A noise behind them, like ragged breathing. From the cash register area. Ricky narrowed his eyes at Kevin, then with a grin stormed past him. He raised his shotgun, pointing it in front of him as he circled the cash register counter.

Kevin's eyes darted to the register. The pistol was missing.

*Crack!* Ricky jerked backward. *Crack!* The woman popped up from behind the counter in a firing stance, both hands gripping the outstretched pistol. Ricky stumbled, toppled over a display case into the water, and thrashed like a hooked fish. *Crack!* Silence.

The woman swiveled the gun to Kevin. He threw his hands up, inadvertently tossing the lab coats into the water. She slowly made her way toward him, the gun pointed at his head.

He ignored the hammering in his chest. "The lab coats are—they're all wet now, but I can get some more in the back if you want."

She said nothing, just kept moving slowly until she stood about six feet in front of him. The gun never wavering.

"I'm taking the boat," she said, not taking her eyes off Kevin.

"I figured." Kevin remained frozen, his arms still up in the air.

The woman leaned over and swiped the flashlight from the counter. She hugged it to her chest. "Nothing funny. You move, I'm blowing your fucking head off." She slowly backed up toward the shattered windows, the gun still trained on him.

Kevin cleared his throat. "Look, I don't know if this makes a difference to you or not, but the way I see it, you were never here."

The woman stopped and blinked at him. It seemed like she was about to say something. Then she lowered the gun, turned and limped outside to the boat tethered to the tree. Kevin lowered his arms and watched her untie the boat, awkwardly stepping into it. A minute later, the engine rattled to life and she disappeared, the flashlight bobbing up and down.

Kevin walked over to where he saw his friend topple into the water by the display case. Nudged Ricky's submerged body with the tip of his boot. He reached down into the water and found an ice-cold hand. Nausea swelled in his gut.

Grabbing onto the wrist, Kevin pulled so Ricky's head and shoulders slowly surfaced, his wide lifeless eyes fixed on something behind Kevin. Blood trickled out of a dark hole in Ricky's pale wet neck. Kevin looked at him for a few more seconds—a mixture of horror and relief surging through him—then released his grip. His friend's face disappeared with a satisfying splash.

\* \* \*

Loree guided the boat back out in the same direction she was headed earlier. She didn't know why. It wasn't like she needed to catch Route 136 now. As she approached her wrecked big rig, she heard shouts and laughter. Several boats surrounded her trailer. The doors had been broken into and people were inside, trying to rip through the shrink-wrapped pallets.

She heard bits and pieces of conversation from the looters as she motored past.

"...driver's dead as fuck..."

"...Ricky blasted the guy's head clean off..."

"....swear I saw a head floating by..."

She never glanced in anyone's direction. The words "Sinbad Trucking" caught her eye as she veered past her truck. Maybe she'd hitch a ride along Route 136 after she dried off and cleaned herself up. The back of her head was bleeding and her arm was pretty messed up from her truck's shattered window. Her leg was in bad shape too.

But she was free. Everyone would assume she was dead now and word would get back to Veto. That Chinese dude swore he wouldn't say anything and Loree believed him. His buddy wasn't going to blab. Yeah, she killed him, but the asshole had it coming.

It's not like she hadn't killed a man once before. Funny, how they both ended up in a watery grave.

Time for Loree to try again. To start fresh, a clean slate. And this time, she had a real good feeling about it.

# THE CHASE
## Elizabeth Heiter

Her brother was going to commit murder today.

The knowledge had been swirling in Kayla Morell's head, eating at her gut, since the moment news hit that Maggie Wilbourne hadn't gotten a last-minute stay of execution. Kayla didn't know why she hadn't realized it earlier, but when Wilbourne's lawyer had stepped out of that jail and read the convicted killer's final words to a salivating group of reporters, fear had struck harder than her dad's fist.

The rapists Wilbourne had killed deserved it. The law had failed her, just like it had failed Kayla and Jacob. But Maggie wasn't a natural killer. She'd been doomed the moment she'd made that choice, even if in her final words she claimed their deaths had finally set her free.

Her older brother Jacob was different. Kayla was certain he'd never get caught. And she knew Maggie's words, combined with the distraction of the flood, would propel him into a choice he could never take back. And he wouldn't be the only one who'd pay for it.

She'd wasted precious time calling Jacob, first his home phone, then his cell, even his work, although she knew his classes were over for the week. She'd started out in her car, before the flood waters had swallowed so much of the town. But she'd pushed it, trying to coast through waters way too deep, and now her car was abandoned in Everton's business district.

She was lucky she wasn't with it, sunk under God knew how many feet of murky water. Her arms and legs still ached from swimming as hard and as fast as she could away from the rapidly swelling floodwater. Her uniform was shredded from running into things beneath the water's surface, so she'd tossed it when she got home.

She'd wanted to hop in a hot shower and stay there for hours, until she felt warm again. But she couldn't. Not only had she returned to find her house looted and trashed and the power dead, she just didn't have time. Instead she'd changed into jeans and a sweatshirt heavy enough to warm her and hide the weapon at her hip. Then she'd hauled her old kayak from the garage and gone out again.

That had been hours ago. She'd made it to the hill where Jacob lived, to his gorgeous white colonial, a present he'd bought himself after making tenure. She'd dragged the kayak behind her and let herself in. But it was empty, unscathed even by the looters.

So she was out again, maneuvering through what had once been streets. The big camping flashlight on her lap lit up her path. Fires in the distance sent a dim yellow glow over things farther away: a woman with long, dark hair striding toward a boarded-up home, a man in a mask trailing behind her; a teenager rowing a canoe, a mutt beside him, a blanket over them both; a man weeping at the edge of the water as it rose slowly around him.

Kayla turned away from them, her arms aching as they rotated in a wide circle, slicing the oars through the water, over and over. Something bobbed in the boat's path, looking suspiciously like a bundle of drugs, heavily wrapped in bright yellow tape. She ignored it, laser-focused on her mission. But when the cell phone in her pocket rang, she dug it out to check the caller. The station. Again.

As soon as the dam blew, they'd called back all officers, whether they were on duty or not, to help with rescue efforts. Kayla had planned to stop her brother and then go in. But that had been hours ago.

Now as her kayak drifted into yet another street sign, hard enough to bounce her cell phone out of her hand and into the water, she figured it was fate. An excuse for why she wasn't there to rescue her friends and neighbors, to protect them from people taking advantage of the tragedy.

The guilt rose up again, hard and insistent. She'd taken an oath to protect and defend and was betraying that promise, the mission that had given her life purpose. But she shoved the guilt down. Jacob had protected her all her life, taken the beatings meant for her, hiding her when their dad's rage became too much. It was her turn to protect him.

She picked up the paddle and kept moving.


Jacob Morell hopped out of the boat onto dry land in the darkness, giving his ears and eyes a minute to adjust. The water sloshing and slapping against his oars exchanged for the distant hum of a generator. The glow of his lantern illuminating a few feet at a time traded for a deeper darkness.

He didn't have to see to know where he was. The water had stopped right at the edge of their old sandbox, a sinking pit of two-by-fours that Jacob once suspected hid the body of his mother. As a teenager, he'd dug the whole sandbox out, gone six feet down, while laughing eyes watched from the kitchen window. So he knew she wasn't there. He'd probably never know where she was buried.

But the sandbox told him something now. Because two hundred feet ahead was the house, miraculously still untouched by the flood waters, as if even nature was afraid of the man who lived inside.

He closed his eyes, listening, trying to adjust to the blackness. When he opened them again, he still couldn't see, but a smile escaped. He didn't need an unguarded noise to tell him. He could sense it, almost smell it. His prey was here. His first kill.

But it wouldn't be his last.

Giving the boat a hard shove, he watched it wobble along the water until it disappeared in the darkness. No sense leaving an escape route.

His target might have been approaching a forced retirement, but he was still savvy and strong. He wasn't going to go easy.

Jacob's heart picked up speed. This was in his genes. He'd been fighting it all his life, but Maggie's final words had set a fire inside of him. It was time for the victims to stop paying over and over again. It was too late to save Maggie, but he could follow her example. There was one more predator Jacob could guarantee would get what he deserved tonight.

Lowering himself into a crouch, Jacob made a run for the line of trees to his left. His fingers grazed over the penlight in his pocket to the weapon his father had bought him so many years ago.

He'd felt an instinctive desire to use a knife, like the old man, but the stirring of excitement when he'd grabbed it, the twitch in his crotch, made him leave it behind. The gun would do, and that was its own kind of irony.

His father's words came back to him now, when he'd handed over that gun the day Jacob had moved out. Jacob had stared at it, shocked at his father's nerve, wondering if he had the courage to fire it.

Bobby had given him a lopsided, knowing smile, then said, "You don't have the guts. But one day, trust me, you're going to want this. The gun is easier. But a knife is so much more fun."

"Head in the game," Jacob whispered to himself, then crept toward the house where he'd grown up. Toward the man he knew was inside.

The blast of a shotgun made Kayla duck, and her kayak see-sawed back and forth. She threw her hands wide, managing to steady it before she toppled into the water. But her lantern wasn't so lucky. It went the way of her cell phone. A new kind of fear prickled on her skin because the distant fires were burning out now, just plumes of gray smoke atop smaller sparks.

The inky night seemed to surround her, the scent of dirty water rising into her nostrils, and she wondered how many people were below her, victims of the flood. Had another one just been added? Who had fired that shotgun? And how close was the shooter?

She stayed perfectly still, fighting not to shiver in the frigid air, straining to hear an approaching boat. Way in the distance, a motor started up and her breath caught. A light bounced, catching on the waves alongside her before moving past. The boat whizzed by, twenty feet away, and the driver never noticed her.

Tears fell as she sat in the darkness, losing sense of direction. How was she going to reach her brother without light to guide her? Last she'd been able to tell, she was a mile away from where he had to be headed.

Wiping the tears with the back of her hand, she gripped her paddle and wrenched it down into the water. The kayak had been pointed in the right direction. There was no choice but to keep moving. Eventually the sun would come up and she'd be able to navigate better, but by then it would be too late.

"You've faced down bank robbers and a murderer," she reminded herself. "You can do this."

Her mind screamed back that the bank robbers had been the stupid Neddle brothers, who'd tried to steal ten thousand dollars with plastic guns. Or that she'd just been one of six cops who'd been there for the raid to bring in Maggie Wilbourne after her short-lived escape three months ago. Kayla had been the rookie in the very back. And if some of the evidence that had been inadmissible at trial was true, Maggie had been a victim long before she'd been a killer.

But none of that mattered. Not that Kayla was a newbie who still felt uncomfortable holding a gun on anyone, who'd never fired once outside of practice. Not the loss of light, meaning a slight shift in any direction and she'd end up on the wrong side of town.

The only thing that mattered was Jacob. Memories propelled her. Images of Jacob standing in front of her, his face so bloody she wasn't sure it would ever heal. Of him getting to his feet over and over again, forcing her to stay behind him, because they both knew what would happen if she didn't.

But the physical beatings Jacob had protected her from were irregular. They stood out in her mind, like mile markers in her life. The emotional thrashing was the slow killer, day after day, leaving her feeling worthless and helpless. Like she'd never escape.

If it hadn't been for Jacob, she never would have.

But he'd been beside her all those years, older, bigger, wiser. Telling her she could create her own future. Making her believe it. Helping mold her into the person she'd become, a police officer who'd earned the badge and upheld the law even when it didn't always seem fair. Even when it hadn't saved her back then. Because deep inside, she knew it was saving her now, giving her purpose and direction.

Kayla paddled harder, until her shoulders felt ready to pop out of their sockets, then she leaned into it, giving even more.

It was like Jacob was lending her his strength as she raced for their childhood home, praying she wasn't already too late.

\* \* \*

The back door creaked as he jimmied it open, and Jacob stepped carefully, quietly, into the kitchen. He'd deferred college four long years, waiting for Kayla in the confines of this hell, but since they'd left, neglect had set in.

A layer of dust coated the counters, two of the cabinets hung low on their hinges, and there was a long, dirty crack in the linoleum floor. Even the walls looked grimy, yellowing with age.

He shouldn't have been surprised. Bobby Morell had always spent more time on the road than at home, and without Jacob and Kayla to keep the place presentable, he'd let it go. Jacob wasn't sure what the old man planned to do now that his work was forcing retirement on him.

It wasn't just that Bobby would be leaving the job he'd held for decades. Or even that Bobby would soon be trapped alone in the house that had once held four. As far as Jacob could tell, Bobby did all his killings while he was on the road, far from home, where he was less likely to become a suspect. Bobby had no personal connection to the victims, except for the one woman whose death haunted Jacob most.

Without him and Kayla there to scream at, home would be nothing for Bobby. It had never been more than a showplace, somewhere people knew him, knew he wasn't capable of murder. Bobby had always loved to put on his neighborly façade and go out in the community, volunteering and socializing. He surely did even more of that now, displayed his carefully constructed "good guy" persona to the world.

Just one more reason no one would ever believe he was a killer. Just like they'd never believed him or Kayla about the beatings, the few times they'd dared to seek help. Their father kept them locked in the basement while the bruises healed. Without evidence, Jacob had learned quickly, no one would look twice at a pillar of the community. But stuck at home, with a father who'd had to explain Jacob's "fantasies" to the police, Jacob had discovered fast how much worse things could get.

He shuddered, the full-body spasm like muscle memory kicking in from being back in this house. He tried not to think about the past, to focus. One wrong move could get him killed, and Jacob knew exactly how much he'd suffer before he died.

So he waited, poised just inside the doorway, forcing patience and letting his eyes adjust even more. He might have age and strength on his side, but his father had home advantage.

By Jacob's best estimate, his father had killed nineteen women. And Bobby Morell didn't choose easy, transient victims along his highway routes. Oh, no. Bobby liked a challenge, so he traveled far off his sales routes and found upper-class women who lived in supposedly secure gated communities. Somehow, he'd figured out how to beat the company's vehicle tracking system, giving him a solid alibi the one time a witness had spotted a company truck near a victim's house.

And maybe Bobby liked the publicity, because that's how Jacob had kept count over the years. Bobby's "airtight alibi" had first made Jacob suspect the extent of his father's evil, because he'd seen a souvenir Bobby had kept. He'd looked for it after the police came, showing a picture of the victim, a locket around her neck just like the one in Bobby's suitcase. But of course, it was nowhere to be found.

Just like it always was with the beatings, there was no evidence. No way to prove the extent of Bobby's evil. And no way to escape it.

After that, he'd watched the media. The Invisible Man—so named because he left nothing behind, just took a personal memento with him when he left—had garnered a lot of news stories over the years. Police never found DNA, prints or any useful forensics, according to the media. But the Invisible Man still had a signature, a specific way of torturing his victims that had shocked Jacob, even knowing the levels of brutality his father could reach.

But now that Bobby was about to leave the job that gave him legitimate reasons to travel, he was going to have to curb his killing impulses. Which meant he had nothing left to lose. So, Jacob wasn't about to underestimate the old man.

He crept forward, avoiding the spots on the floor that bubbled up and might crack under his feet. Nerves made his fingertips tingle, but a different kind of excitement was building in his chest, too.

For so long, he'd fought the depravity inside of him. Fought it for Kayla, who might have looked more like their dad, but had the heart of their mom. Maybe he should have given in and done this a long time ago, because he'd always sensed what the initial taste of blood would unleash. And for the first time in his life, he felt like he could take a full, unconstrained breath.

Genetics at work, he supposed. Maybe it took a monster to destroy a monster.

He slid against the wall and pressed his ear to the doorway into the living room, where his father had always liked to sit at night. Would he be there tonight?

Probably not. Jacob didn't know how, but he was sure his father was expecting him. He eased back and slinked the other way, not wanting to be pulled into a trap.

Only the moment he stepped backward, something hard and cold pressed against his skull and his father's voice whispered in his ear.

"Welcome home, son."

Kayla hauled the kayak onto dry land, not stopping until it was several feet in, tucked up close to the house where she'd never wanted to return. The water was still rising, and she didn't want to drown here. If she had to die, it wasn't going to be in Bobby Morell's house. Not after she'd finally gotten out.

As a kid, she'd been certain she'd never make it. That one day, her father would truly snap or Jacob wouldn't be fast enough, and she'd end up like the rest of Bobby's victims. Like their mother, buried somewhere in an unmarked grave.

But she *had* made it. She'd turned her life into something good, committed herself to stopping other evils, to the law and justice. She'd escaped both her mother's fate and her father's path, and she was determined to help Jacob do the same.

She scanned the edge of the water with eyes that had finally adjusted to the darkness and her shoulders slumped. No sign of another boat. Could she be wrong?

Panic threatened, and with every step toward the door, an old fear slid closer to the surface. A powerlessness she thought she'd finally banished when she earned the badge.

Her feet unintentionally slowed, her breath coming faster and faster at the thought of being near her father after all these years. She'd managed to avoid him since she'd graduated from school and returned to Everton, naively thinking that as a cop, she could finally find justice. Not just for girls like the one she'd been, but also for all the women she knew Bobby had killed.

When she reached the entrance, she pulled her Glock from her pocket. It was her service pistol, so she couldn't even fire warning shots without having to explain things to her chief she wasn't ready to talk about. Things she might never be ready to talk about.

Seconds before she kicked in the front door and gave away her presence, she reconsidered. The lock on the back door had always been questionable. She could pick it silently.

But when she rounded the corner, the back door was hanging open. Her heart ratcheted up speed until she could hear it pounding in her ears. She was right. Jacob was here.

She stepped hesitantly over the threshold, fighting the innate desire for self-preservation screaming at her to run in the other direction. The house was silent. Except...

She strained to listen and there it was again. A distant *thump*. Coming from the basement.

Memories kicked in hard, the first time Jacob had been locked down there without her. She'd run from home, hiding for days until finally she snuck back in during the middle of the night, fear making her entire body shake. She'd opened the door and discovered her brother had broken all his toes trying to kick it open and get to her, thinking she was alone with their father. Thinking she was going to end up like their mother.

A sob broke free and Kayla slapped her hand over her mouth, almost firing her gun as her other hand jerked. Suddenly she was six years old, woken from a dead sleep by her mother jamming a hand under Kayla's chin to keep her from screaming. With quick, sloppy movements, her mom had yanked Kayla out of bed. Then, Kayla found herself tossed in the back of their old station wagon and her mom had hopped into the front seat, still wearing her nightgown. She'd let the car coast out of the driveway silently, as Kayla cried for Jacob.

Then her mother had punched the gas, whispering what she'd surely thought were words of comfort. They were escaping Bobby. The two of them would start over. New town, new names, new lives. Jacob couldn't come, because deep down, her mother knew. Jacob was his father's son.

They'd driven for a full day, only stopping for her mother to buy coffee and food at a drive-through. Then they kept going, until the miles of highway were burned in Kayla's brain. Every few hours, her mother would insist she'd spotted Bobby behind them. Kayla had thought it was exhaustion making her see things that weren't there. Finally, her mother's shoulders had started to slump and they'd pulled into a motel with a flickering vacancy sign to rest.

Kayla had fallen into a deep sleep as soon as she hit the bed, exhausted from nonstop crying for her big brother. She'd woken to a scream, cut off almost before it started. She'd opened her eyes to find Bobby dragging her mother by the hair out of the room and slamming the door behind him.

She'd tried to follow, but he'd blocked it and she couldn't get out. She'd tried to scream, but her mom had purposely chosen a place run-down and deserted where they were less likely to attract attention. Kayla had yelled herself hoarse, but no one heard.

Hours later, Bobby had returned, a single drop of blood on his white button-down. He'd put her in his car and driven her wordlessly back to Jacob, something big rolling in the trunk at every highway turn.

Shaking off the past, Kayla opened the basement door and the near-silence erupted into a full-blown wail of pain.

Jacob watched through eyes partially swollen shut as his father swung back a foot. It felt like slow motion as that steel-toed boot headed for his ribs again, but still connected too fast to block. The gun flew from his pocket and Bobby laughed.

"You should have pulled that upstairs, son. While you still had a chance."

"What do you think of his chances now?"

The voice came from the stairs. Determined and defiant. But underneath, he heard the unease. Kayla.

Jacob's heart lurched and he wanted to scream for her to run the other way.

But she was already descending, her own weapon centered on their father's chest. "Don't move."

Bobby swiveled slowly toward Kayla as Jacob reached for his gun, and something sharp jammed Jacob's lung until he was gasping for breath. He remembered the feeling. Cracked rib. Only this time, he was pretty sure it had punctured his lung.

He still had another one, Jacob reminded himself as his fingers closed clumsily around the weapon. He couldn't believe he'd let his father get the upper hand, couldn't believe he'd followed orders to move into the basement, even with a gun pressed to his head.

It smelled of must and blood and death, even though Jacob was pretty certain his father had never killed in his own house. It made Jacob gag as he rolled awkwardly, trying to get to his feet while Bobby was distracted.

"Kayla," Bobby breathed, and it sounded like happiness.

His sister's gun shook up and down. Or maybe that was Jacob's vision.

"Jacob, are you okay?"

There were tears in Kayla's voice that brought back a thousand memories. He tried to reassure her, but his words were garbled.

In his peripheral vision, Bobby slid sideways a step, toward the weapon he'd set on a workbench, and Kayla took the rest of the stairs fast. Behind her, dirty flood water started to follow.

"I said, don't move. Go for that gun and I'll shoot you."

Bobby lifted his hands, and even through blurry vision, Jacob could tell a smile quirked the very edges of Bobby's lips. "Your brother attacked me. I was defending myself. It's over, now that you're here to protect me with your badge."

Kayla's weapon lowered a fraction of an inch because Bobby knew his daughter well. She was everything he wasn't. She'd never shoot someone out of spite. Only to protect. Bobby knew it as well as Jacob.

But Jacob was different. And Bobby should have known that, too.

Somehow, Jacob got his hand closed around his gun and stumbled to his feet as water started to inch closer and closer. Once he was standing, the pressure on his lung eased and his vision started to clear. He blinked a few times, getting the world back into focus, then leveled his weapon on Bobby.

Jacob barely recognized his own voice as he said, "You can go now, Kayla. I'll do the rest."

"No." Kayla's gun moved toward him, an instinctive jerk probably drilled into her at the police academy— aim at the threat—then back again. "You're not like him, Jacob. We can leave together. I'm not going without you."

"Yes, you are." He used his older brother voice, the one she'd always obeyed when he told her to run or hide.

But this time, she stood her ground, even if her voice wavered. "I can't let you do this. This isn't about protecting anyone anymore. He's finished, and we both know it. This is just vengeance."

"Don't those women deserve vengeance?"

"They deserve *justice*, for what he did to be proven and for him to pay for it the right way. Are they really getting that if their families never know the truth? If they spend the rest of their lives still searching for what happened? Or is it just for you?"

"They're never going to prove it." Jacob's gaze swiveled briefly to her. She didn't need to wear her uniform to look like a cop, and he had a flash of pride at the strength of her convictions, the goodness in her eyes.

Still, it had been so many years since they'd all been in the same room that it surprised him all over again how much Kayla looked like Bobby. Same golden streaks in her brown hair. Same stormy gray eyes. Same stubborn jut to her chin. And yet, it was Jacob who'd inherited his black soul.

"You can't save me. But I can stop him for good this time."

Bobby's lips twitched, a conniving smile hooking the corners before dropping off, and suddenly, Jacob *knew*. Yes, his father had been waiting for him today, but this was the ending Bobby wanted, too. He was going to have to retire soon, but he wasn't interested in a life without killing. He'd figured out how Jacob could be his legacy.

One kill. He was his father's son, so of course Bobby knew that was all it would take to push Jacob over, turn him into Bobby.

He wondered fleetingly if this was how it had been for his father, if Bobby ever had any good in him, or if he'd started out pure evil. Maybe, before Jacob and Kayla had come around, Bobby had been like him. Knowing there was something bad inside of him, but desperate to fight it, not to give in to the urges. Maybe once, he'd been winning that battle, too.

The gun trembled in Jacob's grip, and he bracketed it with his other hand, trying to steady it. Behind him, the window up near the ceiling cracked then shattered, and water began pouring inside. A flash of panic hit Jacob, but his father just kept smiling, smug and sure.

"Jacob," Kayla warned, ignoring the waters rising around them as her weapon sighted on him once more and her voice told him she'd made up her mind. "You can't shoot him. There's nothing left to prevent. And it's what he wants! This is murder. You try to fire and it's my duty to protect him."

Jacob slid his finger under the trigger guard. There was no turning back now. "Maybe that's how it was meant to be. I kill him, and you kill me."

He'd have to be precise, because his sister might not be comfortable with a gun, but he knew her willpower. If she thought it was her moral obligation, she might get him before he took down Bobby.

And before Jacob died, Bobby Morell had to go.


"I forgive you," Jacob told his little sister, sighting his weapon on their father's forehead.

"No." Kayla lowered her weapon, trying to calm him down, not to let him hear the panic in her voice. She needed to reason with him—and fast, before the water sloshing around her knees rose even more and they all drowned down here. "Don't make me do this, Jacob. We both know he's finished killing."

"And he never has to pay for what he did to those women? What he did to Mom?" Jacob shook his head, and even though he looked more like their mother than Bobby, suddenly Kayla saw their father in him.

The feral gleam in his eyes, the bloodlust Jacob was going to set loose by killing Bobby. Once he pulled that trigger, he'd no longer be the Jacob who had protected her all her life, and they both knew it.

She'd be keeping a list of his kills, one more man who shared her blood that she was trying to bring down. And like Bobby, she was sure she'd never be able to prove it.

A sob tickled the back of her throat and she swallowed it down. "It's not worth sacrificing yourself," she whispered. "Please don't make me do this."

Her brother smiled, something dark and ironic. "Now *you* sound like him."

"Do it, son," Bobby taunted. "There's nothing like the power you'll feel. But for the next one, use the knife. I promise, when the blade goes in that very first time, you'll never be the same."

A light came into Jacob's eyes that Kayla had never seen before. His finger tightened on the trigger.

"No!" Kayla screamed. Her sob was swallowed by the sound of her gun firing.

Her weapons instructor would be proud. It was center mass and she didn't even have to double-check to be sure it was a kill shot.

She flung her weapon away from her, knowing she'd never pick one up again as it disappeared into the dark water. She'd betrayed everything she believed in, and it had been almost unconscious, instinct taking over, wanting the retribution for herself.

Maybe there really was no escaping genetics.

Jacob lowered his weapon slowly, and when he blinked, the shock faded, leaving behind something different. Not the older brother who'd raised her, but not a monster, either. Somewhere in between.

Maybe they both were.

Together, their gazes shifted to the man slowly sinking below the floodwater, disbelief frozen in his dead eyes.

# EPILOGUE
### Jennifer Hillier

The news of the dam blowing didn't immediately make national broadcasts. Neither did the flood. It took a few hours for the major outlets to pick up the story, and even then, they were slow to send out their helicopters and news crews until they were certain it was a true disaster. That said a lot about the significance of Everton, Pennsylvania to the rest of the country.

In other words, the small town wasn't significant at all.

Hannah Hayes, rookie reporter for MSNBC, was woken up at three a.m. in her Brooklyn apartment by a series of texts from her producer. A helicopter ride and four hours later, here she was, continuing her broadcast of the flood from the rooftop of downtown Everton's tallest building. The eight-story Bonaventure Hotel, once considered a grand place to stay fifty years ago, was seedy now, even on its best day. But the view was perfect.

The river running through Main Street and all of downtown was surreal, especially to someone who had grown up seeing it in its normal, non-flooded state. Looking down, Hannah saw several smashed storefront windows, a knocked over stop sign, and four cars pushed into each other by the strength of the water surge. The neon sign for Poole's Leatherwear, a shop that sold motorcycle jackets and boots, had half its lights out and was currently blinking "Poo here." She couldn't help but snort. A red Ford F150 floated through the intersection. It reminded her of the truck her high school boyfriend used to drive.

For all she knew, he still lived here, and that was his truck.

It was cold on top of the hotel and she wrapped her arms around herself. Her new Burberry wool coat she'd bought on sale at Saks wasn't warm enough, but it looked good on TV. The sun was barely out, its weak rays casting an orange glow on the water-ravaged town. Otherwise, the sky was clear. Which seemed strange to Hannah. Normally floods were caused by rain, but today there wasn't a storm cloud in sight. This flood was man-made.

Actually, no. It was *woman-made.*

Paul Wong, Hannah's cameraman, offered her his jumbo bag of pretzels. She scarfed down a handful, careful to keep the salt off her perfectly painted lips. Paul always had snacks on hand. He was tall and athletic, and someone Hannah totally would have slept with if he wasn't married. They munched in silence, both hungry and tired, while their producer wrapped up a phone call a few feet away.

"Who's he talking to again?" Paul asked her, nodding toward Jonas, who was standing a little too close to the edge of the roof for Hannah's comfort.

"He's getting official confirmation that the dam blowing up is about Maggie Wilbourne." She reached for another pretzel. "None of the other news outlets have tied it together yet. They're saying it's a cult of some kind, but nobody's actually said Wilbourne's name. Jonas is following up with some person on Twitter who's certain it's linked to The Daughters."

"That's a fucked up name." Paul frowned, waiting for her to elaborate.

Hannah wasn't in the mood to explain. Instead, she looked over at Jonas, who was still speaking into his phone. He caught her eye and grinned, which meant he had something good.

"You grew up here, didn't you?" Paul asked through a mouthful of Rold Gold. "In Everton?"

"Yes, but on the poor side of town." Hannah pointed down Main Street to an area just beyond the downtown. "My mom was a maid at the Sleepy Time Motel, and my dad was a mechanic at Woods Automotive before he got fired for drinking on the job."

The cameraman raised an eyebrow. "This must be difficult for you to see, then. The damage to the town, I mean. Is your family okay?"

"I have no family. Except my Aunt Nora, and she texted last night to say she was fine."

"You know, I never would have taken you for a small-town girl. You look too...expensive." Paul stopped. Blinked. Swallowed.

Hannah barked a laugh. She was neither insulted nor flattered. She fingered a lock of her professionally high-lighted hair, a precise shade of beige blonde that set her back three hundred bucks every eight weeks. *You want to go prime time, you have to look prime time, darling,* her boss had told her last year, prompting her to ditch the box dye she'd been using for regular appointments at a salon she could barely afford.

"So when did you leave Everton?" Paul asked.

"As soon as I could." Hannah's tone was curt. The cameraman got the hint and turned away, busying himself with his equipment.

Jonas disconnected his phone call and approached them.

"Okay." The producer rubbed his hands together, but whether it was from the chill in the air or because he was feeling gleeful, she couldn't tell. "The Daughters are officially claiming responsibility for blowing up the dam. Someone on Twitter posted a link to their blog, and there was a statement."

"*Was?*" Hannah asked.

"The blog is down now. But the Twitter guy grabbed a screenshot and our tech guy at the studio said it was google cached, so we have it. We're going to have you read it on air, live. Be ready. You're on in less than two minutes."

She was ready. Jonas texted the screenshot to her iPhone and she scanned the statement quickly. Paul switched the camera on, illuminating her in bright white light. On Jonas's cue, Hannah started speaking.

"I have here a direct statement from The Daughters, the group that's taking responsibility for blowing up the dam. MSNBC has confirmed it's legitimate." Hannah spoke in her on-air voice, pausing every few words for cadence and effect.

"*Dear Townspeople of Everton:*

"*I don't know how many of you are left. Some of you died last night. Some of you managed to make it out of*

*this town, never to return again. The rest of you will
stick around and rebuild this place, but if you think that
makes you a hero, think again. Where were you when
Maggie was raped?"*

Hannah took a deep breath to calm herself, then
continued.

*"We blew up the dam, and we washed away the sins of
this town. But it's not over. It will never be over. Everywhere you go, we will be there. Waiting. Watching. We
are the Daughters. We are the women who serve your
food. We make your coffee. We cut your hair. We cash
your checks. We fix your teeth. We operate on you at the
hospital."*

Hannah looked up, directly into the camera's lens.
Her hand, and the phone in it, dropped to her side. She
was no longer reading. Her next words were enunciated
slowly, purposefully.

"We broadcast your news."

Paul's head poked out from behind the camera, his
mouth dropping open. Jonas, alarmed, stepped forward,
but the cameraman held him back, mesmerized. The producer made a rapid slicing motion across his neck with his
finger. He wanted Hannah to stop talking. But there was
no way she was going to shut up. Not now, not when she
had a captive audience. Nobody had been listening before.

They were sure as shit listening now.

"This is your fresh start," Hannah said to the camera.
She was speaking to the people of Everton, to the town
she had left behind but had never forgotten, to the
goddamned world. "So don't fuck it up."

"Cut!" Jonas yelled.

The camera light went dark.

# ABOUT THE CONTRIBUTORS

**E.A. AYMAR'S** latest novel is *You're as Good as Dead*. He writes a monthly column for the *Washington Indepen-dent Review of Books* and is the Managing Editor of *The Thrill Begins* (for the International Thriller Writers). Aymar is also involved in a collaboration with DJ Alkimist, a NY and DC-based DJ, where his stories are set to her music. For more information about that project, visit eaalkimist.com.

**ROB BRUNET** laces character-driven crime fiction with dark humor. His short stories regularly appear in *Ellery Queen Mystery Magazine*, *Out of the Gutter*, and *Shotgun Honey*. He bounces between Toronto and the Kawarthas, teaches creative writing, co-hosts Noir at the Bar Toronto, and spends as much time down dirt roads as life allows.

**SARAH M. CHEN** juggles several jobs including indie bookseller, transcriber, and insurance adjuster. She has published over twenty crime fiction short stories with *Shotgun Honey*, *Crime Factory*, *Betty Fedora*, *Out of the Gutter*, and *Dead Guns Press*, among others. *Cleaning Up Finn*, her noir novella with All Due Respect Books, was shortlisted for an Anthony and an IPPY award winner.

**ANGEL LUIS COLÓN** is the Anthony and Derringer Award-nominated author of *No Happy Endings*, the "Blacky Jaguar" series of novellas, and the short story anthology *Meat City on Fire (and Other Assorted Debacles)*. His fiction has appeared in multiple web and print publications including *Thuglit*, *Literary Orphans*, and *Great Jones Street*.

**HILARY DAVIDSON** won the 2011 Anthony Award for Best First Novel for *The Damage Done*. The book also earned a Crimespree Award and was a finalist for the Arthur Ellis and Macavity awards. The sequel, *The Next One To Fall*, a mystery set in Peru, was published by Tor/-Forge in 2012, and the third novel in the series, *Evil in All Its Disguises*—about a missing journalist in Mexico—came in 2013. Hilary's first standalone novel, *Blood Always Tells*, was published by Tor/Forge in 2014. Hilary's widely acclaimed short stories have won a Derringer Award, a Spine-tingler Award, and two Ellery Queen Reader's Choice Awards. A Toronto-born travel journalist and the author of eighteen nonfiction books, she has lived in New York City since October 2001.

**MARK EDWARDS** writes psychological thrillers in which scary things happen to ordinary people. He has topped the Amazon UK chart five times and sold over two million books. He lives in the West Midlands, England, with his wife and three children.

Longtime journalist **GWEN FLORIO** writes the Lola Wicks mystery series. The fifth novel in that series, *Under the Shadows*, is set for release in 2018, as well as *Women of Stone*, a standalone novel set in Afghanistan. She lives in Missoula, Montana.

Critically acclaimed and award-winning author **ELIZABETH HEITER** likes her suspense to feature strong heroines, chilling villains, psychological twists, and a little bit (or a lot!) of romance. Her research has taken her into the minds of serial killers, through murder investigations, and onto the FBI Academy's shooting range. Her novels have been published in more than a dozen countries and translated into eight languages; they've also been shortlisted for the HOLT Medallion, the Daphne Du Maurier award, the National Readers' Choice award and the Booksellers' Best award and won the RT Reviewers' Choice award.

**J.J. HENSLEY** is a former police officer and former Special Agent with the U.S. Secret Service. He is the author of the novels *Resolve, Measure Twice, Chalk's Outline, Bolt Action Remedy* and several shorter works. J.J. gradu-ated from Penn State University with a B.S. in Administra-tion of Justice and has a M.S. degree in Criminal Justice Administration from Columbia Southern University. Mr. Hensley's first novel *Resolve* was named one of the "Best Books of 2013" by Suspense Magazine and was a Thriller Award finalist. He is a member of the International Thriller Writers and Sisters in Crime.

**JENNIFER HILLIER** is a novelist who writes about dark, twisted people who do dark, twisted things. She was born and raised in Toronto but spent eight years in Seattle, which is where all her books are set. She loves her son, her husband, the Seahawks, and Stephen King (not equally, but close) and is the author of five psychological thrillers.

**SHANNON KIRK** is the international best-selling author of *Method 15/33* and award-winning author of *The Extraordinary Journey of Vivienne Marshall*. Her debut, *Method 15/33*, garnered numerous awards and is optioned for a major motion film. When not writing, Shannon is a practicing attorney in Massachusetts.

**JENNY MILCHMAN** is the *USA Today* bestselling author

of three critically acclaimed and award-winning psychological thrillers, as well as the forthcoming *Wicked River*. In 2010 she founded the holiday Take Your Child to a Bookstore Day, now celebrated in all fifty states and on five continents. (Antarctica, we're coming!) She is known for going on very, very long book tours.

**ALAN ORLOFF'S** debut mystery, *Diamonds for the Dead*, was an Agatha Award finalist, and his seventh novel, *Running from the Past*, was an Amazon Kindle Scout selection. His short fiction has appeared in numerous publications, including *Jewish Noir, Alfred Hitchcock Mystery Magazine, Chesapeake Crimes: Storm Warning, Mystery Weekly, Noir at the Salad Bar, Black Cat Mystery Magazine*, and *Windward: Best New England Crime Stories 2016*. Alan lives in Northern Virginia and teaches fiction-writing at The Writer's Center (Bethesda, MD). He loves cake and arugula, but not together.

**WENDY TYSON** is an author, lawyer, and former therapist from the Philadelphia area. In addition to her two series, The Allison Campbell Mystery Series and The Greenhouse Mystery Series, Wendy's work has been published in literary journals and anthologies. Wendy's a member of Sisters in Crime, Penn Writers, and International Thriller Writers, and she's a columnist and contributing editor for *The Thrill Begins* and *The Big Thrill*, International Thriller Writers' e-zines.

BOOKS

On the following pages are a few
more great titles from the
Down & Out Books publishing family.

For a complete list of books and to
sign up for our newsletter,
go to DownAndOutBooks.com.

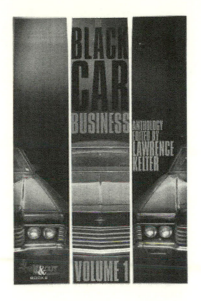

*The Black Car Business Volume 1*
Lawrence Kelter, Editor

Down & Out Books
April 2018
978-1-946502-53-7

It's the sedan just within sight that seems to be mimicking your speed and movements as you walk down the dark deserted street late at night. As the hairs rise on the back of your neck you wonder, who is behind the wheel and what is the driver's intent? It's The Black Car Business and its presence means your life is about to abruptly change.

Contributors: Eric Beetner, J. Carson Black, Cheryl Bradshaw, Diane Capri, Jeffery Hess, Lawrence Kelter, Dana King, Allan Leverone, Simon Wood, and Vincent Zandri.

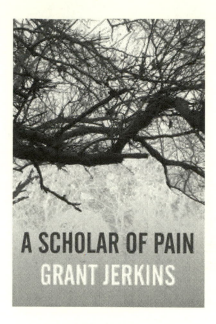

*A Scholar of Pain*
Grant Jerkins

ABC Group Documentation
an imprint of Down & Out Books
February 2018
978-1-946502-15-5

In his debut short fiction collection, Grant Jerkins remains—as the *Washington Post* put it—"Determined to peer into the darkness and tell us exactly what he sees." Here, the depth of that darkness is on evident, oftentimes poetic, display. Read all sixteen of these deviant diversions. Peer into the darkness.

*Dead Guy in the Bathtub*
Stories by Paul Greenberg

All Due Respect, an imprint of
Down & Out Books
March 2018
978-1-946502-87-2

Crime stories with a dark sense of humor and irony. These characters are on the edge and spiraling out of control. Bad situations become serious circumstances that double down on worst-case scenarios. A Lou Reed fan gets himself caught on the wild side. A couple goes on a short and deadly crime spree. A collector of debts collecting a little too much for himself. A vintage Elvis collection to lose your head over. A local high school legend with a well-endowed reputation comes home.

This debut collection is nothing but quick shots of crime fiction.

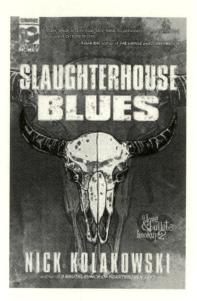

*Slaughterhouse Blues*
A Love & Bullets Hookup
Nick Kolakowski

Shotgun Honey, an imprint of
Down & Out Books
February 2018
978-1-946502-40-7

Holed up in Havana, Bill and Fiona know the Mob is coming for them. But they're not prepared for who the Mob sends: a pair of assassins so utterly amoral and demented, their behavior pushes the boundaries of sanity. Seriously, what kind of killers pause in mid-hunt to discuss the finer points of thread count and luxury automobiles? If they want to survive, our fine young criminals can't retreat anymore: they'll need to pull off a massive (and massively weird) heist—and the loot has some very dark history...

Made in the USA
Middletown, DE
25 April 2018